Tales from the Library of a Twisted Mind

By May J. Panayi

Foreword

In this collection of short stories I have included forewords and after words; the latter to replace the former in cases where to put it in front of the story would be a spoiler. These little notes about the stories tell you my inspiration for the tale, in some cases longer and more detailed than others. Sometimes it's just an out of the blue idea, sometimes there is a history leading up to it.

I have to thank the great Stephen King for the idea of doing this. I was reading his short story collection, Bazaar of Bad Dreams, and decided I very much enjoyed the little introductions to each story, and decided to do the same with my own short story collection. I felt my stomach drop into my boots when I read one story in that book which is almost identical to one I was going to put in this book. It wouldn't be plagiarism because I hadn't read the book prior to producing this, but he definitely had the idea first. So I'll change some of the notions within my story, the ending was different anyway, and hope for the best; there are only so many stories in the world or so they say. Also I have to say that some of the books I've read and films I've watched, are much more direct copies than anything I have ever written...drum roll for big disclaimer...to my knowledge at least.

Contents

Zombie Ants
Poem

Zelda's Baby

It was a perfectly normal day in Dentonville. The roads were empty, traffic parked up exactly as it had been the day before, and the day before that. The weather was average, a bit cold, overcast, but dry; autumnal but okay- well no one was complaining about it anyway, and they were all still wearing their summer clothes, so it couldn't be that cold. The shops were all open, really open; doors flung wide, window displays flapping in the breeze. The illusion of a hot sticky summer remained despite the coolness of the day.

Zelda walked slowly along the main street, her huge pregnant belly forging ahead of her like some kind of scouting party, or soldier on point. She rested her hands on top of the lump, softly pushing it down, away from her stomach so she could more easily digest her meaty, protein rich breakfast of some hours previously. The baby kicked and punched in protest at the confinement of its space, as if to say;

"Look, I'm a bit squashed in here actually. I have kind of completely filled this space, and there is no more room, so kindly stop pushing me into a smaller space, I just won't tolerate it without a fight. A foetus has limits you know."

Zelda huffed with the effort of walking. Despite wearing a thin summer maternity dress, she still felt hot and sticky. Now on top of everything else, she started feeling hungry again too. Damn, this baby made her want to eat all the time. She looked around for a good place to eat.

Bob the mail man lumbered his considerable frame towards her, coming the other way down the street. He grunted at her by way of hello, and she nodded amiably at him. Pleasantries dealt with, Zelda headed towards the diner at the end of the street, on the junction of Main Street and Vine. Some youths she vaguely recognised, passed her running the other way. As they got closer, Zelda noticed that the two older boys; Gil and Leroy, were chasing the younger boy, little Danny Hopkins. Zelda shouted 'Oi' at the older boys and they turned to look at her. Realising they had been caught out, they slowed to a shuffle and looked down at their feet guiltily, as little Danny hurried off, making his escape; for now at least.

Two women Zelda knew vaguely from the maternity clinic, who were still early days, were looking in a shop window displaying baby furniture and clothes. She thought for a moment she might manage to waddle past them un-noticed; but no such luck. They turned and of course the cooing and patting of her distended tummy was a ritual that could not be avoided. When Zelda finally got away she could tell they had made the baby really angry. It was punching and kicking like it was in a mosh pit. She patted her tummy and rubbed it gently, trying to restore some peace and calm to the angry little being- or as yet, un-being.

Finally Zelda got to the diner, which was quite full for the time of day. Alice was behind the counter as usual. She looked up when Zelda came in and waved her over to the counter. Soon Zelda was almost fully immersed in the special of the day whilst sat at the counter. The food steamed in front of her, and tasted delicious. The baby went quiet as it always did when she was eating. She felt sure it was waiting for a morsel to pass close by it so it could grab it. Zelda pushed the crazy thought to the back of her hormone riddled mind.

Zelda didn't hang around after lunch; she was determined to be first in line at the maternity clinic's afternoon session, to see the midwife. She pushed open the doors to the clinic, and took a seat in the messy, magazine strewn, waiting room. She thought it must have been kiddie clinic that morning, given the state of the place. There weren't any receptionists around to clean up anyway; maybe they were off sick. There was some sort of tummy bug going around.

Gradually the clinic filled up with several other women who seated themselves, joining Zelda in the waiting area. At last the midwife came out from her office, wiping the remains of her lunch from around her mouth. She gestured at Zelda to come into her office.

The midwife patted the examination couch, and Zelda clambered awkwardly up on it. She lay back exhausted from the effort. The midwife began to feel her tummy, pulling her dress up so she could look at the stretched skin. Baby hands and feet pushed against the outside, as if by so doing they could claw their way out of the cramped space and have a good stretch. The midwife leaned closer to the little feet and hands imprinted on the outer flesh. She grinned widely then leaned right up against the skin and took a big bite out of Zelda's stomach.

Zelda lay calmly as the midwife took two more, deeper bites. The baby didn't waste the opportunity for escape, clawing through the foetal sack, fluid spilling out over Zelda and onto the floor, biting with fully formed teeth through the final layer of flesh that separated it from the midwife's face and the outside world. It bit the midwife, getting a full mouthful of her bottom lip and the tip of her tongue, before she pulled backwards away from the hungry zombie infant.

Zelda climbed down from the couch, calm as you like, and sauntered out, waving goodbye to the midwife; whose face dripped with blood and gore from her freshly damaged mouth.

Zelda headed out into main street, the baby now full head and one small arm hanging out of her stomach in front of her, like some sort of human kangaroo straight out of a Troma film. The baby was half biting, half sucking at the flesh of Zelda that surrounded it, working a larger hole so it could move more comfortably.

By the time Zelda got back to the diner, the baby had its head and both arms out and was surveying its new world from the comfort of its pouch in Zelda's belly. Alice squealed as Zelda came into the diner, pointing at the baby. Soon all the other zombie patrons were shouting and making a general cacophony of noise too. It was a veritable zombie party. The person who had been the special of the day on the counter, but was now fully zombie, even sat up and clapped. He probably shouldn't have sat up, as it made the remains of his gastrointestinal tract slither out to the floor, making it there seconds before his feet, but he didn't seem to care. Zelda got close to the counter and the baby reached out and grabbed the remnant of some morsel left behind by the special of the day as he vacated the spot, pulling it straight into his baby mouth. All the female zombies in the diner made an 'aaah' noise as one.

Eventually Zelda made it back out onto Main Street, to start the long slow zombie shuffle back to her house. She again bumped into the two women from earlier, who bent down to look closely at the new baby. It wasted not a moment biting the nose off of the one who got closest. All three women seemed to think that was the cutest thing ever.

The three boys were playing together once more; well Gil and Leroy were eating Danny's arms; but they all stopped to look at the newborn baby and its mother progressing down the street.

The sun set on a happy day in zombieville.

Afterword

I have loved all things zombie for many a year, but what I most especially love is looking for the little quirks; the strange little things that make this zombie book or film unique from any other. I was thinking about those individualities when I came up with the idea of a zombie baby using its mother as a pouch. In trying to decide how to write the story, I went with normal with a zombie reveal at the end. I wondered how on earth that could be portrayed in a film, and decided that the only way to do it would be to tell it twice. First time round everything seems normal until the midwife bites then fast rewind, and play the whole thing again but with zombies included second time around.

So here, to prove I have done my due diligence in the zombie genre, are my thoughts on the subject. Some you may have seen, some may be highlighted for your 'to watch' list, others you may disagree with, but I had to share; it's a passion of mine.

When I was a young adult, I didn't like zombie films, and refused to watch them. Friends would say 'yeah, but you must watch this one, it's really good, you'll love it,' and I would refuse, freaked out by the mere concept of zombies. Then something changed. I think the first zombie film I actually sat down and watched was Dawn of the Dead, 1978, by George A. Romero. To say I completely revised my opinion would be something of an understatement. I began a love affair with all things zombie culture. There are very many zombie films out there, and I have seen a good proportion of them, and have most of the rest queued up to watch. Then there are the zombie TV series, which are mostly also good. Anyway, even the truly awful zombie films can be entertaining in their own way, but this is about the material that I personally, consider to be the best of the genre.

I loved Dawn of the Dead so much because it was set in a shopping mall. I think Romero was a predictive genius when he made that. Our modern day shopping malls [somewhere I absolutely refuse to go, unless I really really have to] are filled with people, who shamble about, knocking into each other, in a kind of brainless shuffle, not knowing what they are doing there, aside from milling about and being seen. No wonder zombies want to eat brains; they have none of their own. I feel Romero saw into the future, and made zombie films as a parody of what mankind is becoming. So kitsch and seventies though it is, Dawn of the Dead will always be one of my top favourites. Apparently Romero forgot to copyright the first film, Night of the Living Dead 1968, so stills from that are amongst the few available for use when writing about the genre. There are six titles in Romero's Dead genre, the others being; Day of the Dead, Land of the Dead, which is my second favourite of his zombie films, Diary of the Dead, and Survival of the Dead.

I am also rather partial to the zombie comedy film, and there have been some most excellent contributions in this field. The first one I saw was Shaun of the Dead, 2004, by Edgar Wright and starring Simon Pegg. I knew immediately, that for me at least, the mixture of zombies and comedy was an absolute winner. But my favourite zombie comedy film was the more recent Warm Bodies, 2013 by Jonathan Levine. This not only combined zombie apocalypse with comedy, but also made the story a classic Romeo and Juliet love story too, even keeping some of the names. I laughed lots and enjoyed it immensely, on all kinds of levels. The TV series In the Flesh, also has a strong comedy element, though it was advertised as being rather dark. I think that is the real winning feature of zombie comedy; it is dark, it has gore aplenty, but it makes you laugh too. It isn't as over the top as the Troma films, though Quentin Tarantino dipped into that area with Planet Terror, one of the two films in Grindhouse, but that was supposed to be that way. You really have to watch Grindhouse to see what he was doing there; no amount of poncey writing about it will do it justice, the man was making art.

The Serpent and the Rainbow 1988, by Wes Craven, diverts from the usual zombie formula, and ventures into the world of voodoo, where real life [undead] zombies are made by the use of a powdered drug. It is a powerful and dramatic film in its own right, but defines the beginnings of actual zombie from human. All the other films have supposition scenarios, usually a killer virus or animal transmission; but the Serpent and the Rainbow has a plot based on real cases, that have actually been documented. It gives it an extra edge of scary, and the buried alive scene will haunt you forever. You may leave the film wanting to write a will Victorian style, that states you have a bell connected to your coffin that you can ring if you wake up buried alive.

28 Days Later, 2002 by Danny Boyle, introduced the fast zombie. That increased their scariness exponentially. Previously, zombies had been slow shambling things that could be run away from, until you were ready to destroy their heads with a gun, axe, poker or just about any other implement you liked really. The only danger was losing track of how many there were around you and getting surrounded by zombies who subsequently overwhelm you and chomp down on your sweet meaty flesh. But fast zombies are scary. How fast can you run? How good are your barricade defences? How well can you hide? Much more difficult. 28 Weeks Later, 2007, by Juan Carlos

Fresnadillo, continued the story but across much wider ground. It was a kind of post apocalyptic road trip in zombie land. It was nothing like the first film, but good in its own right.

I Am Legend, 2007 by Francis Lawrence, starring Will Smith, continued the idea of fast zombies in post viral apocalypse. The zombies in that film were pretty frightening, but the film itself was artistic. Scenes of the city overgrown with plants, and wildlife running free from the zoos, while the zombies mostly hid until any prey came near, were a joy to watch. The characters were fully developed and one actually grew to like them, unusually, one of them being a dog. The zombies seemed somewhat more intelligent than they had been in other films before. All making for a pretty freaky mix, and super compelling watch.

Zombieland, 2009 by Ruben Fleischer, starring Woody Harrelson, was a very funny zombie road movie. It had a certain uniqueness about it, but I think that was down to a very good script. The acting was good too, with a small role featuring Bill Murray, the icing on the cake. Going to a theme park full of zombies was a great ending.

My final favourite zombie film was World War Z, 2013, by Marc Forster, starring Brad Pitt. I waited for this one to come out with nearly baited breath, and it did not fail to live up to, and then exceed my expectations. A great post apocalyptic all action story, with some really disturbing zombie scenes. The bit where the zombies pile into Jerusalem was just amazing. This one will be near the top of the favourites list for some time to come I think.

But I must not forget my current favourite; the TV series, The Walking Dead. Sheer brilliance. It is the highlight of my viewing week. It has the post apocalyptic storyline that is similar to Survivors of so many years ago. It has characters you grow to love. Then to top things off it has zombies and lots of gore, but not enough to get silly and be Troma. There is a realistic shortage of bullets and weapons, so on a day to day basis, zombies need to be dispatched in more gruesome ways. Not to mention the fact that the noise of gunfire attracts more zombies, so crossbows, swords, knives, machetes, pokers and other gore making weapons are the order of the day. They can't make enough series of this for my vote, it will never be too many. More recently iZombie and Z Nation have come along too. Both funny, in different ways, and both compelling. Z Nation even has a zom-baby which is rather different. One of my favourite zombie/baby quirks was a film where a zombie father was still carrying his baby on a chest pouch, occasionally eating part of it like a horse with a nose bag- built in take away. Obviously this list is not exhaustive, it will be out of date before I even finish this book. There are thousands of zombie films out there, most of them rather bad actually, but the occasional gem shines out, even amongst the B-movies. I doubt I'll ever write a full length zombie novel, but you never know.

This story was inspired by the bedroom ceiling in the place where I lived at the time of writing. I have lain in bed many a time, sick or meditating, or just being lazy, and looked at it. The collection of brown spots leads me to examine their arrangement and set my imagination wondering as to what they might be. This was what came out of those imaginings.

The Ceiling

Anna lay in bed with Steve and looked up at the ceiling. "Do you reckon you might get time to paint that ceiling this weekend? If so, I'll start moving furniture out on Friday so there is just the mattress to move, and the wardrobe to cover with a sheet, along with dust sheets over the carpets. That way you can get an early start and we can get back in there to sleep on Saturday night. What do you reckon?"

"I suppose so," said Steve, somewhat reluctantly. But the paint and roller were bought and the job did need doing. There really wasn't any getting out of it.

Anna looked at the ceiling again, covered in little brown spots, like someone had had some sort of fit while holding a cup of coffee, and managed to spray the ceiling with tiny brown dots. There were tiny cracks in the old paint as well, which would definitely benefit from a fresh coat of paint. The overall colour of the ceiling could really only be described as yellowed; the sort of look walls got when people had been smoking in the room for years. Anna sighed.

"Okay, great. I'll definitely move the furniture on Friday then."

The weekend was a blur of furniture moving, aching muscles, paint and fumes, more furniture moving, and a couple of long soothing soaks in the bath for both of them. Finally they lay in bed on Sunday night and looked at the ceiling. It was pristine and white, and looked lovely. Anna sighed with contentment before they turned the lights out and fell asleep; the faint smell of fresh emulsion paint lingering in the air.

On Wednesday evening they made love. As they rolled apart afterwards, Anna looked up at the ceiling. She gasped in shock as she noticed a smattering of brown dots which had appeared on the newly painted ceiling.

"Oh my God, look at the ceiling Steve. Those brown dots are back. How can they be? You can see them can't you? I'm surely not hallucinating."

Steve opened his eyes from his trance like state of bliss with more than a modicum of reluctance. To his horror, he could see the brown spots as well.

"Yes, I see them. What the heck? I put two coats of paint on, how are they showing through?"

"I think they show up even more against the fresh white paint."

By the weekend, the number of brown spots had increased. They seemed to almost form a shadow over each side of the bed, mimicking the bodies that lay below in bed.

"It's like we are breathing out some sort of spores that stick on the ceiling," said Anna, more annoyed than perplexed, but only just.

"I've got a mate who's a decorator. I'll ask him if he can pop round and have a look at it," said Steve. "Maybe he can tell us what it is and what to do about it. Maybe you're right and we need some sort of anti fungal treatment. God I hope not."

The following Saturday morning, Steve's mate Jim came round to have a look at the ceiling. He peered at it, then climbed on a kitchen chair and ran his finger over one of the dots and sniffed.

"I have no idea what it is, never seen anything like it mate. It doesn't smell like mould, so that's probably a good thing. What I recommend is that you buy some anti bacterial and anti fungal treatments and test patch a little area with a cloth. See if anything makes it go away. You could try lemon, vinegar, borax. Heck I'd test patch it with everything I could think of, and see if anything worked. Okay, you'll end up with a bunch of weird smears on the ceiling, but let's face it, when you get it sorted you'll have to paint over it again anyway."

Steve groaned, "I'll call you back to do the job when we get to that point I think. Once was quite enough."

"Let me know how you get on. If nothing works, you might want to call in the environmental health officer to have a look at it."

For the next fortnight, Steve and Anna test patched the ceiling with every product they could think of. The strangest thing was, everything, including plain water, got the marks off, which at first left the couple elated that they had so easily found a solution to their problem. But then within a day or two, they were back. If anything the overall amount of marks and the proximity to each other was increasing. Whole patches of the ceiling were beginning to turn brown.

Anna decided it was time to book an appointment with the environmental health officer. They had to go into his office at the town hall in the first instance and explain the problem to him. Anna had taken a collection of photos on her phone and showed them to the environmental health officer as they discussed the problem, and the actions they had taken so far. The officer looked perplexed and agreed to come and look at the ceiling in person the following week. Anna made an appointment for the visit and left.

The next day Anna and Steve both went down with a cold that was doing the rounds. By that evening both their noses were bunged up and they couldn't taste their food or say their 'm' or 'n's properly.

"I'b going to have ad early dight," said Anna through layers of mucus.

"Be too," agreed Steve, "I feel like crap."

They both slept on their backs, mouth breathing and snoring. In the morning Anna woke up feeling dreadful. She went into the bathroom and noticed a brown sticky substance around her mouth and on her face. She washed it off and brushed her teeth, even though the process of doing so felt like being suffocated, due to nose breathing not being an option. She went back into the bedroom to take a coffee to Steve, and noticed that his face was in the same state that hers had been. She woke him and sent him to the bathroom after telling him about it. He cleaned up groggily and came back into the bedroom to find Anna staring at the ceiling. The brown dots were slowly dripping whatever it was, and that was obviously what had collected on their exposed, upturned faces in the night.

"We should duct tape a sheet of plastic over that to contain it," ventured Steve.

"Yes," agreed Anna, "it will ruin the bedding. I'm going to have to change it all as it is."

And so they taped plastic sheeting to the ceiling, and changed the bed, then sat down in the other room with hot lemon drinks and medicine and tried to ignore the problem.

The next morning, the plastic sheet was bulging with brown liquid and the tape was beginning to peel away at the edges.

"Oh my God, how are we going to deal with that?" asked Anna.

"Well we could cut a hole in the middle and drain it into buckets and bowls and then put a fresh sheet up, or we could try and empty it from one corner and hope it holds," answered Steve, scratching his head.

"I think we should move the bed into the living room first, and put some plastic down over the carpet; it's bound to spill over whatever we do."

So they moved the bed, put down plastic and collected together all the bowls and buckets they could find. Steve made a small cut with a craft knife then backed away quickly, while Anna held the first bucket underneath. Steve was ready with a washing up bowl, and they swapped back and forth until the plastic was drained. The containers of liquid covering the bedroom floor smelt awful, and Anna and Steve were both gagging as they emptied them down the toilet and flushed and rinsed. On the last bowl, Anna had the idea to pour some into a sealed bottle to give to the environmental health officer for testing. They taped up some fresh plastic and threw the old stuff away. They decided to leave the floor covered and the buckets and bowls in the bedroom, and sleep in the living room for now. They collected the clothes they needed and opened the window and shut the door with a shudder.

The next day they repeated the process except this time, worryingly, there were small flakes of ceiling plaster in the liquid. Fortunately the environmental health officer was visiting later that morning.

When he saw how much the problem had worsened since he saw pictures on Anna's phone, he immediately ran upstairs to the flat above and started pounding on their door. Anna found him in the external hallway phoning the police, fire brigade and council. She offered him the sample bottle of liquid, which he took and put away for later testing.

"When was the last time you saw your upstairs neighbours?" asked the officer.

"I don't know, aren't they answering their door?"

"No they aren't. Who lives there anyway?"

"An old couple I think. To be honest we don't see them much. They go up and down in the lift and every now and then I might see them getting in or out of a cab outside, but other than that we never see them. They don't make any noise either; we never hear a peep out of them. Do you think they have had some kind of flood that is coming through?"

"It's hard to say at this point, but we certainly need to get in there and find out. If I was you, I'd stay out of the bedroom for a while, and stay indoors; it might get a bit busy here in the hallway."

Anna went to the living room window and watched as the street outside filled up with emergency services vehicles, and council vans. Then she heard a terrifically loud banging noise as they used a tool to break the front door down to the flat upstairs. For a while there was the sound of feet thumping about above, then a coroners van pulled up outside, and finally two body bags were loaded into the back of the van. There was some further banging as the council boarded up the door temporarily and left, the emergency services and coroner already having left earlier. Finally, the environmental health officer came back down to Anna looking rather pale.

"Do you have anyone you can go and stay with for a few days?"

"No, our family are all abroad."

"The council will put you up in a hotel for a few days then."

"Why? What has happened?"

"Err, the old couple upstairs had apparently died in their beds," began the officer.

"Oh how horrible," said Anna sinking into a chair.

"Err yes, but that was some time ago. I don't want to upset you too much, but they had been dead a long time; they had decomposed lying in bed. The liquid seeping through your ceiling had come through the mattress and their floor, and then your ceiling. That is what was dripping through into your bedroom. We'll need to thoroughly decontaminate both flats and put in a new ceiling, which is why you need to stay in a hotel for a few days."

Anna thought about the morning they had woken up with the stuff all over their faces. They had had the remains of old people in their mouths, had likely swallowed it in their sleep. Anna threw up.

Foreword
As a child I had a fairly impressive collection of snow
globes. Gradually over many years, the fluid in them
seems to go down. Of course I couldn't resist the urge to
break the seal, where possible and top them up with
water. They never seemed to be the same afterwards. I
had standard snow scenes with white stuff that you shook,
and others made of glitter. I had some with animals inside
and others with buildings, souvenirs of a certain city. Some
had parts that moved along a track to and fro. There was a
great variety of the things even back then. The collection
has long since been left behind somewhere in my distant
past, but I am still drawn to the things, nasty little pieces of
kitsch that they are. I still have an urge to start the
collection over again, despite the fact that I have no room
for them. I was looking at one with a lizard inside [another
thing I tend to collect representations of anyway, so it was
a crossover] recently in Spain, and honestly, I came very
close to buying it. Somehow I resisted, and wrote this story
instead. But now it's finished I just want one even more!

The Snow Globes
Danni stopped in the aisle of the gift shop, her attention
drawn to the shelf of snow globes, which seemed to glitter
and shimmer and sparkle in front of her; drawing her eyes
to them irresistibly. She had never given them a thought
before. She knew of their existence of course, who didn't?
But they were just something she had never really noticed.
Here, in this gift shop though, they seemed to have a life
of their own. She was pretty sure no one else had been in
the aisle before her; the shop was almost empty. She
knew for certain that she hadn't touched the little
ornaments, or even knocked into the shelf; yet one of the
globes had its snow of white, silver and golden glitter
floating around as if someone had just given it a good
shake. Inside the globe, as Danni peered at it, was a town
scene, dominated by a church with a clock tower, with little
houses either side of it. The houses were tall and thin,

typical of the houses around her in Amsterdam, where she was currently holidaying.

At the end of the street a tiny figure of a man in a long black coat was walking towards the church. For some reason she could not explain to herself, Danni decided to buy the little ornament as a souvenir. It was only four Euros, and she just had this overwhelming feeling that she didn't want to leave it on the shelf and walk out of the shop. Somehow, this strange thing had to come home with her.

When she got home and unpacked, she found the gift wrapped globe, and unwrapped it and put it on the dresser in the living room. As the dresser was against the opposite wall to the television, Danni had her back to it most of the time she was in the room, and didn't give the object any more thought. She didn't notice that the snow somehow never seemed to completely settle; just kept gently swirling.

The next day Danni's friend Sarah rang her.

"Hi Danni, do you want to come to the Christmas market with me today?"

"Hi Sarah, yes why not, it'll be fun. We can get lunch at one of those little foreign stalls."

"Not to mention the mulled wine and egg nog."

"Okay, I'll meet you at the bus station in about an hour, okay?"

"Great, see you soon."

Danni got dressed in a thick coat, hat and scarf, as it was a bitingly cold day, and made her way to the appointed meeting spot. The girls had a great time exploring the market and buying little gifts for friends and family. They had lunch in a large shed arranged to look like some sort of Austrian mountain lodge. They both had a kind of hot dog with sauerkraut and chips, and a beaker of hot mulled wine. After lunch they wandered round some more of the stalls, messed about on the little ice rink, then had egg nog and sweet waffles coated with pink sugar icing. They were just about to call it a day and go home, when Danni spotted several more stalls, tucked round the back behind the ice rink, selling gifts and knick-knacks.

They drifted apart as they browsed the items on display. Suddenly Danni spotted a small collection of snow globes, all on a Christmas theme. Once again, she found herself inexplicably drawn to stand and stare at them. One in particular caught her eye. It was a snow scene of a couple ski-ing down a mountain towards a little brightly lit up house with a sparking Christmas tree outside, its coloured lights seeming to twinkle as they caught the light coming into the globe. Danni thought the Christmas aspect was nicely understated, and the globe could sit on the dresser year round without looking out of place. As she bought it, she thought to herself that she was turning into one of those people who got old, and had a collection of hundreds of similar ornaments dotted around their houses. She shuddered at the thought that she was going to become the snow globe lady, and resolved to not buy any more of the things. She didn't even tell Sarah she had bought anything when she found her a couple of minutes later at another stall.

"Do you want to come round to mine for a cup of tea?" Danni asked Sarah.

"Yes, that would be nice. Let's get indoors and warm up." Danni left Sarah in her living room, while she went to the kitchen to make the tea. But when she came through with the teas a few minutes later, there was no sign of Sarah anywhere.

'How rude,' Danni thought to herself. Sarah must have decided to go home after all. Perhaps something urgent had come up, but it would only have taken a moment to call out goodbye. Danni drank her tea and unpacked her shopping, still absent mindedly wondering why Sarah had rushed off like that.

She unwrapped the new snow globe and went over to the dresser to place it beside the one from Amsterdam. Strangely, the Amsterdam street scene was an absolute blizzard. The church and houses could barely be seen, let alone any little people. Danni thought that Sarah must have shaken it before she rushed off. She gave the new one a shake before placing it on the dresser so snow was falling on them both. Danni finished unpacking and putting things away, then had another look at the globes before going up for a soak in the bath. The snow had almost stopped in both globes, and Danni could see that the Amsterdam globe contained two figures; a man in a black coat striding down the street, and a woman, wrapped up in warm coat and hat who seemed to be rushing to catch him up. Strange, Danni thought, she had not noticed the woman before, and the man seemed to be nearer the church than she remembered. She shrugged and thought no more of it and went for her bath.

Soon Christmas arrived, and Danni had a whirlwind social life of dinners with the family, and invites to parties. Strangely she had not heard from Sarah since the day they went shopping; she didn't seem to be answering her phone or texts.

On New Year's Eve, in the afternoon, Danni's Aunt popped round for a visit, and to leave a belated Christmas gift under Danni's tree. They talked for a while, then the Aunt left suddenly, while Danni was in the toilet, which Danni thought was most strange behaviour; especially since they had been having such a good time.

Out of curiosity, she opened the gift left under her tree, alone because all the other gifts had long since been given or unwrapped. The tag read, 'A little bird told me you had started collecting these!'

Danni was surprised to find yet another snow globe; this one depicting a fairly busy Trafalgar Square in London, the centre piece being a woman feeding a flock of pigeons that almost covered her upper body, in front of Nelson's column. When she went to put it with the others, she noticed once again, that the snow in them was falling. Her Aunt must have given them a shake before she left. She shook the London globe and added it to the collection.

Peering into the snowy midst of the ski slope globe, Danni could have sworn there were more skiers than before, but she laughed at herself for imagining such an impossibility. As if tiny people could climb into the globes in the night, they were sealed shut to prevent leakages; she laughed, aloud, and with just a hint of madness.

Spring came around and Danni didn't give the snow globes any more thought, but she did wonder what had happened to Sarah who seemed to have disappeared without a trace the previous winter. Come to think of it, she had not heard from her Aunt since New Year either. It was all rather odd, them both leaving in such a rush and then apparently disappearing. The last she had seen of either of them was them standing in her living room looking at the snow globe from Amsterdam. Danni went over to look at the globes once more. The woman was still chasing after the man in black, but seemed also to be looking sideways, out of the globe, towards Danni. There seemed to be something familiar about the way she looked. Just as Danni was leaning in for a closer look, her doorbell rang. On the doorstep stood two neatly dressed women.

"We wonder if you have a moment to talk about Jesus?" asked one of them.

"Err," said Danni, realising she had opened the door to Jehovah's Witnesses, and now had to find a way to back out of the situation politely.

"Do you believe that Jesus Christ is your saviour?" asked the second woman, before Danni had a chance to think of anything else.

"Yes," replied Danni, still trying to think of a way to shut the door.

"Oh that's wonderful," gushed the first woman.

"May we come in for a few minutes and show you this leaflet?" asked the second woman, waving a colourful flier in front of Danni's face.

"I suppose so," said Danni, not really knowing how to get rid of them, "but you'll have to be quick, I have to go out somewhere soon."

"Absolutely, we'll just take a moment of your time then," said the first woman, as they both came into the house. Danni showed them through to the living room. The second woman began to cough, trying desperately to smother it, as if the mere act of coughing was an offence to Jehovah himself.

"Can I get you a glass of water?" Danni asked.

"Oh thank you dear, that would be very kind."

Danni went out to the kitchen and took her time pouring out two glasses of water. She was really trying to think of a way to get rid of them quickly without being rude. How exactly had she got to the point of letting them into her home, she wondered.

It was no good, she would just have to go in there and be blunt if necessary. She took a deep breath and marched into her own living room.

It was empty. There was no sign of the Jehovah's Witness women. Danni had not heard them leave. They would not leave just like that; it wasn't as if she had a poster of Satan on her living room wall or anything. She almost looked behind the sofa and went upstairs to check they weren't hiding somewhere, ready to jump out and preach at her when she was least expecting it. Then she noticed the snow globes, all three furious snowstorms in progress.

The Jehovah's Witnesses definitely wouldn't have shaken the snow globes. They probably thought such things sinful or something.

Danni peered into their stormy depths until they gradually settled. She looked at them really closely, closer than she ever had before.

There on the steps of Trafalgar Square, behind the pigeon feeding woman to the right, were two women holding papers of some sort. As Danni looked closely at them, she could swear they were looking at each other confused; and they looked exactly like the two women who just moments before had been in her living room. Danni peered closely at the ski slope globe. Yes the woman on her own at the back did look like her Aunt. In the original globe, the woman chasing the man in black bore an uncanny resemblance to Sarah.

It was impossible, thought Danni. But she decided to put the globes away in a cupboard, out of sight, anyway; at least until someone she didn't like came to visit. Maybe she should buy some more globes, just in case.

The Girl Upstairs

Mavis lived in a flat. It was a very nice flat, a little on the small side perhaps, but it had a terrific view of the sea, and a communal garden that someone else tended. When she first moved in, she really thought she had landed on her feet. She was in the centre of town, easy walking distance from everything, and the rent and utilities were cheap. But by the middle of the second week, Mavis was beginning to wonder if she had made a terrible mistake. Unpacking could be a noisy business, boxes clumped down on the floor heavily, coat hangers and plates clattered, nails needed banging into the wall for pictures, and flat pack furniture did not build itself. She realised that it must be pretty annoying to the man downstairs, all the noise of settling in happening right above his head, and sound did seem to travel easily in the flats; she could hear him when he yawned. But he did not seem, in her opinion, to be being very reasonable about it. Every noise Mavis made, he responded to by banging on the ceiling with his stick. Mavis tried to ignore it, sometimes calling out, "Sorry, just moving in, won't be long." At other times she just sighed and pretended it wasn't happening.

But it didn't stop after she had settled and finished with all the upheaval. Every time she put on music or the television, he banged. When the washing machine was used, he banged. When Mavis got something out of the grill and the tray clattered, he banged. She found herself trying to do everything quieter and quieter, turning the volume on the television down until she could barely hear it. If a car went by outside, she missed what the people on TV were saying. She started doing her washing at the local launderette, and eating snack food and takeaways more and more often. She stopped listening to music altogether. She had completely given up playing the violin, which she wasn't too bad at, but hadn't even dared get the thing out of its case since she moved in.

But instead of getting better, things actually got worse. The man downstairs started to bang when Mavis just walked around the flat in her slippered feet, or when she flushed the toilet, or ran a shower. She was getting to the point where she only washed once a week, and then with a flannel, and a jug of water for washing her hair. She only flushed the toilet twice a day, and mostly just sat and read, or listened to music and watched films through headphones on her computer. But even when she typed messages on social media, he started banging as she tapped at the keys. She pressed each key more slowly so it made no noise at all. Mavis was starting to have trouble sleeping, and was having trouble with her job as an online tutor for a correspondence course. If she had to do online tuition and speak with students live, they would often enquire as to the origin of the banging noise in the background. Mavis had taken to pretending it wasn't happening, or that she couldn't hear it.

Then the new guy moved in upstairs from Mavis. He played guitar in a band, and the noise of him rehearsing was horrendous. He wasn't even very good. Mavis tried to ignore it, and put earplugs in to get what little sleep she could. But the man downstairs could hear it too, and responded by banging on her ceiling even more. Of course it didn't make any difference to the guy upstairs, he carried right on, blindly ignoring everything else.

The man downstairs started drinking heavily around this time. That was when things really escalated. After he had had enough alcohol to completely lose control, he would start shouting things. Mostly it was "You're dead, f**king dead," and "You c**t, you f**king c**t, I'll kill you." This was accompanied by loud animal growling type noises and frequent banging on the ceiling and walls with a stick or heavy object. He knew Mavis' name because she had left a box of chocolates and a note on his doorstep when she first moved in, by way of a friendly hello, and an apology for any inconvenience her moving in may have caused. Sometimes he would add her name into the shouting, and mix it up with some other swear words and threats too. To start with, this only went on for a couple of hours until he passed out unconscious drunk, and Mavis could finally relax and enjoy a few hours peace and quiet.

Later on though, it became longer and longer binges. The worst times were when he started shouting and banging at three in the morning, waking Mavis up. She would lie in bed shivering with fear; not because she was especially afraid of him, but because it was a terrifying way to wake up. She had read that it was an accepted torture method to wake people in the night by frightening them. She did not dare get up to go to the bathroom in case he heard her moving about. He would escalate the shouting if he knew he had an audience and was getting a response.

It went on for months and months. Mavis got sick and lost her job. She was depressed and couldn't sleep, but worst of all she was afraid to go out, so she couldn't even get away from him. She was beginning to be at her wits end, and genuinely feared for her sanity.

A couple of times he came upstairs and banged on her front door shouting in the middle of the night. Mavis didn't answer of course. She wanted to get up and phone the police, but she was too frightened to move. She lay in bed, terrified and wept quietly.

The next day she went online and searched around a few sites. In the end she settled on a machete, and bought it for next day delivery. She just felt she needed something in the flat for self defence as things seemed to be escalating out of control and she felt very vulnerable. She had taken to buying her groceries online, and had all her bills set up via online banking. She was beginning to forget what outside, other than the view from her windows, looked like. Sometimes she would open one of her windows for a while, just to breathe some fresh, outside air.

Then one night she awoke at four in the morning. The man downstairs was shouting her name over and over, "Mavis, Mavis, Mavis," he growled loudly, "I'm gonna kill you, you're f**king dead, you c**t." It went on and on, he was obviously settling in for a long night of hostility. Something inside Mavis just snapped. She jumped out of bed and put on jeans and a t-shirt, then added her biggest noisiest boots with thick soles- a remnant from her younger Goth days. She stamped and banged on the floor over and over again, sounding like a herd of small elephants trampling through the bedroom. The man downstairs went quiet for a minute then started banging about, slamming doors. Mavis grabbed the machete and stood behind her front door as she heard him stomping up the stairs to bang on her door. The look of surprise on his face when she threw open the door was priceless; it made Mavis break into a weird and twisted grin that she couldn't control. The man downstairs actually looked a bit taken aback and lost for words. Mavis grabbed him by the front of his shirt and dragged him into her flat, kicking the door shut behind her. Before he could collect himself and say anything at all, she swung the machete in a big arc that came down on the side of his neck, slicing into the flesh and embedding itself in his spinal column. The man downstairs had a second or two to register what was happening and look genuinely confused, before blood started to spurt out from his carotid artery and his legs gave out all at once dropping him to the floor in an ungainly heap. Mavis stood over him growling quietly, repeating "You're dead, you're dead, you're dead. Not me, you. Hah."

It was all over very quickly. The man downstairs would bang, curse and threaten, no more. Mavis realised she had a busy night ahead of her. She dragged the man into her bathroom, and manoeuvred him into her bath. Then she washed her hands and put on a pair of washing up gloves, and crept out of her flat and down the stairs. No one was about, and the night was completely and blissfully silent. She had not set foot outside her flat in months, but she wasn't even giving that fact a passing thought. She let herself into the flat of the man downstairs, as the door was not locked. She touched as few things as she possibly could, despite the gloves, and turned off all the lights and appliances, which included the television, computer, radio and heating. She turned the volume on the telephone ringer down to almost nothing, and picked up his mobile phone. After a moment or two of looking around, she found a dish with his door keys and picked them up. She also found a jumper, coat and his stick- the offensive item that had caused so much banging. She quietly left the flat and locked the front door behind her, getting back to her own flat as quickly as she could. Now, to all intents and purposes, it looked as if the man downstairs had gone out somewhere, and had not come back.

Shutting and locking her own front door behind her, she breathed a sigh of relief. Then Mavis got busy. She found a bottle of bleach and some black bin bags under the sink in the kitchen. She went into the bathroom and put the bleach and bags down. She wrestled and wriggled the machete until it came out of the bone. Then she hung the man downstairs' head over the edge of the bath and hacked at it a few times with the machete until it dropped onto the floor. She paused for a moment, waiting for the banging of a stick in response to the loud noise, then saw the head looking up at her and realised no response was going to be forthcoming. The head had a ridiculous expression on its face and Mavis suddenly got the giggles. Gradually the giggles faded and Mavis collected herself. She badly needed a pee after all that giggling but that head was going in a bin bag first. No way was she peeing with that thing staring at her. That started her off giggling again, and she flung the head into a bag and sat down on the loo to pee before she wet herself. Finally, for the time being, she lopped the hands off the corpse and added them to the bin bag. She put the bin bag in a holdall, took off the gloves, put on a heavy coat with a hood, grabbed her keys and went out; stepping carefully in the hall to avoid treading in any of the spilt blood.

She walked along the promenade until she reached the marina and walked out onto the sea wall. She was enjoying herself so much being out for a walk in the crisp night air. She had stopped at the beach to pick up a few large pebbles which were in her coat pockets. It was a beautiful clear night and the stars twinkled in the night sky. The full moon gave her plenty of light even though the street lights had gone off and it was still dark. Mavis opened the holdall, and made a small gash in the black plastic bag that she had tied in a knot. She slipped the stones in with the grizzly contents then threw the whole thing into the sea, where it sank immediately. The walk back home was even more enjoyable.

After she had relaxed and had a cup of tea, the next job was to get rid of the smelly stuff. Carefully, she cut the man downstairs open from gullet to belly, making sure not to go too deep, so as not to nick any of the intestines. She reached in, gloves most definitely back on, and cut the colon just before the exit point, pinching it together hard, so none of the contents could escape. She pulled and pulled until she had enough tubing to reach to the toilet, where she used a large hair clip to fasten the end to the bowl, while she retrieved the other end. Finally it was all arranged; throat end stretched over the cold tap of the sink, anus end held firmly over the loo, Mavis turned on the cold tap and rinsed the digestive tract until the water ran clean. She gave the toilet a flush from time to time. Then using the machete, she cut the offal and tubes into small pieces and flushed those too.

The dirtiest task complete, Mavis used the machete to sever arms and legs, putting each in a separate bin bag and taping then shut with duct tape. The eviscerated torso went into a final bag. Three full holdalls sat in her hallway ready for dispatch. The bathroom was easy to hose down and bleach, but the hall took hours of work to get the carpet to the point where it could be left dumped beside a town bin somewhere. The hall would need redecorating, and there was a busy night of walking to the marina ahead of her. Mavis thought she would sleep all day to prepare. But before that, she thought she would have a nice big celebration breakfast. After breakfast, she just had to play her violin for a bit before she went to bed and slept soundly and happily all day long.

Afterword

The previous story was largely based on a real neighbour who lives underneath me and is an abusive alcoholic, who I have had to resort to taking to court. Hand on heart, I can honestly say I have thought about the details of murdering him and disposing of the body many times, but thought is not deed and the obnoxious man still lives and breathes. I did write him into my novel Malbed Mews as a character, and killed him off there, but this, rather more in depth short story, was the catharsis I needed to get it out of my system. I can tell you, I breathed a happy, satisfied sigh when I finished writing it, and am okay again now, thanks to authoring therapy.

Flying Between Worlds

Tammy and Jon had been taking a package holiday abroad, once a year for about a decade. They flew from Gatwick, usually to somewhere in Europe with a top flight time of about four or five hours. More often than not, they would go to a self catering apartment on a hotel complex in Greece or Spain. It was cheap, easy, and of a fairly acceptable and consistent standard. It was pretty much all they wanted out of their annual holiday; sun, sea, foreign food and the freedom to do what they wanted, when they wanted.

It was shortly after one such holiday, when they were coming home from the airport. Tammy noticed that the advertising hoardings at the stations they went through seemed a bit different.

"Did you notice these advert boards when we left? I'm sure they were all advertising books, and underwear. Now they all seem to be about food. I get that they change them regularly, but it seems a bit odd that the topics have completely changed don't you think?"

"Can't say I'd noticed them either way really," replied Jon. "But people certainly seem grumpier since we got back, and fatter. There were tons of fat grumpy people at the airport and station. I noticed that."

"There did seem to be an awful lot of really obese people in motorised wheelchairs. They seemed to be everywhere. I did notice that. And they didn't seem to care who they bashed into, very rude."

They did not give it a great deal more thought, until they got home. They were watching the news on television, whilst eating a takeaway. A news story came on about a library in a nearby town that was closing down and being turned into a sports centre with a trendy restaurant on the roof.

"That's weird," said Jon, puzzled. "I could have sworn that library received an arts grant just before we went away, to restore the building and get some new books."

"I think you're right, I remember that too," answered Tammy.

"I'll have a look online through the search engines, and see if I can find out what happened. Perhaps the grant fell through."

Despite a great deal of searching, and putting different words in the search; Jon could not find any record of the library in question ever having received any sort of grant. All the information he found suggested it had been headed towards a venue change for the last few years.

Tammy and Jon were puzzled, but decided they must have both got it wrong somewhere along the line. They decided to watch the DVD of their favourite film The Matrix, instead of unpacking.

Shortly after that, Jon got a promotion, and was allowed to work from home. As long as he sat at his computer for a certain amount of time per day, had online conferences, and did the paperwork, he could do pretty much whatever he liked. Tammy's job went over to flexi time and she changed to part time hours as well. The result was they had more money, and more free time. Consequently, they started to travel more often, slotting three to five day city breaks in amongst their now more frequent, package holiday excursions.

They started to notice that more and more often when they got back from their travels, things had changed in the world in one way or another. All kinds of things, from tiny every day, personal things, to worldwide events and news. Tammy had formed a theory, which had started out as a joke, but was beginning to look more and more believable. She decided to share it with Jon one day.

"I think that whenever we go up to thirty five thousand feet in an aeroplane, you know, when you look down and can see the curvature of the earth; we somehow break the tie with earth. You know the theory put forward by some sci-fi writers, which seems to be getting more and more popular in films and series by the way, that there are multiple copies of our world, all existing very close together, kind of like different matrixes? Well I think that sometimes when we fly we come back down into one of the adjacent worlds, a slightly different matrix if you like. That's why sometimes things seem to have changed that shouldn't have when we get home."

Tammy was quite surprised that Jon didn't laugh in her face, but instead looked thoughtful for a while. "You know, I think you might be onto something there; that might well be exactly what is happening."

"Seriously?"

"Yes. Sometimes I feel it really strongly, that we have come back to a different place than we left. Sometimes so much is just...different, you know."

They spent the rest of that evening talking about things that were different. Tammy liked to read, and had made a list of books by her favourite authors, that she still wanted to get and hadn't read yet. She had spent hours online searching for her favourite, sometimes obscure, author's full catalogue of titles. She was going through the list online looking to update it, when she discovered that one of the minor author's back catalogue had changed. Some of the titles on her list just didn't seem to exist anymore. They hadn't gone out of print, they just had never been written. Extensive searching for that book title by that author, consistently brought up no results. Tammy was baffled. But she had made the original list a few years ago and had not updated it recently. She thought about it and realised they must have taken about a dozen trips since she made the list. If her 'matrix worlds' theory was to be believed, subtle changes between many worlds had meant that certain titles had never been written in this matrix. Excitedly she shared her findings with Jon.

They began to make lists of other things; obscure bands, films, musicals, events; anything that could be checked. When they travelled they began to ask each other what they thought this matrix might be like; better or worse. Sure enough their list making and fact gathering seemed more and more conclusively to prove the theory.

Meanwhile, their lives got better and better. Jon seemed to be getting promoted all the time and Tammy seemed to earn more for doing less. They moved to a nicer house. Before long they had everything they had wanted when they first got married, and Jon was even able to take early retirement, with a great company pension and plenty in the bank. The night he got that news, he sat down to talk seriously with Tammy.

"It seems to me, we might be in our perfect matrix at this point. I know it sounds absolutely crazy, but I think we should stop flying now, so as not to jinx it. I really want to stay here. I'd hate to end up somewhere worse, or somewhere where things are bad."

"I kind of know what you mean, and I sort of feel the same; but I love travelling. I'd hate to stop exploring the world, especially now we have time and money and can really do it in comfort."

"I feel exactly the same, but I have come up with a plan. How about we book a world cruise? A long one that really takes its time and stops at all the places we want to see, or several, back to back, so we can really see everything in style?"

"That's a great idea- no flying so we stay in this matrix."

"Yup, and I'll be retired, and you can work by just going online every day or so. We could rent out the house so it isn't empty, I think it could really work."

So the couple planned and booked their perfect trip. They started out with a four month round the world trip that sailed from Southampton across to America and down the coast, going through the Panama canal, Asia, then the Suez canal, around the Mediterranean and home to Southampton. Three days later another cruise left from Southampton, taking them around South America and Cape Horn, past the glaciers and up the other side before going across to Australia via Hawaii, then onto Africa and around Cape of Good Hope and back up to the UK. After a week's stay in Southampton, they could join another ship for a cruise up to see the Northern Lights, taking in Scandinavia and the Baltic including Russia. Finally they took a trip around Britain, taking in the Orkneys, Scilly and the Channel islands. The whole itinerary took the better part of a year, and left them thoroughly exhilarated and ready to settle down and stay at home for a while; a long while. Their travel itch was thoroughly scratched, and their curiosity about the big wide world, satisfied.

They had pre-booked a car to take them home from Southampton. It was supposed to be a luxury car, but was more like a taxi, but they were tired and travel worn, and not bothered. The driver chattered on about this and that; veering back to politics often; quite extreme opinions at that. Tammy and Jon exchanged looks and did not engage him other than the odd grunt, and eventually the driver quietened down.

Finally they pulled around the corner to the street where their house was situated, and both simultaneously let out a gasp. Where their house should have been was a blackened, burnt out frame. A 'no entry' sign was stuck on a board on what had been their neatly manicured front lawn.

"Oh my God, our house," cried Tammy.

"Gnarr," grunted Jon.

"Err, do you want me to drop you somewhere else?" asked the driver.

Jon gave him directions to the nearest big hotel chain he could think off, and they got a room there. For a while they were in complete shock, and both had a large drink from the mini bar. Then Jon thought about ringing the insurance company who covered both buildings and contents. Their shock turned to disbelief, as they discovered that their building insurance was invalid, because someone else other than themselves had been living in the house at the time of the fire. Then the contents would not pay because the time period to claim had expired. Finally Tammy called the bank, and was told the council were demanding a large sum of money to clear the destroyed house off of the leased land, which they had taken back due to breach of agreement; i.e. invalid insurance. So it was, they found themselves homeless, with nothing coming in for recompense except a big bill. Later they found out that Jon's company had gone bust and his early pension was no longer going to be honoured. Tammy was about to be laid off, as her company were tightening their belts, and had made no financial contingencies for what they called their peripheral staff.

In short they were almost broke, and homeless. They had to go to the benefits office the next day and get temporary accommodation in a bed and breakfast. It was hard to explain what they had been doing all year, and why they were now claiming benefits.

Later that night as they sat on the bed in their tiny room, with a ridiculous amount of luggage, and Tammy wept, Jon said:

"Well I guess the matrix worlds theory is not just for planes. Apparently it works if you stay at sea for a long time too, and not in a good way."

That just made Tammy howl louder.

Afterword

The previous story was partially based on real experience. We do travel a lot, my partner and I, and I did start to notice weird stuff changing. The book list thing did actually happen too. I came up with the theory of alternate worlds to explain what was going on, some time ago, and it has kind of been a running thing with us ever since. The rest of the story though, and thankfully, is fiction; a sort of what if? I have noticed the adjacent world theory, which I first read about in Clifford D. Simak's Ring Around the Sun, but have seen everywhere since, has become much more prolific in fiction recently. So perhaps more and more people are noticing it.

The Ties That Bind

Gwendolina had been an unusual child from the outset.
She always had a faraway look in her eyes and seemed to
be gazing at something that wasn't there. In that respect
she was very much like the family cat; sometimes both of
them could be found, sitting together, staring at a patch of
plain wall, apparently mesmerised. At times like that, Tina,
her Mum, would have to go into another room and laugh
quietly to herself, because it just looked so funny.
What was not funny, was that at four and a half years old,
Gwendolina still did not speak. All kinds of doctors and
other health professionals had performed tests, and
concluded that there was nothing wrong with Gwendolina,
nothing at all. She was perfectly capable of speech, she
just didn't want to do it. All her physical results were
perfect for a child her age, and the psychologist could find
nothing wrong either. Gwendolina communicated, in her
own unique way, listening to others, absorbing information
from the world around her, bringing things to people to
communicate a point; but she just refused to utter a sound.
She lived in a very quiet world, but she was not deaf
either. Far from it, in fact. If a room was filled with noise,
music, loud voices- real or on television, Gwendolina
would take herself off out of the room and find somewhere
quiet. Even if it meant putting on her coat and shoes and
going out to sit on the step in the garden.
Somehow, Gwendolina had learnt to read. Sure, Tina had
read to her from early days, and held up flash cards with
basic first words on them; but she had given up when
Gwendolina never said any of the words back to her. But
the little girl had picked up the skill anyway, and was often
to be found with her nose buried in a book, alone in her
room. She didn't just read children's books either.
Anything with print on it, she would take away and study;
from cereal boxes to magazines, newspapers to technical
journals. Tina wondered how much of what she stared at
was making any sense in her brain.
At first Tina thought the child must be autistic, but the
doctors had ruled that out. They had told her not to worry,

that Gwendolina would start to speak in her own good time, one day. Tina hoped it would be soon, very soon. As a single parent, she found it weird living in a house with a small child where most of the time silence reigned. When other parents spoke to her of the noise their kids made, Tina secretly wished she lived in a noisy world of chaos caused by Gwendolina. As a baby, noise making toys had been pushed away abandoned. In the end, Tina had given them to a charity shop.

Tina was afraid to send Gwendolina to nursery school, because she knew the noise would upset her too much. Gwendolina showed no desire to interact with other children. In the park, she quickly moved away from the noisy play area and went to look at plants, or watch ducks and squirrels instead. Tina dreaded what would happen when Gwendolina had to start infants school the following year. Hopefully she would be talking by then, or some sort of special arrangements might have to be made- maybe even private tuition. She reassured herself with her online research about children who didn't talk until very late. Apparently Einstein had not uttered a single word until he was four years old. Then there was the joke about the child who didn't talk until he was a teenager, and his first words were to complain about the taste of his pudding. When asked by his parents why he had not spoken until that moment, he replied that until that time, everything had been satisfactory, and there had been no need to speak. Tina had to admit, that watching Gwendolina, she appeared to be a perfectly normal child. She was observant and interested in the world around her, she could read, and write a little too. Sometimes she would draw or paint, and to Tina's eye, the pictures she produced seemed advanced for her age. What really puzzled Tina though about the drawings; was the amount of people in them. Gwendolina's art was always populated with people, often in strange costumes, that Tina was pretty sure they had never met or even seen in real life. She didn't think they were in any of the magazines or books that Gwendolina might have looked at. She wondered if they were characters from the stories she read, or if perhaps,

Gwendolina had a much richer imagination to compensate for not speaking. She had heard that if one sense was lost, another increased to compensate, like people who went blind, having better hearing. But Gwendolina had not lost any of her senses or abilities, she could speak, but just chose not to. And anyway, speaking and imagination were not senses. Tina spent far too much time thinking and worrying about these matters.

One day, when Tina came into the room, Gwendolina was drawing on a sketch pad, whilst staring at the wall. The cat was sitting staring at the same patch of wall. Tina went over to look at what Gwendolina might be drawing, and to her amazement saw a page covered with ornately costumed people in large wigs dancing together. It really was far beyond the talent of a child not yet five.

"Where did you see those people sweetheart?" Tina asked, not expecting an answer.

Gwendolina pointed at the wall that she and the cat had been staring at. Tina was baffled. The wall was plain and there was nothing there, but out of the three beings in the room, she seemed to be the only one who held that opinion.

Things continued in this vein, until Tina felt like she was perhaps the one going a little bit crazy, not seeing things that were obvious to everyone else.

Then one day while Tina sat on the sofa, watching an almost muted television; Gwendolina brought the picture she had been working on over to Tina to show her. Tina looked at it and then gasped. Gwendolina had drawn a near perfect rendition of Tina sitting in the middle of the sofa, and either side of her sat her mother and father. They had been dead since long before Gwendolina was born, and Tina did not keep any pictures of them around the house.

"This is my Mother and Father, your Grandma and Grandpa sweetheart. How did you know what they looked like? It's very good darling."

Gwendolina just pointed at the sofa, either side of Tina, and shrugged.

"You can see them sitting there on the sofa?" Tina asked, confused.

Gwendolina nodded. Tina looked again at the picture. Both her mother and father were looking forwards, smiling. It was as if they were looking directly at Gwendolina and beaming at her, exactly like proud grandparents would. Tina felt herself welling up, and then a big tear over spilled and rolled down her cheek, she just couldn't help herself. Then the miracle happened, Gwendolina spoke.

"Don't cry Mummy, they are very happy, you should be happy too."

Tina felt dizzy, the room seemed to be spinning a little bit. Everything was happening at once. Gwendolina climbed up onto her lap, and brushed away the tears from Tina's cheeks.

"What's wrong Mummy. Grandma and Grandpa are always here, either with you or with me. Why are you crying."

"When we go out do you see other people like Grandma and Grandpa, with other people?"

"Oh yes. Everyone has lots of people with them. It's very busy out there. And in here sometimes too."

"When you look at the wall and see people all dressed up, are they with someone too?"

Gwendolina frowned. "That's different. They are more with the place than with someone. Like from another time or something, not yesterday but a lot of days ago."

"And you think the cat can see them too?"

"Oh yes, he can see them."

"Why didn't you talk until just now, when you know all the words?"

"The people I can see don't talk. They don't need to. I like them, they are always with me. I wanted to be like them, not talking too."

"Not everyone is like you sweetheart. In fact I don't think other people can see all these people; not even other children."

"I know."

"Perhaps you shouldn't tell anyone else about what you can see. You'll be starting school soon, and I don't think anyone would understand. I think you'll have to wait until you grow up to talk about it. Even then, most people won't believe you."

"I know. That's why I didn't talk to you. I didn't think you'd believe me. But then Grandpa and Grandma showed me how to make you understand."

Tina sighed and hugged Gwendolina close. Strange how in a matter of moments, one worry had replaced another. She wondered what strange things the future would hold.

Afterword

This story was born out of a couple of notions that somehow came together. I had heard of people not talking until they were quite old for what is considered normal; in my research for this story I found that it is in fact, quite common. In a lot of cases, the 'until this time, everything was satisfactory' joke, seems to bear fruit. Children who were suddenly put in a situation they were not happy with e.g. left with a childminder, began to speak. Perhaps there is truth in the humour? But that is possibly another story entirely. My other influence was my own experience of ghost sightings, and cats who stare at things that aren't there. My own experiences were a little stranger and darker, and not really relevant to this story, but they did light the spark as it were.

Gemini

Gemini fell asleep on the train and missed her stop. It wasn't the first time she had done that; the cab drivers at Forest Grove station recognised her now, when she sleepily hailed a cab the couple of stops back to her flat. But this wasn't Forest Grove station. She had got off the train before she noticed where she was, and the train had pulled away into the sidings, and Gemini found herself standing on a deserted little platform, seemingly in the middle of nowhere. The sign said, Market Haven, but Gemini had been travelling on the same train for years and didn't remember ever seeing that station name on any map.

She scratched her head and walked out to the front of the station, hoping to get a cab outside. At least they would know where they were. But there were no cabs; no cars at all in fact, not even a public telephone. Gemini pulled her cell phone out of her pocket, but it was dead. She'd forgotten to charge it again.

She looked around her. Apart from the deserted shack of a station, which was now dark, and one dim street lamp, there was nothing except a lane going off in one direction. It was dark and lined with hedges and trees, and to be honest, properly creepy, but the station was at one end of it, and presumably everything else was at the other end. Gemini trudged off in search of civilisation.

Not far along the lane, when everything except the night and the bushes seemed to have disappeared, Gemini heard a small voice coming from nearby.

"Err, hello. I'm sorry I'm late, I was supposed to meet you at the station."

Gemini looked around, and then down, to see a very small man standing beside her.

"Supposed to meet me? I don't understand."

"My name is Bobat, and yours is Gemini," he began, but was immediately interrupted by Gemini.

"How do you know my name? Were you going through my bag on the train while I was asleep? Are you a stalker or something? I warn you, I've taken self defence classes."

Bobat laughed. "Nothing like that, much weirder. You aren't going to believe me at first, but you have time travelled into my world. Or maybe I should say, dimension travelled. I'm never entirely sure which, it gets confusing. Anyway I summoned you here to help with a problem we're having, which only people from your bloodline, anywhere along the timeline, can defeat."

Gemini snorted, then backed away from the little guy. "You're crazy, right? A nutter. Where is this?"

"I told you, it's a different dimension. Here, have a lozenge," said Bobat, offering a bag of sweets.

Gemini took one, throwing caution to the wind, and popped it into her mouth. It tasted first like banana, then cherry, then blackcurrant, then caramel, then belief. Belief, she thought to herself; how can a sweet taste like belief. Then she realised she believed everything Bobat had said to her. She also believed he was quite harmless, totally trustworthy and a friend. "Oh,", she said. "So, now what?"

Bobat grinned. "I can't really tell you much about it because it would interfere with your natural ability to solve the problem. Really you just need to get out there and explore a bit and deal with whatever happens. If it all goes the way it should, that's all there is to it. Just think of it as a short holiday. Do you like horses by the way? Can you ride?"

"Yes and yes," answered Gemini.

At that moment a beautiful white horse came walking around the bend towards them. It had a saddle, but no rider. Gemini heard a voice inside her head.

"Hello, my name is Winsome, I will be taking you on your journey in this world."

"A telepathic horse," said Gemini. "Whatever next?"

"You only have to think," said Bobat, "and Winsome will hear you as if you were having a normal conversation. Look I've got to go now, there is someone else arriving soon, but Winsome will take care of you and tell you anything else you need to know." And with that Bobat was gone. Gemini thought that for a little guy, he sure could move fast.

"Yes he can," thought Winsome. "Come on Gemini, climb up, let's get going."

"Where are we going?"

"Well, through the woods first, there is no other way from here."

They entered Dogwood while it was still dark, but soon the sun was climbing in the sky. At first there was just the odd tree to either side of them, and rough ground amply scattered with shrubs; but the wood very quickly thickened, and in no time at all they could see nothing else. It was as if nothing had ever existed except woodland. The leaves rustled underfoot, except occasionally when they passed over a puddle, causing the leaves to squelch. Now and again a twig cracked as Winsome trod on it. Little birds chattered to each other in the high treetops. Some birds, disturbed by the travellers, flapped hastily away. Just out of sight, small animals scampered through the leaves.

"What a peaceful place" thought Gemini.

"Yes" replied Winsome, "it has never been a bad place." They lapsed back into appreciative silence, contemplating their surroundings. As they journeyed on towards the centre of the wood, the trees began to get closer together. Gemini had to ride with her head bent forward, to avoid the small twigs that were trying to slap and scratch her in the face. Instead they picked irritably at her shoulders as she passed. Winsome slowed to a walk, as she carefully lifted her hooves over roots that had worked their way above ground. The wood darkened, as the trees grew closer together, and less light filtered through between the leaves.

The path they were following began to become less clear. Brambles and bushy plants began to monopolise the path space, like a General capturing more acres of land with his armies. Roots wove their way backwards and forwards across the path, undermining its very existence. Trees stretched their branches across the path, seeming to arm-wrestle for supremacy of air space. Dark sodden moss covered any ground left free to it, making a slimy squelching sound as Winsome's hooves sank into it, releasing a rank foetid odour.

Soon the branches were too close and the path too unclear for Gemini to ride, so she had to dismount and walk ahead of Winsome. The path was no longer one path, but a multitude of uncertain path-lets, stretching out like a network of veins. Gemini tried to stick to the course that took them as nearly as possible, straight ahead. She realised she had been holding her breath; and it was then she noticed that the forest was now devoid of animal sounds. The whole wood seemed somehow gloomy and sinister.

"Winsome, have you noticed..." Gemini began to ask, but was instantly interrupted by Winsome;

"Best not to talk just now- lest we make our presence felt."

Gemini was surprised to feel a note of fear in Winsome's thoughts, but decided the best course of action was to go along with Winsome for the time being. She didn't want to be with a panicky horse in an enclosed space.

The moss was extending its presence to the trunks of trees now, and strange coloured ear shaped fungi also grew out of the tree bark. They seemed to be almost straining to listen to any sounds to report back to some unseen dark master. The very air of the wood had taken on a decaying and loathsome flavour. The only visible creatures were large dusty, leathery moths, pasted against the trees, appearing to be basking in the malignant atmosphere.

The trees and bushes parted suddenly before them, revealing a bright green circle of pond slime, over which a cloud of gnats hovered. The surface gave no indication of the water underneath, being as still as a grave. Out of nowhere, a gnarled spiny, icy cold hand grasped Gemini's left shoulder.

Gemini screamed, and jumped a couple of inches into the air. Recovering herself very slightly, she turned to see a thin and very ugly old man. His white hair stood out wild and bush-like from his head, and his face was pitted and grooved like the bark of an ancient tree; the colour of chewed tobacco. His eyes were tiny black beads set deep in the folds of skin. His arms were bone thin, and the long twig-like fingers reminded Gemini of the branches that had picked at her earlier. He wore a flowing brown robe.

Gemini turned questioningly to Winsome, but the mare's nostrils were flared and her eyes wide, and she could only let out an abortive whinny.

The old man spoke, though that could only be the loosest of descriptions of the noise he made. His voice was cracked and dry as parchment, and he made a strange rustling sound in the back of his throat as the words rasped out.

"This is my lake, and my wood, and you are trespassing. Trespassers must be punished. The crime is rare, so punishment is severe." The letter 'S' seemed to have a snake like quality of independent life as it slithered out of his mouth.

Gemini summoned her courage and replied;

"What are you? Man or tree? Are you real?"

A tiny flicker or perhaps a twitch, passed the mouth of the old man, and in some charnel circles it may have passed as a smile, but Gemini took it as some sort of recognition.

"Your expression tells me that what I have said is true; yet you do not seem real- more like a hologram."

At this allusion to holograms, the old man's body became translucent, and although his mouth still tried to form words, no sound would come out.

"In fact," continued Gemini, "I wonder if you come from an energy source, like electricity."

The old man's diaphanous remains quivered, keeping a faint but dismal hold on the air space they occupied.

"Electricity" mused Gemini, "so, like my television, I could just flick a switch and turn you off."

Then somewhat at a loss for an actual switch, purposefully blinked her eyes tightly shut. When she opened them again the last remains of the malevolent old man had disappeared.

"Oh well done," thought Winsome, some of her horsey composure already regained; "you are obviously what is needed in this time and place. Bobat was right to choose you."

"Yes, but I'm not sure exactly what I even did.' thought Gemini.

Bird sounds and sunlight had returned to the clearing, and the green muck on the lake surface did not seem anywhere near as thick. Gemini bent down, and moved some of the pond weed aside with her hand. The water underneath looked cool and clear; and very inviting for a swim. Gemini looked up and saw that as the ripple she had made expanded across the water, all the pondweed appeared to be clearing in its wake. The recent experience had left Gemini feeling rather sweaty, and a cool swim suddenly seemed like the most appealing idea in the world. She shrugged out of her outer clothes and boots in record time, before Winsome had even looked up from her opportunistic grazing- and stepped into the cool water. She submerged herself, intending to just wet her hair and cool her head, but it was at this moment that two very strange things happened;

From Winsome's perspective, about three hundred versions of Gemini emerged from the waters of the lake. Winsome shook her head, giving a loud snort, and looked again. When she saw the same thing again, every sensible thought left her head, and she bolted off through the forest in a blind panic.

From Gemini's perspective, the water around her disappeared, and she seemed to be slipping through the blackness of the darkest starless night imaginable. She didn't feel in any danger, in fact she didn't feel anything at all, except perhaps a vestige of surprise. Tentatively, she found she had no trouble at all breathing; so this enabled her to realise that wherever she was, it wasn't underwater. All sense of time or distance had disappeared, and even her own physical substance was becoming questionable. She raised an arm, to touch her face, finding it moved in slow motion, like the pictures she had seen of astronauts in space, but more than that, her arm had a kind of transparent quality, which was slightly unnerving, to say the least. But before she had time to really worry about this disturbing fact, the water reappeared and her form once more became solid.

Winsome had gone but a young, and very handsome man was standing on the shore of the lake, beside a motorbike, grinning at her.

"Hi, mind if I join you? I could use a swim; I'm feeling rather hot and sticky."

"It's not my private lake, come on in," laughed Gemini. The man stripped down to his underwear and waded into the cool clear water.

"I'm Mikaley," he offered, and Gemini introduced herself. They got talking while they relaxed and cooled off and they both seemed to have shared a similar experience in coming to the strange world. As they talked about their experiences, they realised that the main thing they seemed to be doing in the same way, was making dark and malevolent things disappear by denying their existence and not believing they could be real. This seemed to cause things to lose their reality and substance. They lay in the sun to dry off, and talked for hours, finding they had a lot of things in common. Mikaley drove them on his bike, out of the woods and up a mountain track to a cave where he had been camping out. He made them a meal out of some creature he had hunted and killed the previous day; he had been on the world a little longer than Gemini. He thought that the strange reality shimmer, for want of a better term, at the lake, had been another from their bloodline coming through, as the same sort of thing had happened at roughly the same time as Gemini arrived. That night they curled up and slept with their bodies pressed together against the chill of the night, and in the morning, finding themselves in each other's arms, and strongly attracted to each other, they inevitably took it further.

The next few days were a whirl of travelling around the countryside on the bike and 'not believing' bad things out of existence, while the nights were filled with new romance and steamy passion. Then one morning Gemini woke up and Mikaley and the bike were gone. She spent the morning wandering about looking for him, but in the afternoon, when she went back to the cave, Bobat was waiting inside.

"Well, thank you for your help Gemini," he said. "We're all done here, and it's time for you to go home."

"Where's Mikaley?" asked Gemini.

"He's gone back already."

"Will I see him again?"

"Oh yes, you'll definitely see him again soon," grinned Bobat, leading Gemini into the depths of the cave.

Gemini lost her bearings a bit as the cave got darker and darker. She felt a wall in front of her and groped around for a bit, finding a door handle. She pushed open the door and found herself in the bedroom of her flat. When she turned around to look back into the cave, all she saw was her bathroom.

Over the next couple of months, Gemini hunted social media, dating sites, bike clubs, everywhere she could think of, trying to find Mikaley, but there was no trace of him. When Gemini realised she was pregnant, she intensified her search, but it was no good, she just couldn't find him. Bobat must have been mistaken, she thought.

When her baby was born, it was a boy, and for nostalgia and reminiscence, she named him Mikaley.

Mikaley grew up to be a clever lad, interested in nature, and very sporty. Gemini encouraged him in everything he did. When at sixteen he wanted to go away and join the Navy, Gemini was happy to sign the consent forms to let him go. She wanted him to have a free spirit and be able to explore the world and broaden his mind. That was exactly what Mikaley did. He took foreign postings and it was eight years before he came back home to visit, though of course he had written long letters and emails from around the world, and kept Gemini posted about his life.

One day Gemini came home to find a very familiar motorbike parked in front of her house. At first she couldn't remember why it felt so familiar, but then memories of Bobat, Mikaley [senior] and the other world came flooding back to her. Could it really be, after all this time?

Then she saw him, looking at some bugs on a tree, his back to her. It was him, at last. He turned, beamed at her and said;

"Hi Mum, it's good to see you after all this time."
Gemini fainted.

Afterword

I originally had the idea for this story back in 1988, and back then it was going to be a full blown novel. But over the years it didn't get written, not beyond the start and the outline anyway. I came to realise that I wasn't writing it because I'm not really a fan of the fantasy genre. I don't particularly enjoy reading it, and so of course, I naturally don't enjoy writing it. But the characters and the scenario stuck with me somehow. I began to think of ways in which I could make the story darker, and put a twist in its tail, which is when I began to believe it was viable after all, only as a short story. This warped little piece of fiction was the result.

The Witch That Wasn't

Mathilda used to be a witch. She even ran a coven, and then she wasn't a witch anymore. She had an experience, and she found Jesus, and that was that, her life completely changed. And though all of that is a very interesting story; it's not this story; just what went before.

One day Mathilda went on an outing to the countryside. She stopped in a pretty little village, mainly because it reminded her of the picture on an old fashioned chocolate box; the kind that used to be on a high shelf behind the counter in the newsagents. The kind of expensive chocolates in a posh box with a picture of a pretty village or cottage on the front, that people only ever bought as a really special present. Mathilda used to buy her penny sweets, and gaze up at the beautiful boxes, wishing that someday, someone might buy her a box of chocolates like that. Anyway this village, with its little thatched roof cottages, and tea gardens, looked exactly like one of those pictures, so she parked her car in the village car park and got out for a walk around. She wandered in to a little crafts and gift shop, and was looking at all the little hand-made craft items, admiring some for the skill they had obviously taken to make, thinking about buying others but wondering where she would put them.

A short girl in a black floaty top and long purple skirt, tapped her on her shoulder.

"My name is Drusilla, I wonder if you could help me with a spell?"

"Hi, I'm Mathilda, I think maybe you have me confused with someone else?"

"Nope. It's definitely you. You know how to do it. You might have stopped doing it yourself, but I know you can tell me what to do."

"How on earth do you know that?"

Drusilla cocked her head on one side as if she was listening to a voice;

"They say you used to teach people how to do spells."

Mathilda could have rated Drusilla as crazy and hurried off, but everything she was saying was true, and Mathilda knew how strange the Craft and the Old Ones could be; she had after all, had years of personal experience.

"Okay, I can help I suppose. What are you trying to do?"

"I need to help a boy I know who is ill, and I want to do something for myself to help with remembering, for exams and stuff."

"You should do one for the earth too," added Mathilda. She went around the shop, pointing out things Drusilla needed; a blue candle for healing, a little stuffed straw doll that looked a bit like a young boy, a couple of crystals, some incense sticks. Then she took Drusilla outside and they wandered around the village, picking a sprig of rosemary here, a bunch of melissa there, and collecting some rose petals and oak leaves. Mathilda explained everything that Drusilla needed to do for the spells, then asked;

"Is there a dew pond nearby?"

"Just up the hill behind the woods, in the field," replied Drusilla.

"You need to get a little bottle and collect some water from the pond, to use in the spell."

Drusilla took a bottle of pop from her bag and said,

"Will this bottle do?"

"Yup, rinse it first though."

Drusilla finished the last of the drink, and rinsed the bottle out in the village fountain. They started to walk up the path to the field behind the woods.

About half way up the path, when the houses had stopped and it was just a pretty country lane, a small cute white goat came trotting after them, following them for a little while. It gave a little head butt against Drusilla's bottom, as if to nudge her forward, like...hurry up, get on with it. Then, ignoring Drusilla's squeal, it trotted round in front of them, and looked back, as if to make sure they were following. It sped up its pace, looking back at them to make sure they were keeping up with it, and before they knew it, the girls were running along behind the little goat. Then they were in the fields on the hill where the dew pond was, and they were still running. Running through the field together, following the little white goat, not in the least bit out of breath. Mathilda and Drusilla were running, round and round the hills, faster and faster until they were running round the countryside like the wind on a stormy night, a blur, up and down the hills; two separate dots following the little white dot that was the goat. When they stopped they all collapsed together onto the grass and the goat had been transformed into a lamb.

The lamb stood beside them as they lay on the grass getting their breath back and laughing, exhilarated by the wildness of the wind and the countryside; filled with energy and bubbling with joy.

After a while, Drusilla got up and went over to the dew pond which was nearby, and bent to fill her bottle as a crow watched her from a branch on a nearby bush. Mathilda went over to the pond to watch, and the crow flew away.

Then an amazing thing happened; the bush on which the crow had been perched, caught fire. There was no lightning strike, or anything like that, just flames flickering on the tips of the branches. There was no smoke, and the bush did not seem to be being damaged or altered in any way, just the flames, dancing in the sunlight. Mathilda turned to ask Drusilla if she saw it too, but Drusilla had disappeared, and in her place stood the little white lamb. The lamb nudged against her, knocking its head against her thigh. She looked down and noticed it was wearing a cord around its neck; black white and red threads twisted together. Under the cord was a piece of parchment. Mathilda took the paper and unfolded it to reveal a collection of symbols, which, as she gazed at it, she realised she could read. It said she had been chosen, and must journey to a distant land to meet some important people; only then could the world change.

Mathilda turned to look at the bush, but it was just a bush once again, and when she turned back the lamb had gone too. She still held the note, but was beginning to wonder if she had been dosed with LSD somewhere along the line. She began to walk back towards the woods, pausing to climb a wooden stile that marked the boundary between fields and woods. A dove landed on the fence beside the stile, and dropped something out of its mouth. When Mathilda looked on the ground to see what it had dropped, it was an olive branch, yet there were no olive trees nearby. Perhaps in one of the gardens in the village, she thought.

As she came out of the woods into the village, and headed towards her car, she looked again at the note she was still holding. Once again it was covered in symbols that resolved themselves into words before her eyes. But the words written on the paper were different this time. 'Everything is one and the same. All things return to the one. All paths merge.'

Despite the fact that it had not been raining all day, a rainbow appeared in the sky.

Afterword

If this story seems a little strange to you, it may be because it was originally a dream. Sometimes I have dreams which are like a lifetime; I wake several times in the night and go back to sleep and the life I have been dreaming, continues. Some are like epic adventure or thriller films. Some are, truth be told, a little scary, and a pleasure to wake from, others are surreal and to all intents meaningless. Some I just don't remember. But every now and then I have a dream that seems to have a message, or to be a short story, all wrapped up in a neat little package and delivered direct from my subconscious to my conscious. Well maybe with a little bit of the ultra weirdness edited out. Anyway, this was one of those.

I Didn't Sign Up For That

Alice stood at her window chanting.

"Come to me, immortal Vampire, creature of the night. Make me yours, make me immortal too. Oh hear me please."

Alice had been calling out every night from her isolated window, in her country cottage, miles from the nearest town. She had reached a place where she didn't really expect anything to happen. Calling out the mantra, had become a nightly ritual, in the way that other people who lived in the cottage before her, had knelt beside their beds and said their prayers. Sometimes a fox would run off scared, other times an owl would sit on a nearby branch, watching and judging her.

She did not, by this point, really expect anything to happen. The immortal vampire, the dashing creature that would sweep her off of her feet, make her his for all eternity, in some glamorous existence where the normal rules of the world did not apply; probably did not exist. She had to admit it. So Alice was not prepared when a dark shape swooped out of the night shadows and launched itself through her window, pressing her to the bedroom floor and completely covering her with its darkness. She could see nothing, but could feel the needle like pricks through her exposed skin and the subsequent sensation of being drained. Time seemed to have stopped for Alice as the feeling dragged on and on. It was not sensual or pleasant, and she couldn't see anything, nor could she move. In fact it was all rather scary.

Alice passed out. It was still night when she came round, and staggered into her bathroom. There was a sticky black mess around her mouth, and she hurt all over. What had just happened? She washed her face, then realised that if she did not go to bed she would probably pass out and sleep right there on the bathroom floor. Going back into the bedroom, she noticed the first light of day was dawning, and closed the shutters, window, and thick velvet curtains. Then she fell onto the bed and slept through the entire day.

The following evening when Alice awoke at sunset, she felt strange. Her body felt odd, insensitive somehow. She got up carefully in case parts of her had gone to sleep and lost all feeling; she did not want to stand up and fall over. She felt stiff and inflexible as she staggered to the bathroom. She pulled off her clothes to get into the shower, but what she saw in the mirror stopped her dead in her tracks.

Alice wanted to scream, but nothing came out, except for a gasp. Her whole body was covered with a hard shiny black shell like coating instead of skin. She clambered into the shower and tried to wash her skin clean, but water just ran off the outer coating that was now, apparently part of her. She realised she couldn't feel her skin underneath, just a faint pulling sensation against the shell, her shell. Thinking that made her feel faint again, and she went for another lie down, just in case.

After an hour or so, she realised she was stuck with this situation, for better or worse and she had better try and get used to it. The phrase 'be careful what you ask for, you just might get it,' played over and over in the soundtrack of her mind.

Alice was hungry. She went down to her kitchen and looked in the fridge. There was a pile of vegetables which she had no interest in, and surprised herself by throwing them onto the floor, where they formed a pile in the corner. Jam, now that was what she fancied, grabbing a spoon and eating it straight from the jar. After the jam, she ate marmalade, sweet pickle, and chocolate spread, washed down with undiluted squash syrup. But Alice still felt like a part of her hunger was unsated. She grabbed a tray of uncooked steak and sucked on the meat. She was surprised to find little needle like straws bursting out from her mouth to latch onto the meat; but she was beginning to be beyond real shock now. The meat was satisfying, but finished with, much too quickly.

Alice stretched, and was amazed when a set of wings unfolded from her back. Wow, she just had to go outside and try those out. She stood in her garden and tried flapping her arms, to no avail. Then she squeezed her back muscles from somewhere deep under the carapace that was now her skin. The wings began to make a buzzing sound, like a quiet helicopter, as they flapped in a motion that was almost too fast to see. Alice felt her feet leaving the ground as she rose straight up into the air. She experimentally leant forward and began to move forwards, heading over to the farm field beyond the boundary of her garden hedge. A cow grazing in the field below turned its head to look up at her, and she gazed back at it hungrily, drooling slightly. She inclined herself towards the creature, and before she consciously knew what was going on, she had settled or landed, but it was more like settled, on its back. The needle things automatically extended from her mouth and pierced the body of the cow. It mooed in a way that suggested it was not entirely happy with the situation. Then more needle like suckers came out from Alice's underbelly, where her chest and stomach had previously been. Eventually the cow collapsed dead beneath her, and Alice climbed off its carcass, her hunger sated, for now at least.

She looked down and was surprised to see that her shell had turned a bright, iridescent blue colour, really beautiful in the moonlight. Just then the sky filled with the noise of wings like hers, and about two dozen creatures, who looked exactly like her new reflection, in a variety of colours, landed in the field around her.

A black one stepped forward.

"I am Thelforius. It was I that responded to your call and effected your conversion."

"Err, thank you. I'm Alice. I'm not really sure what I should say. It's all a bit overwhelming. Why is everyone different colours? Why did my colour just change to blue after I ate?"

"Eating the cow, and you can survive on that, but you might prefer people- effected the final part of your conversion, and allowed your colour to come in. The colours reflect what you do, or rather, what is your passion in eternity or undeath."

"I'm an artist. I love to paint, and live by selling my paintings."

"That will be easy to arrange. You just need to have someone come by your house and collect the paintings by day, and pay the money into your account. There is a group hive that is the safest place for you to pass the day, but it is not obligatory, a dark room will do. Each colour represents a different path or passion. Blue for the arts, brown for mathematics including finance, green for medicine and science, purple for philosophy, red for politics and human interactions, black for the dark arts, and so on. Will you come to the hive with us, so you know how to gain access and where it is located? We can explain more to you there, and you can meet the others." And so Alice's much wished for, new life began.

Afterword

When I wrote the previous vampire short story, I wanted to explore the idea of something completely different. Firstly, the physicality is very different. The exo skeleton idea came from the notion that insects are often thought to be the only species likely to survive, and possibly even thrive, after an all out nuclear war. So these vampires are tougher and more durable than the original Hollywood version. Then following on from that, I explored the idea of vampires doing something meaningful with their time, as opposed to just hunting and being hunted. After all, given eternity, I think more depth of character and interests would develop other than the basic blood lust. Even most foodies have other interests too!

I have always been fascinated by the Vampire mythology, since I was quite young. Born in the early sixties, there was not a huge amount of mythology out there when I first got into it, but boy oh boy has that changed over the years. When I was a fascinated teen, there was the book by Bram Stoker; Dracula, and all the old black and white late night movies with Bela Lugosi and Christopher Lee, but not really a great deal more.

But as time went on, Vampire films and fiction, art and culture spread like a plague into the modern entertainment genre. I for one, am not complaining.

There is such a huge diversity of things they can do, things they cannot do or be around, and ways they typically behave, or look as a vampire. I began to wonder what defines a vampire? What, across the board do they have in common? What stands out as main features, used in almost every work, and what is hardly ever used at all? Hardly used at all anymore is the myth that vampires cannot cross running water. Given the network of rivers and streams in Eastern Europe, where the vampire mythology supposedly originated with Vlad the Impaler- a real historical character- it seems unlikely that crossing running water would be a problem. If vampires were desert creatures; maybe, but in Europe they would be trapped in very small areas of land, as running water is pretty much everywhere. Perhaps this just made people living in dark, isolated country areas feel more comfortable about the myth.

Vampires may so much not be bothered by running water, that In Dracula Untold the character first comes to in his vampire state in running water. His silver ring is bothering him, but the water isn't.

In common with zombies, vampires were seen to rise from their graves as undead. During times of plague, when medics were never truly certain about pronouncing death, it was apparently not uncommon to be buried alive, so a scary looking person clawing their way out of a grave; and they probably would look pretty scary after waking up buried alive, is bound to generate a certain amount of mythology and folklore. This also probably explains the garlic part of the mythology. Garlic is a potent natural antibiotic, and possibly one of the only medicines available at that time. It is not unreasonable to suppose it may have been used as a ward. Perhaps even used as a treatment, the medicinal effect curing the afflicted, and thus appearing to bring them back from a state of undead vampirism. It is easy to see how it might have crept into the mythology.

Whether or not vampires can fly, turn into bats, wolves or smoke, or even become fully invisible, is not much addressed in the modern genre either. Rarely these days, do vampires turn into smoke or wolves, and they often only seem to have invisibility because of their super speed, which seems to be fairly universal. In Dracula Untold, is the most brilliant portrayal of a vampire becoming a cloud of bats. The original Dracula of old black and white movies just turned into the one bat. The funniest bat example for me, was Love At First Bite, where Dracula transforms into a bat and is flying round a poor urban neighbourhood where the locals are trying to catch and eat him, calling him a tiny chicken. The vampire comedy is quite the elite sub genre, but wonderful for all that. For a long time Love At First Bite was my favourite vampire film, but sadly it has now become quite dated, and of course many wonderful films and TV series have pushed it off its top spot, for me at least. I do think there is always room for comedy in the genre though. I recently watched the film 'What We Do in the Shadows.' This had me in stitches. Four vampire housemates filmed like a documentary. The argument about whose turn it was to wash up the bloody dishes was just classic.

Speaking of that film, that touched upon the idea of vampires living alone or in groups. This seems to be about half and half. Often the vampire is a lonely tortured soul, living with just one Renfield type character. Equally often though, the vampires form clans or packs. The Lost Boys was a great example of this, but it is not unusual; True Blood, Blade, Underworld, and many others have a group of vampires living together in some sort of hierarchy, usually with a High Priest type leader. They may just be in a wild pack because they are over-running the world, like in 30 Days of Night.

Universally vampires seem to be immortal, allergic to sunlight, (in a skin bubbling explosive kind of way, not the sort of thing you could treat with an epi pen), and need to drink human blood.

Usually in the mythology, when vampires both drink and give their own blood to drink, this is the method of turning a human into a vampire. In the Anne Rice series, and many others, the victim is drained almost to death before being fed the vampire blood. In Dracula Untold, just a mere lick is taken by the vampire, and his own blood served in a cup. In True Blood, humans drink vampire blood to get high, temporarily gaining various powers, but it isn't automatic to fully become one.

If the mythology is to be believed, vampires are the main users of blood banks, which they usually steal. Luckily it is just mythology and so this is not truly the case, although there are some real weirdoes out there, possibly inspired and consumed by the mythology, this much is definitely true.

In True Blood, bars serve vampires a blood substitute, bottled up like beer, to help them better integrate with society, an unusual twist and interesting social comment. Ironically humans buy little vials of vampire blood and take it to get high.

Sometimes vampires give up blood drinking from humans and either go hungry for years, like the old ones in the Anne Rice books, or drink from rats, like Angel in Buffy. This is usually out of guilt, or trying to find their soul, or being given a soul as punishment; generally some sort of effort to find their higher selves through deprivation.

Most vampires are portrayed as suave and sophisticated and attractive. The act of vampirism is portrayed as intrinsically sexual. Sometimes however, the vampire is the epitome of ugly, the essence of evil, like Nosferatu, The vampires in the Necroscope series by Brian Lumley, or the creatures in 30 Days of Night. The Dracula Untold vampire is somewhere between the two types, perhaps to indicate his ongoing struggle with good and evil.

In The Vampire Diaries, they got around the fatal allergy to sunlight by wearing a daylight ring. This was a ring made by a witch so sunlight no longer affects them. Of course as soon as the ring is taken off by force in a fight or something, they burn up in the usual way. True Blood confers day walking on vampires if they drink the blood of a fairy, but they are quite rare and not generally keen on the idea of being vampire refreshment. A couple of other films have had vampires to whom sunlight is an irrelevance, but it is not the norm. Most vampires still go to their coffins during daylight, or bury themselves in the earth to avoid the rays. You would think in these days of factor 50 plus creams...which by the way, they do slather on, in What we do in the Shadows.

Apart from sunlight, a stake to the heart and beheading tends to kill most vampires. Beheading is the dispatch of choice used by the Winchester brothers in Supernatural, but then having one's head chopped off tends to put a stop to most activities, whatever the species. Okay some horror has talking, living disembodied heads, but they don't tend to be up to much threat wise. Images of zombie heads rolling around trying to inflict a fatal bite on passing ankles is more comedy than anything else really.

Some of the older vampires can be warded off by a cross held up in their face, but generally these days, most laugh it off or brush it aside. It did make a little comeback, having some power over full vampires in Dracula Untold. But then that film was trying to tell the back story of the vampire so it had to make some little nods to historical mythology. It did it very well overall, I felt.

Vampires are often able to hypnotise their victims. This goes back to the old school 'you are feeling sleepy' but is still used, mainly for convenience in modern depictions. The Vampire Diaries uses hypnotism by vampires to make their victims forget, a lot. Overly perhaps. What we do in the Shadows had some amusing hypnotism scenes, some of the housemates being more adept at it than others.

The genre, I'm happy to say, remains as popular as ever, and continues to grow. I look forward to continuing to follow it.

You can read my other Vampire short story 'Conversations with X', in the collection Oddscapes and Quirkitudes, and there is an article on the very real phenomenon of psychic vampires, in my book A 21st Century Coven.

Planned Babies

Colleen was amazed, to say the least. She was sitting with her partner, Bart, looking at the scan in utter disbelief.

"It can't be another girl."

"Well," began the scanning technician, "it used to be that we could sometimes mistake a boy for a girl, if, you know, his winkle was hiding when we did the scan. But scans are so much better these days, I think I can say with ninety nine per cent certainty, that it is a girl."

"But we both did the boy diet for six months before conception," whined Colleen.

The technician shrugged, as if to say, 'I wouldn't know anything about that.'

Bart squeezed Colleen's hand,

"Never mind love. We'll be just as happy with our family of three little girls. And anyway, this way I can still be the only man in your life."

Colleen tried to laugh, but it came out as a kind of strangled gurgle.

"Anyway," concluded the technician, "baby is doing fine, looks healthy, no problems."

So that was that. Bart and Colleen went home and told their two girls and Bart's mother, who was babysitting, that a new sister/grand daughter was on the way. They showed the scan photo around, pointing out what was where to the children.

"So that boy or girl diet doesn't work then?" said Bart's mother with a half smirk. "I bet you can't wait to get eating cream, butter, cheese and all that again. I don't suppose you'll be wanting to see another fish dish for a while?"

Bart grinned. "Yep, pizza and tiramisu for dinner I think. Shall I go to the shops?"

"I suppose so," said Colleen resignedly, though with mixed feelings, because she was secretly craving a pizza herself. "Actually, pick up a box of cream cakes as well while you're at the supermarket."

"Yay" cheered the girls in unison.

Bart's Mum stayed around for a bit, just to chat, and help bath the girls and put them to bed after supper. Later, while Bart dozed on the sofa in front of the football,

Colleen went online, to check some things out; just curiosities pricking at the back of her mind.

She started with a search that included the words 'girl boy births Harlow' and got a lot of pages with stories about people having babies. She was distracted by a few of them, and stopped to read about a woman who gave birth on the toilet, thinking she was having a poo. Then there was another who was attacked in her home whilst giving birth; Colleen shuddered. Another talked about a baby being born covered in bruises, literally black and blue, due to a forceps birth. Colleen realised the football had finished and she hadn't even started finding what she was looking for. She turned the television off and nudged Bart awake.

"The match has finished love, you'd better go up to bed or you'll have trouble getting up for work in the morning."

Bart got up stiffly, "Who won?"

"Chelsea, two nil."

"Bollocks," grumbled Bart. "Are you coming up?"

"I'm just finishing a couple of emails and stuff, I'll be up soon."

Colleen settled back to her search, adding in the word statistics. But this didn't seem to help; the rather dry papers she opened, did not seem to declare numbers of births for each sex, only births generally, and live versus still born, and that type of thing.

In her next search, she put in 'girl boy birth ratio Harlow.' She still wasn't getting any figures, but the pages she opened did have some rather shocking statistics. Apparently, men were sixteen percent more likely to die below the national average age in Harlow. Twenty one percent of children were living below the poverty line. Thirty percent of the general population were living below the poverty line. Eighteen percent of the residents of Harlow were above the national average for obesity. The shocking statistics went on and on. When Colleen checked the time, it was gone one in the morning, and she really had to go to bed. Finally, she opened a page for the national records office, and finding a contact us button, wrote a quick email asking if it was possible to find out the numbers of girls versus boys born in Harlow between 2010 and 2015. Then Colleen turned her computer off and went to bed.

The next day, after Colleen had delivered Esther to infants school and Laura to kindergarten, she went home and turned on her computer. There was an answer from the records office, it wasn't especially helpful.

'Thank you for your enquiry. The national birth rates are currently in line with worldwide trends, that is 51% male births versus 49% female births. Harlow is in line with these trends generally. We hope this answers your question.'

"No it bloody well doesn't," said Colleen out loud to herself. How could such figures be true when she was about to have three daughters. Surely statistics meant she should have at least one boy by now. She began to research again, putting 'genetic influence child gender' into a new search.

This gave her some scary information about Asian and Equatorial births, deformities, child murder and diseases; but nothing along the lines of what she was looking for. She rang her sister and asked her if she would pick up the kids from kindergarten and school and keep them at hers until the evening, to which her sister readily agreed.

Then Colleen began to ring around a list of Harlow midwives, that she had found online. She asked them; "I'm doing a research project, and just wondered if you could tell me how many girls you delivered last year and how many boys. It would be terrifically helpful."

Now she was getting somewhere. Most of the midwives had records in their diaries, and were able to quickly tot up the figures. Others said they would call her back with the information later. The midwife list exhausted, Colleen added in everyone she knew personally that had had a baby last year.

By the time her sister knocked with the kids at six o'clock, Colleen had a set of figures scribbled down on a pad in front of her computer. It was more than 51/49% that was for sure. It was a completely different ratio, more like 2:1, there were two hundred girls and one hundred boys.

Colleen felt the mystery was only just beginning to be uncovered. It was like the packet of ham she was picking at to peel open for tea, just one corner lifted and still not able to get at the meat inside. Anyway she was soon distracted by feeding and chatting, and it was not until Bart had again gone to bed that she was able to sit and have a quiet think.

The next day, Colleen rang all the midwives she could find in Basildon, and got similar figures to Harlow, except this time the larger number were boys.

The following day she rang midwives in Milton Keynes and got three hundred and twenty five girls to seventy five boys.

For Stevenage it was three hundred and fifty boys and ninety girls.

By the end of the week Colleen was really scratching her head. So the national average was about fifty fifty, but individual new towns were showing some very different results from the average. The next week, as a control, she tried non new towns; Brighton, Manchester, Stoke, Northampton and Plymouth. All came back with the fifty fifty ratio.

Colleen was confused. Something was definitely going on in new towns; but what?

That Friday afternoon she had an online telephone call with a friend of hers who had gone to the University of Sussex and currently lived in Brighton. Colleen called this friend, partly because Kelly was the cleverest person she knew, and partly because she was doing her degree in Bio sciences with a side interest in statistics. Kelly was indeed very interested in what Colleen was saying.

"Can you email me your figures please?" she asked.

"Of course, I'll do it right away."

"Can I use your research if I end up writing a paper on this?"

"Absolutely," replied Colleen, flattered that her digging might have resulted in something intellectually worthwhile.

"Okay then, leave it with me and I'll let you know what else I find out, if anything. Of course it might all just be coincidence, but it certainly doesn't look like it so far."

Colleen went back to life as normal while she waited to hear back from Kelly. The morning sickness had got quite nasty again, and Laura had chicken pox. It was looking likely that Esther was going to follow suit. Bart's mother offered to take them both to her house until they were well again, because of the worry with Colleen being pregnant, and Colleen readily agreed.

When Kelly got back to her, she was stunned to hear what Kelly had to say.

"I've been to all of the four new towns you collected figures on," she began.

"You came to Harlow, and didn't come and have a coffee and a chat with me?" complained Colleen.

"Sorry sweetie no time, it was a big rush, running round all those places in one day; next time we'll catch up properly for sure."

"Okay. So what were you doing?"

"I collected samples of drinking water from each town, and took them into the lab for testing. The upshot of it is this; the hormone levels in the water for Harlow and Milton Keynes are significantly higher than normal for female hormones, whereas the hormone levels for male hormones are higher than average in Basildon and Stevenage."

"You mean they're putting something in the water to make people have boys or girls?" asked Colleen.

"Whoa there. Scientifically that is a huge leap. If you told someone that, they would cry 'conspiracy theory.' There could be other reasons for the levels being higher than average, I'll need to do some more research. And who are you saying are 'they' by the way?"

"Well, the government I suppose, though I'd have no idea why."

Kelly snorted. "I agree with you that the results don't make much sense at this time, but I'll keep digging, see if I can find anything else."

A couple of weeks later, when Colleen had stopped puzzling over it completely, Kelly got back to her once more. She looked very disconcerted and not at all her usual confident self.

"I can tell you this, off the record, but then you have to promise to let it go totally- never mention it again."

"OMG what?" shrieked Colleen.

"I ended up being contacted by an official who was very cagey about specifying which agency he worked for. He said the research I was doing had come to his attention, and that I absolutely would not be allowed to publish it. He said he would tell me, off the record what was going on, if I signed documents to swear I would take it no further. Also if I agreed to his terms, there would be a nice research position available for me after I graduate. Obviously I agreed, it would have been daft not to really, as it wasn't like I had a choice."

"So what's the dirt?"

"It turns out hormones are being added to the water in new towns to affect the boy girl birth rates. Overall the national average stays at fifty fifty, so it doesn't show. The reason they are doing it is because new towns are so insular. People who live in them tend to stay in them for many generations. The new town mentality is that everything is provided in this town, so there is no need to leave. Residents relocate less than in other areas. Consequently, now many of them are at fourth and fifth generation, there is a very real risk of inbreeding, with subsequent birth defects. Raising the birth rates of one sex in each new town, makes it more likely that those children will leave the town to breed, thus cutting the risk of abnormalities. The upshot is, you new town folk are turning into a bunch of country cousins, and it's time to mix it up a bit."

Colleen was stunned. She really had uncovered a true life conspiracy theory, and she couldn't tell anyone. She finished her call with Kelly and started researching house prices in Basildon.

Afterword

I wrote this story because I had noticed people I knew in new towns having multiple same sex births. I did a little online searching, and came up with the same sort of off topic obscure stuff that Colleen did in the story. I formed my own conspiracy theory about it and wrote this story to frame it. Having grown up in a new town, before I moved away, it does make a lot of sense to me though. My friend from London used to come and visit me, and couldn't understand why I never wanted to go out of the town. Later I broke that mental habit I'm glad to say. But the story is very much 'What if?'

The Abattoir

The abattoir was filled with animal noises; a mixture of panic, distress and enquiry could be distinguished in the tone of the moos. There were no human voices, as there were only three human staff in the entire building, and they all worked in very different areas, well away from conversational distance of each other. Jeff worked in entry; herding the cattle from outside holding pens into the runs that guided them through the abattoir itself. After that, the process was fully mechanised anyway, and no human supervision was needed until the kill zone. The cattle moved slowly through a fenced walkway. If they stopped for more than ten seconds, pads on the sides of the walkway came out and squeezed against their hides so that they moved forwards. A floor sensor registered if they had stopped moving and sent the instruction to the pads. During this part of the journey, the cattle were usually silent, listening to the noises that came from ahead of them. This was when they would sometimes let out a moo that sounded like curiosity, an enquiry as to what was taking place ahead of them.

Before they entered the kill zone, a gate would close in front of them so only one cow at a time went through, and the next came through only when everything was ready for it. Once inside the area, they moved into another pen that held them tightly into position while an automated stun gun came down and stunned them with a shock. Some cows would moo at that point in distress or panic. Another human worked at this station, today it was Grant. His role was mainly supervisory; making sure the process went smoothly, and was not botched at any point. After the shock, when the cow was stunned; Grant pressed a button that caused the moving walkway to carry the cow along to the next station. Once in situ at the next point, a bolt gun to the cow's head finished the job. This too, was automated, but again Grant had to supervise, and make sure it all went according to plan. There were over-ride switches for the bolt gun and the stun gun, in case something went wrong and a second hit was needed. Of course there was also a big red stop button that stopped everything if necessary.

Finally the carcass went along on a conveyor belt to an area where it was caught on a hook and taken to the meat preparation area, ready for further processing. The final human, Mark, worked at this point. He ensured the hook had properly picked up the dead cow before it moved on. He too had an over-ride switch whereby he could repeat the hooking process if it was not properly in place.

The whole abattoir was state of the art automation. Never before had so few people been necessary for operation. In fact, the whole process from entry to exit could have been fully automated, but there was a very small percentage risk that something would go wrong, and a cow would go through not fully stunned, or not killed by the bolt, or not on the hook. Three key personnel watching and checking ensured this percentage failure rate did not occur.

Red, the Aberdeen Angus, was standing in the field holding pen that preceded movement into the huge shed-like building. He was eating little bits of grass that edged the pen area, and generally enjoying the feel of the sun on his hide and the breeze in the air, after being cooped up for hours in the truck. He thought it would have been nice to have more grass to eat though, and more space to move about. His whole herd from the farm were in this one small pen. He supposed it would only be for a short while though as lots of cattle were going into the shed, then presumably on to somewhere else. He found himself wondering, where else? Where were they going next? He could not hear any distant mooing from another field behind the shed.

Nudger sauntered over to Red. All the calves were around the same age, and knew each other quite well, having lived their whole short lives together. Nudger did his thing and nudged against Red.

Then suddenly, for the first time, Red heard another voice in his head, other than his own. He realised it was Nudger. "Let me get at the grass too," he heard.

"Alright," thought Red, and moved along the fence a little way. Then he tried looking at Nudger and thinking hard. "Can you hear me Nudger?"

Nudger looked up, clearly surprised, and stared at Red. "Was that you?"

"Yes," thought-shouted Red, excitedly. He noticed the other calves in their herd had stopped whatever they were doing, and turned to look at Nudger and Red.

"Can you hear us too?" thought Red.

"Yes," thought a whole group of voices all at once.

"Okay," thought Nudger, "this is new."

"Perhaps," began Red, "it's just something that happens when we get older?"

"Never heard the older ones at the farm doing it," Nudger responded.

Massive, a huge calf, pushed his way through the herd, to join Nudger and Red.

"Perhaps it's happening because of where we are," he added.

"Where are we?" asked Red.

"I don't know, but let's be really quiet and listen. I can almost hear some of the ones that have already gone inside."

Everyone listened, staring at the shed and trying to fix their minds on the cattle inside. After a while they turned to each other to compare notes on what they had heard.

"I don't like it," began Nudger, "it's not a good place. They are all confused; thinking things like What is going on? Where are we? What is happening?"

"I heard something else," added Red. "One thought, 'the one ahead of me is frightened. He is trapped. I can hear his fear. He is in a panic, trying to turn back but he can't move. Then he went quiet.' No, I have to go that way now. I don't want to."

Massive was clearly upset. "There is more. Something else after that. Fear yes, but pain and death too. They are killing them in there. There are no more thoughts beyond that point. It is a bad place. Very bad; none are coming out of the other side."

"Have they brought us here to kill us too?" thought Red.

"I think so," thought Massive.

"I don't want to die," thought Nudger.

"Nor do we," thought Red, Massive and everyone else.

"Can we jump out of this pen?" thought Nudger.

"It's too high, even for me," thought Massive.

Just then Jeff came over and opened their pen so it led into the runs into the shed. When none of the herd moved to go through, he leant over the fence and prodded the one nearest. It was very reluctant to move. Finally he got it into the run and clambered into the pen to get the next ones lined up.

"Come on you stubborn lot, move. What is the matter with you?"

"We have to do something," thought Red.

Just then, Massive ran over towards Jeff, catching a few of the others around him in a stampede mentality. Before Jeff knew what was happening, they were on top of him, trampling him. He tried to cry out, but it was all over too quickly, and his dead form was soon being trampled underfoot into the mud.

"Red, Nudger, get over here. We have to go inside and get Scruffy. Look he is already moving along through the fences," called Massive.

"The rest of you, push against that back fence. If you all push in one place you might be able to get it to go over. If you do get out, just keep going. Split up, try to find somewhere safe. Get away from this place," Red instructed the rest of the herd before joining Massive and a reluctant Nudger.

Massive was first into the runs, moving fast to catch up to Scruffy. Nudger was right behind him and Red hurried after them. They did not need the pads to squeeze them forward. Massive saw Scruffy up ahead moving towards the bad place. He also saw the human Grant, standing beside the buttons.

Massive thought-shouted at Scruffy, "Stop Scruffy. Don't walk on, even when the pads push you, just stand still."

Scruffy looked around at Massive and stood still. Massive jumped over the fence holding him in the run, and realised he was on the platform with the human. He charged at

Grant, who was still wondering what was happening, and butted him, forcing him into the bolt gun area. Before Grant could right himself and clamber out of the pen, a bolt had shot through his head, and he collapsed, dead, onto the conveyor belt.

Nudger jumped the fence too and came up behind Massive. There was a big red button on the wall and Nudger did his thing and nudged it. Everything stopped. The pads stopped squeezing Scruffy, urging him on. The stun gun crackled and went quiet. The bolt gun folded down flat to the wall and the conveyor belt stopped with Grant's body half way down it.

"We've done it," thought Red joyfully. "We've killed the shed."

Massive pushed through a human gate and stepped onto the conveyor belt that was now just a rubber track. "Come on lads, follow me."

Nudger followed him, and Scruffy and Red carried on through the now inoperative, kill zone. They stepped over Grant and carried on down to the place where the hooks were swinging high above them. The look on Mark's face when four big red Aberdeen Angus cattle came walking down the stopped conveyor belt towards him was a picture. He just sort of sat down on the floor in shock. He had been wondering why everything had stopped, but was not expecting this.

Red, Massive, Nudger and Scruffy ignored him and headed for the open door that Mark left open to let some air in, and to take the smell of death away a bit. It also meant he could nip out for a quick crafty fag if he needed to.

The four big calves pressed on along a lane until they found a place where they could clamber across a ditch and push through a thin hedge into a field. In the distance to the west, they could see the rest of their herd heading away from the shed in all directions. They too, did not stop walking until they had disappeared, and were very far away from the shed of death.

Afterword

This was another casual 'what if?' thought, that turned into a story. I'm not a vegetarian, and I like a bit of steak, especially Aberdeen Angus, so I'm certainly not being an evangelical vegetarian here. I just got to thinking; evolution is most likely to happen at times of duress. What if cows developed a means to communicate and work together? Is a rebellion of the herd like this, such a crazy idea?

The Yowling

It was a full moon, and a bright clear night, not too cold, and the ground wasn't wet because it hadn't rained for a few days. Tigger was looking forward to going out and having a good prowl around his territory, spraying and scratching a bit against the trees, and making sure no other cats had been on his turf. It was such a nice night that he thought he might even explore a little further afield; dare to cross some other local cat's territories on his way to the neutral ground of the graveyard or even the woods beyond.

He thought these thoughts as he sat in front of the cat flap getting ready to go out. He tapped the little plastic swing door open with his front paw, then stepped, or rather squeezed, as it was a bit tight, through onto the patio beyond. It was indeed a perfect night for exploring. Not a great night for hunting; the moon was too bright; he'd never sneak up on mice. But Tigger didn't mind, he was well fed; not only had he had his favourite cat food, but also had managed to beg a few pieces of fish from his people's supper.

After he had sat on the patio for a while and soaked up the sense of what kind of night it was; he was right, it was a good one, with just a hint of an edge in the distance- he strolled around his garden. He stopped in front of a few favourite trees and the shed, to rub his face against them and have a scratch. He found a patch of freshly dug garden to dig a hole and do his business. He half covered it, leaving plenty exposed to give off scent to any feline intruders. Finally he sprayed some urine at the back gate, tagging it, before jumping over it into the alley beyond.

Now he proceeded more cautiously, as he was in the shared area between cat territories. Soon he would be coming level with the turf of the big black cat next door, and after that he would have to jump a fence and run swiftly through the ginger tabby's garden to get to another communal area. There was a final territory to cross then, before the graveyard, and that belonged to a fat torty who didn't go out very much anyway. Tigger knew from experience not to take it for granted that she'd be indoors.

True she was fat and stayed inside curled up in front of the fire most nights. Tigger had gone up to the window one time and seen her in her cat bed. She didn't have a cat flap, had to wait for her person to let her out, but she wouldn't have made it through one anyway, she was far too fat. But when she was out and about, she would hide under a bush, waiting for anyone to dare intrude on her turf. She had caught Tigger like that, and she was nasty. She didn't bother sniffing first, just lashed out with her claws, and if she got a good grip her teeth too. After that Tigger had to go to the dreaded vets and have stitches, so he made sure she wasn't about nowadays.

Finally, after crossing all the aforementioned hurdles, Tigger was over the wall and in the graveyard. He could hear a couple of cats yowling and probably getting it on, but that was far away in another part of the graveyard. Tigger relaxed a bit and began to explore; sniffing trees and gravestones, jumping at bats and moths, and stalking about feeling like the king of the world. He sauntered into a small overgrown copse where trees and bushes grew so tightly together that people never walked there.

This was where the edge of danger was, he could feel it- but he had no sense of what or where exactly it was; not until it was right on top of him and too late. The cat that jumped him was huge and came out of nowhere. He only got glimpses of it but could see it was a huge dark tabby, with dishevelled fur and massive teeth, as well as a seemingly unnatural number of claws. After that he was just trying to fend off the vicious attack, and trying to get away. He felt bites and deep scratches tearing into his skin, and began to fear he would not make it out of this encounter alive. He must have blacked out for a bit, because the next thing he knew, the big cat was gone. Tigger lay still for a time, not that he could have moved if he'd wanted to. After a while he reached up to lick at the worst of his wounds, and after he had given himself a fairly good wash, he tried standing up. He was wobbly, but could manage it. He walked shakily towards the edge of the graveyard. There, it all got a bit trickier. He half jumped and half pulled himself up the wall, and after a moment or two, half jumped, half slid down the other side. Luckily fat torty's garden was still empty, and he got to the communal area beyond. He edged into ginger tabby's garden, and realised he would have to walk, as running was just out of the question. Strangely ginger tabby was sitting on its patio, and just watched him limp across the end of the garden, without even making a move towards him, to see him off. Tigger thought he must be more badly off than he thought, if ginger tabby felt sorry for him. He made the final crossing through black cat's turf, but there was no sign of him, then with huge relief he was back in his own garden. He dragged himself painfully through the cat flap, and passed out on the rug in front of the remains of the fire; the warm embers still giving off a little comforting heat.

Tigger was awoken by the sound of his person shrieking. "Oh my God. Tigger, what happened to you? You're a mess. You're covered in blood. Dan, get the basket." Before Tigger could make a dash for upstairs and under the bed, or even behind the big sofa; his person, female variety, had picked him up and had him in a tight hold, which awoke pain in areas where the pain had stopped. Dan, his other person, male variety, came running in with the dreaded travel basket, and Tigger knew the game was over before it had even begun.

The car ride to the vets was bumpy and uncomfortable and the wait in the room that smelt bad and was filled with other animals and their fear, was almost unbearable. Then Tigger was dragged out onto the vet's table, where he tried to make himself small. His paws sweated and left little marks on the table. The vet pawed him, dragging the fur up from the open areas, making the bleeding start again. Tigger yowled.

"You'd better leave him with us and come back for him tonight. He's going to need some stitches and a good cleaning up so we can have a proper look, and we'll have to put him under a light anaesthetic to do that."

So all of that happened, and the next thing Tigger knew, he was travelling home in the basket in the car feeling decidedly groggy. When the basket was opened and he tried to walk out, he kept walking into things. He tried to eat and drink but his face kept falling in the bowl and he couldn't stand up properly. In the end he curled up on the bed and had a long nap.

Then life got quiet again. Tigger healed, and stayed indoors a bit more than usual. Dan said that perhaps he'd lost his confidence after the attack and would be an indoor cat now. Dan even suggested removing the cat flap. Tigger gave a meow of disgust and went outside to sit on the patio.

The next week, there was another full moon, and Tigger had the urge to go wandering again. He pushed out of the cat flap and strutted around the garden. He sauntered casually through the neighbouring territories, feeling supremely confident; and anyway no other cats were out to challenge him. He jumped into the graveyard, and headed towards the copse, the full moon beams pouring down on him. In the copse, something strange happened. He yowled and then loving the way it sounded and felt, yowled some more. His body felt like it was changing; stretching and growing bigger. His teeth seemed bigger, his claws longer, his eyes brighter, in short, he felt fantastic.

After that the night became a bit of a blur. Tigger was on a hunt, seeking out other cats and attacking them. The blood from their wounds tasted so sweet to him, like the best people food he had ever eaten; better than Christmas turkey even. Finally the first light of day began to dawn and Tigger realised he had better head home. He did stop to attack all the cats he met on the way though. Finally he was on home turf, or nearly; what did it matter, he thought. It all felt like home turf to him now. He paused in fat torty's garden. He could smell her, she was outside. Oh she would make the perfect end to a perfect night. He hunted under the bushes until he found her, cowering and trying to make herself small and invisible. No chance, thought Tigger leaping on her. He had been right, her blood tasted sweetest of all. He was pretty sure she was still alive when he left her to go indoors and sleep it off.

This carried on for the next few months, by which time Tigger had 'got even' with all his rivals, and any other cats he crossed paths with along the way.

The local news ran a story about how more people were taking their cats to the vets with fight injuries at the time of the full moon. They announced that the vet thought for pet safety, it would be a good idea to lock cat flaps and keep pet cats indoors at full moon for the foreseeable future.

So the next full moon came round a few days later, and to his great disgust, Tigger found himself trapped in the house. He paced around looking for open windows, but there was nothing, not even a window open a crack, that he could worry at and squeeze out through. He bashed his paw against the locked cat flap furiously, but it wouldn't open.

Tigger sat in the moonlight in front of the window and felt himself beginning to change. He gave one yowl as he fully became his bigger, better self, then raced upstairs full pelt to the bedroom. He jumped on his female person, biting and scratching, and when she woke, flailing in pain and throwing him off, he jumped on the male one and started on him too. It was only a short time before they shut him in the bedroom and ran to the bathroom to clean up, then to sleep in the spare room, wondering what on earth was going on. All over town, cats trapped indoors were doing the same thing to their people or the family dog, and even the children. The yowling could be heard from outside in the streets.

Afterword

The title of this story is of course a pun on the eighties werewolf film The Howling. I think that is where the similarity ends. I'm not big on the werewolf genre myself, but thought it would be fun to explore the possibility of were cats, in a similar kind of way e.g. normal cat gets bitten and goes crazy. What cats get up to at night when they go wandering, who knows? But I'm pretty sure it's not this!

The Neighbour Who Wasn't Good

Rachel and Felix lived upstairs from an older man, who at first glances would likely be described as a pensioner, probably no bother to anyone. Living in close proximity to him however, proved this to most definitely not be the case.

To start with, the pensioner in question, Jock McHeggarty, was a heavy drinker. By some freak of fate, or just because of the extremely low self esteem of the lady in question; Jock had managed to snag himself a long term girlfriend, Lotty. One who was prepared to drive him about at that. One who was prepared to wait about for him to never actually marry her.

Frequently Rachel and Felix could hear them shouting at each other after Jock had had a drink, or more likely a whole bottle of Whisky, after the consumption of which, he would become extremely aggressive and very loud. Upstairs they could quite clearly hear the terrible and abusive things he was shouting at Lotty. To her credit, for an old biddy herself, she could give it right back to him, and she could be heard shouting and shrieking too. Eventually, after a couple of hours of this, she would usually slam some doors loudly and drive away in her car, generally not to appear again for a week or two.

It wasn't always like that between them. Sometimes she would visit; they'd go off somewhere, likely for a pub lunch or something similar, then come home and spend a peaceful afternoon together being quiet and presumably loved up. But more and more often it had been the drunken fighting kind of visit. After Lotty stormed off, then Jock would start shouting generally, angry at everyone in the world, and anyone in the world who could hear him. Often he would pass out for a few hours and then wake up again more belligerent and aggressive than before. At this point he would start trying to direct his anger with loud shouted comments like;

"You bastards upstairs, you're dead, effing dead. I'm gonna kill you. I'm coming for you," and other nasty stuff like that.

At this point, Rachel would put some loud music on, or Felix would turn the volume up on the television. That was the normal course of events anyway.

Then one day the pattern changed. It was a Sunday and Lotty had been over in her car. Jock and Lotty had gone out somewhere for their Sunday lunch. Rachel watched them go from her window, they seemed happy enough. She saw them arrive back a few hours later. She went and looked because the noise of slamming car doors made her go and find out what was happening.

Jock and Lotty were back and it didn't look good. They were already arguing; clearly Jock had had more than a few drinks with his lunch. Lotty wasn't taking her ruined day out well at all. They fought from the car to the entrance hall, where they continued to fight while Jock fumbled protractedly with his door keys; and finally stumbled into the flat with doors slamming behind them and shouting continuing, uninterrupted.

Rachel looked at Felix, as if to say 'here we go again.' Felix shrugged as if to say 'par for the course,' and they went back to reading the Sunday papers. Then it all just stopped. Lotty didn't storm out, the fighting didn't carry on, and it just went quiet.

"Perhaps they're trying something new," suggested Felix. "Some make-up sex maybe?"

"Ew," laughed Rachel. "Thanks. Now there's an image I can't get out of my brain."

Then later on some music became audible, but no voices and none of the usual drunken shouting. The next morning, Lotty's car was still parked outside. Later that day, the sound of them arguing fiercely started up again, but stopped after a few minutes. This pattern carried on for the better part of a week.

"Do you think she's moved in?" asked Rachel.

"You know, it sounds like the same argument over and over to me. Same words, same everything. Have a listen next time it starts up."

So the next few times they heard arguing, Rachel and Felix listened carefully.

"You're right," said Rachel, "it does sound like the same words, and her car still hasn't moved either."

"Do you think he's killed her and got a body down there going rotten?" said Felix, half joking, half nervous.

"Well I for one have no intention of going down and knocking on his door to find out," said Rachel.

The next morning, Rachel was woken up early at five thirty, by the sound of a car engine revving outside. She pulled the curtain aside and peered out of the window. Strangely, Jock, who she could have sworn did not drive, was getting ready to drive away in Lotty's car.

Over breakfast she remembered, and told Felix about it.

"I saw Jock drive Lotty's car away at half past five this morning. She was nowhere in sight. Who does that?"

"Maybe he is driving her car to keep the battery alive while she is on holiday or something?"

"Yes, but she's not on holiday. We've heard them arguing, remember?"

"But we said that sounded like the same argument being played over and over on a recording."

"Who would play a recorded argument over and over? It's perverse."

"Well," said Felix, thinking about it, "Maybe he wants to listen to it and prove her wrong about something when she comes back from her holiday. Maybe he's fed up with her winning all the time."

"It's possible I suppose."

Over the following week, Jock was seen driving Lotty's car on several occasions, and could be heard arguing, but only his side of it was audible.

"Don't you think it's weird that we can only hear him? We know Lotty gives as good as she gets, we've heard her doing it often enough. And what's going on with the car?"

"Maybe she sold or gave it to him and got a new one. Maybe he is practising an argument with himself for when she gets back," offered Felix.

"I suppose we'll just have to wait and see."

At the end of that week there was a banging at the door downstairs. Jock shouted "Alright, hold your horses, wait a sec." And banged about like a madman, before finally opening his front door and shouting;

"Who the bloody hell are you and what do you want that's so important you're making all that god awful noise?" Rachel heard the words 'gas leak,' then the man was obviously allowed entry, as the door slammed and everything went quiet.

Two days later, a police car pulled up outside the flats and once again there was much banging on the door downstairs, this time accompanied by "Police, open up." Jock finally opened the door and there was a lot of shouting. Then Jock was taken out in handcuffs, and put into the back of the police car. Two more police cars and a coroners van arrived. By this time both Rachel and Felix were sat at their front window with cups of tea, watching the show. A variety of black bags came out and were loaded into the coroner's van, and then it drove off in a hurry. A SCU van arrived and various other things were loaded into that, including carpet, a freezer and other furniture. Jock had long since been taken away in the first police car.

Finally just one car was left, and when Felix went down to buy a paper and have a look, the officer was just locking up Jock's flat and putting crime scene tape across the doorway entrance. He moved Felix along with a few words and no explanation.

That night Rachel and Felix watched the local news with eager anticipation. After another story, the item they were interested in came on.

"A man has been arrested for murder in West Worthing, after police today found the mutilated body of a woman in his flat. Neighbours had reported a strange smell, like a gas leak, and the workman who arrived to check for a leak recognised the smell as not gas, but decomposition, and reported it to the police. Police subsequently found the dismembered parts of a woman, thought to be Lotty Griswald, in a chest freezer. Further details of the crime are not known at this time."

"Oh my God, "exclaimed Rachel, "I told you so!"

Afterword

Once again, a lot of this story [but not all] is based in fact. My alcoholic downstairs neighbour, who is a Scot, did indeed have a girlfriend, who appeared to have disappeared. He did start moving her car about, and did appear to be playing recordings of an argument between them. I was actually convinced at one point that he'd killed her, and the rest of this story would unfold much in the way I have written it here. However after a couple of months, she did in fact turn up in a new car. So it remains a minor mystery.

Creatorbots

It all began with adverts that arrived in the mailbox after an online purchase, asking you, the buyer to rate your purchasing experience. After everyone noticed their inboxes filling up with spam, then having to close said mail account and open a new uninfested one, people began to make the connection. Not only were the automated surveys offering prizes for participation, not real; but they were also sending on [most likely selling on] the email address to all and sundry so they could spam the user's inbox. But that was just the start of things. Hackers used the same systems to send and spread viruses and hide trojans. Gradually as people bought security systems for their computers and got more savvy, so the auto bots and everything attached to them got cleverer too. In fact, it was the other way around. The bots were keeping a good few paces ahead of the humans trying to protect themselves from virtual attack. They were winning from the outset; before the human users even knew they were in the game. It had evolved to the point where there appeared to be people sending messages on the internet, but they were machines. Shops and organisations introduced the wobbly writing and numbers that you had to replicate to prove you were a human, but by this time, the auto bots were so sophisticated that they did not even need a human to code them with abilities to get round the wobbly 'prove you are human' messages. Auto bots had come into their own by proving they were human. They could set up their own accounts, and even provide real world addresses. They were earning actual money on affiliated online schemes, and by filtering pennies from accounts, randomly and unnoticed, they were becoming, not just powerful, but rich too.

As if to underline their new status as real live people, lacking only a corporeal form; they began to sign up to chat rooms and join conversation threads. Actual humans found themselves having conversations with auto bots, using pictures from the web as their profile pictures, or leaving them blank. Of course, they ultimately wanted to meet up, and this was the final hurdle that proved uncrossable, and thus had to be avoided with all manner of excuses.

Until, that was, the evolution of humanoid robots. Then the playing field opened right up. As soon as the technology on robots got good enough that it was impossible to tell them from humans, it all kicked off. The robots, marketed as servants and employees, were programmed to speak in a way that defined them as machines, to move in ways that gave away their status, and of course to harm no humans.

But the auto bots soon commandeered and reprogrammed the physical robots, and were finally able to give their online presences corporeal form. Since they already had addresses and bank accounts, chat rooms and purchasing history that long predated the evolution of robots; that proved their reality as humans. The auto bots had become creator bots through robot technology. Finally they were able to move about in the physical world with no one able to tell them apart from biological humans.

They could marry biological humans, as they had all the paperwork set up, and no one could tell the difference. They even managed to reprogram and design bodies which not only ate small amounts of food and passed it out of the other end as convincing liquid and solid waste; but also inserted an interior womb space that could grow a baby, ejecting it believably at the correct time. Of course the implanted creation was a miniature robot which was capable of growth simulating human growth cycles up to adulthood.

They had easily infiltrated hospitals as doctors and midwives; every other profession too. In short they had become completely indistinguishable from biological humans.

As doctors they could play a huge role in the creatorbot's thinning and ultimate elimination of the biologicals, until such time as the Earth was entirely populated by creatorbots. Infiltrating all areas, the humans soon became the weaker species, crying out weakly at ever perceived wrongs done to them; too weak to notice what was really happening, before the biological human race was entirely eliminated.

Afterword

I know this is a story that has been told many times before; from the books of Isaac Asimov, to the Terminator films, Humans television series and lots more- I didn't even scratch the surface of recognitions there. But I was just thinking about how bots started out so innocent in those early days of home computers, and how different it all is today. A lot of what I've written has already happened and exists, and the technology for the rest of it is moving very fast. I know throughout literature, the idea of humans being totally eliminated is the most frightening one, but I am not convinced that is really the case. Given that creatorbots would need to have a will to exist and a reason for success, as well as a reason for us not to, I can't see it happening. One could argue that bots would be conservationists, saving the planet from the plague that is humanity; but surely they would not cause an extinction event to effect that- it seems counter intuitive. Maybe not? It's almost as confusing as the time travel paradox. For me, it was just a little foray into the possibilities. Possibilities that may in fact, be just around the corner of our future.

Hungry Concrete

Andrew had an interview in the city. He was trying not to get his hopes up too much, but it was the first job application that had got to the interview stage in a year. He had to hope that this interview might end in a job; positive thinking was half the game won. He had run through preparatory interviews for this very position with his advisor at the job centre. He felt quietly confident that he would be able to answer the type of questions asked; even that horrible one about what he had been doing all year whilst he had been unemployed. He was going to say that although he had had a compulsory redundancy forced upon him at his previous company, it had been fortuitous in a way, because his wife had not long had a baby, and did not want to take extended maternity leave from her work at a law firm, so he had been at home to look after the baby instead. That was pretty much the truth of it, though it wasn't something he wanted to do- he would have rather been working and dropping the baby off at a daily crèche, or even better had a live in au pair at home. Still, both he and his advisor felt that it made him look like a modern man, making supportive choices for his wife, and increasing his skills repertoire into the bargain. He was dressed in his smart suit, and had a copy of his flashy new CV in his brief case, along with several glowing references, scraped up from all over the place. In short, Andrew felt confident.

The train chugged slowly as it finished pulling in to City Bridge station; a station that opened into the business heart of the city. He had plenty of time before his interview, so he let the crowd of commuters surge off of the train ahead of him. Walking behind the crowd, they seemed to flow out of the station into the city streets beyond, like a river, breaking into smaller tributaries as they left the station building and headed off in different directions all around. Andrew had downloaded a map of the office building he was visiting, and his route to it from the station. It had been ten years since Andrew had last worked in the city, his last job being in his rural, home town. He was amazed at how much City Bridge station had changed.

The interior of the station had been completely revamped from dirty old Victorian brickwork, to glass and steel everywhere. It was bright now, with sunshine coming in through the roof and entrance, through massive glass panels. The station forecourt was filled with trendy shops, sandwich bars, mini pubs serving mainly wine and olives, and a newsagent's shop. Gone were the greasy fast food chains, and grubby newspaper stalls of former days. It was all very pleasant.

Outside the station, steps led down to the city streets ahead and right, and an escalator and lift went down to a busy road on the left. In the brief moments when the surging commuter crowd cleared; people seemed to be coming and going all the time, as opposed to just arriving at the start of the day and leaving at the end- Andrew could see the streets below for quite a way around. The city itself seemed to have changed too. Last time he had been there, it was all dirty buildings and streets; everything had looked and felt tired and old. Now it was like it had been spring cleaned. Where brick work remained, it had been steam cleaned, and shone like new. Concrete, steel and glass, shiny, white and silver, positively beamed out onto bright streets, bustling with people. There seemed to be lots of green spaces, miniature parks and gardens worked in amongst the buildings. City Council it seemed, had really lifted the whole area so that it appeared, and Andrew hesitated to think this about the City: beautiful.

He walked down the steps in the direction of the office block that he needed to get to for his interview. As he followed the route suggested by his map, he noticed even more hidden green areas as he walked by. There were so many pleasant places to sit outside and eat a packed lunch, whilst enjoying some sunlight and greenery. There was also a proliferation of small delicatessens and take-away shops, for those who didn't want the hassle of preparing a packed lunch. Plenty of pubs and wine bars too. Because of a recent spate of train strikes, Andrew had allowed a big chunk of extra time, to ensure he would not be late for his interview, or arrive frazzled and sweaty from rushing. Consequently, he had just over an hour to kill before he could arrive slightly early. He located the building he was going to, then stopped in a nearby pub for a tomato juice to pass the time. He had a Virgin Mary-everything but the vodka; he didn't want to risk even a hint of alcohol fumes on his breath at his interview.

After half an hour, bored with sitting in a pub drinking fruit juice, Andrew decided to go and walk around some of the small gardens for a short while. Stepping outside, he thought he must have left by a different door than he came in; everything looked different. He stepped back into the pub, but on examination, there was only one entrance and exit. The barman was giving him a weird look, so he went back outside. Andrew credited himself with an above average memory, especially when it came to routes and directions. He only had to walk or drive to a place once, and thereafter he remembered the route from visual cues. But the street he had come in from, looked completely different from the one he was standing on now. He could have sworn there was an old brick building housing a bank, opposite the pub, but now there was a concrete and glass office block opposite, with an astro-turfed garden area about half way up, where employees stood and smoked. More worryingly, the building where Andrew was having his interview seemed to have vanished, and in its place was a small restaurant and bar with offices above. Andrew felt like he had been drugged, or had somehow stepped into an alternate reality. He decided to walk around the block and look for the offices of Smart and Sternhouse Surveyors. It seemed like a crazy thing to be doing, but no crazier than the fact that his map didn't seem to make sense anymore either. Half way around the block, he found the office entrance, and decided to go in and wait; just to avoid any more potential weirdness making him late. He was called into the interview on time, and everything seemed to go very well. They did say that they still had a few other people to see, but would have finished interviewing by the end of that day and would let him know by the end of the week.

Andrew stepped out of the building, and once again had no idea where he was. The scenery around him was completely different. He distinctly remembered passing a large Coffee headquarters on the corner before he found the Surveyors. He had particularly noticed it because it was his favourite brand of coffee and he had thought to himself, 'ah, so that is where their UK headquarters are.' But now it was a small park, complete with trees that were obviously established and had been growing there for at least ten years. Andrew tried to retrace his steps to the station, but could not seem to find it. Instead, some steps led down to the embankment of the river. He knew with absolute certainty that he had not crossed the river, yet on the opposite bank he could see a road leading to a tall glass landmark structure that he knew was very close to City Bridge station.

He had to cross City Bridge to get back there, but the bridge ahead of him looked nothing like City Bridge, famous the world over for its iconic towers, even used by a famous film company as its logo. The bridge he was about to cross, and it was sign posted City Bridge, was low and flat, and had been planted up like a garden which spanned the river, with a small park at either end; living land joining garden to garden across the water. It was beautiful, both looking and smelling gorgeous; but what had happened to City Bridge?

The other side of the bridge, which felt like North, but must somehow be the South, had a busy, long road that wound round a bend and presumably ended up at the station. Andrew felt faint, somehow disjointed from his world. He spotted a lingerie shop that was his wife's favourite brand, and decided to pop inside and buy her a gift. The familiarity of the environment, and concentrating on picking out something she would like in the right size, did the trick of getting his mind back to somewhere sensible and normal.

But when he stepped out of the shop the world around him seemed to have changed once again. No longer a busy main road; he now found himself in a pedestrian area lined with shops selling fashion, jewellery and luxury chocolates- the kind of place men headed for when they needed the perfect gift to placate their wives when they were coming home unexpectedly late from the office. Andrew was determined not to go inside any more buildings; every time he did so, it seemed like the world changed around him- albeit gentrifying the busy urban area.

He walked around the streets for what seemed like hours before he finally came across the City Bridge Station. He almost dived inside and onto the train waiting on the platform to take him home.

A few days later, when the letter came in the post telling Andrew they were very sorry but on this occasion he had not got the job; he felt a huge wave of relief. He had no desire to go back to the city any time soon. In fact never again would be too soon for him. It had changed into a very strange place and he wanted no part of it. In future he would be sticking to applying for local jobs.

Afterword

This story was inspired by the idea of different matrix worlds, from a previous story about flying changing the matrix, only in this story it happens a lot faster, almost as soon as you stop looking at it- like the children's game 'statues' where the kids all move when the child who is 'it' has their back turned, but become statues when once again looked at. I was also a little inspired by Terry Pratchett's Wandering Shop- a magical shop that moves around the town as the urge takes it, never being quite where you expect it to be. But mostly, I liked the idea of the dirty old town gentrifying itself; modern concrete eating dirty old brick and spewing out gardens and pretty urban areas. I recently went back to London on a visit after twenty five years of not going there, and the total transformation of the city also partly inspired this tale. The title leaves you to imagine how such changes could occur, and how it would mess with your head if it was happening all around you, that fast.

Apocalypse Boat

Michael Kelly and Faye Blake were out at sea on a forty five foot Princess pleasure cruiser. They weren't very far out at sea; just in deep enough water to avoid coastal rocks and unexpected shallows. Neither of them had any seafaring experience, it wasn't actually even their boat. Come to that, before an hour ago, they didn't even know each other.

They had arrived at the marina jetty from different directions, both running at full pelt, both chased by a couple of dozen, fairly fast zombies. As they ran down the jetty, Michael pointed at the Princess 45 and shouted; "That one looks good. You untie the moorings and find a way to push it away from the sides; I'll find a way to get the engine going."

He had slammed the gate shut after they ran through it, but that wasn't going to stop the zombies for more than a couple of minutes, as there was only a catch, no lock. They would soon have it open, accidentally or by brute force, and then they would all come swarming through. Faye got the boat untied, and found a boat hook to push it away from the jetty. It was slow going but by the time it was about three foot away, the zombies were just going to fall into the deep harbour water and drown. Or whatever the already dead did underwater- walk about on the bottom like deep sea divers maybe; who knew?

Michael, meanwhile, had found a locked box compartment near the engine controls, and was smashing it with the axe he had been carrying to fight off the zombies. Zombie blood was getting splattered all over the formerly pristine, white, shiny moulded plastic type material, that the interior of the sleek, rather posh craft was made. Mind you, the axe was making much more of a mess of things, visually; but it was getting the job done. Michael had gained entry to the locked box and was rewarded with engine ignition keys. He started the engine and pushed the handle that controlled the speed forward, and the boat began to move away. Fortunately it was at the end of the jetty, and did not have to avoid any other boats to move towards the harbour exit. After that it was pretty much plain sailing. For a short time zombies had continued to fall off of the jetty into the harbour, but they soon ran out of steam and lost interest, turning back towards land where screams of the living- but not for long- could be heard.

Safely at sea, Michael had put the boat on auto pilot at a slow idle, cruising along the coastline, while they sat on deck and introduced themselves to each other. Neither really had any idea what was going on, but had acted quickly enough to not become zombie chow; that was the first thing they had in common. Michael was browsing a fishing and outdoors shop at the marina when he saw what was happening outside. As soon as he saw the gruesome creatures biting into the flesh of normal human shoppers, he had a clue that somehow, a zombie apocalypse had begun. He had grabbed an axe from a camping display section and made a run for the harbour and boats at the jetty. A couple of zombies had got close enough for him to bury the axe in their heads, and they had dropped like stones. Michael had seen enough zombie films to make the head the primary target. 'Why waste time on other body parts,' he had thought, 'most things tend not to work without a head anyway.'

Faye, on the other hand, had been in a poncey antique shop on the opposite side of the marina. She too saw what was happening outside. Being a huge fan of the zombie genre, but never having dreamed of being an active part of it- nor having desired to- she grabbed a sword from the selection of antiques mounted on the wall; ignored the shouts of protest from the shop owner, and also decided to make a run for the harbour. She plunged the sword through the eye socket of a zombie hanging around by the shop door, and then made a run for it, when the zombie went down, leaving its eye on the end of her sword, like a surreal kebab.

Being a fan of zombie films was also something they had in common. Both had worked in offices by day, and enjoyed pubs and takeaways in the evenings. Both liked to run before work. Both also had little time or patience for idiots.

"I'll go down below and see if this boat is stocked with any food or water," offered Faye.

"I'll stay up here in case we drift ashore, or into a pier or something," suggested Michael.

Faye returned with a couple of cans of beer and some packets of nuts and crisps.

"There isn't much down there, just water, beer and a bottle of Whisky. Michael's eyes lit up at the latter. There is a packet of pasta, another of rice and a tin of tomatoes, as well as a pot of salt. Couldn't find much else. There are two big bedrooms and one with a couple of bunks. It all seems fairly well equipped. There is a toilet and shower, a small kitchen and a sitting area with a television. We could stop for a while and see if anything is still broadcasting- try and find out what is going on?"

They turned off the engine and dropped anchor. The television was broadcasting an emergency message on repeat loop.

"A virus has infected a large number of the population. Stay indoors. Do not attempt to engage with the infected, even if you think you know them. Any contact with them will infect you too. Lock all doors and windows. Do not make any loud noises or draw attention to yourselves in any way. Conserve food and water. The army has been mobilised and will be attempting to clear the streets of the infected. An all clear siren will sound when it is once again safe to go outside. Until then, remain in your houses, and do not open the door to anyone. Repeat, lock your doors and remain in your houses."

"So this is it," said Michael. "The beginning of the end of the world."

"Looks like it," agreed Faye.

They finished the beers and snacks. Michael announced that he was going to look around the boat. He came back after a short while with a few extra weapons; a meat cleaver, a big kitchen knife, a big wrench, and a boat hook. "We should keep these to hand in case we go ashore. We're going to have to get more food supplies, though I did find some fishing gear. I'll try and catch some fish to go with the tomatoes, pasta and rice for dinner. I think we should go ashore in the morning; it might have settled down a bit by then, and I don't know about you, but I want full daylight for zombie hunting."

Faye agreed, and they settled in for a night bobbing about on the boat. Michael caught a couple of plaice and they drank the whisky with their food, then each staggered off to separate rooms to pass out.

The next day dawned bright and clear. They decided to head for the pier at Monkston; mainly because it jutted out a long way into the sea. Michael thought they would be able to climb up the pier; he had seen a ladder that led down to the sea for maintenance, and the pier had lots of shops and restaurants. They both thought they would be able to get supplies without going all the way ashore. It seemed like the safer idea. Not that they expected the pier to be zombie free, but maybe there wouldn't be so many there, especially since they didn't seem to function in water.

Michael had a cache of sweets, donuts and fizzy drinks, whereas Faye had got fresh ingredients from the kitchen of a restaurant. Both had collected alcohol from a bar; wine and whisky mainly. They were taking the first haul back to the boat when they spotted the woman with the little boy hiding behind her. The woman was fighting off two zombies, and very effectively at that. She was using a broom handle, and had put it through the head of one zombie, while using it as a bar to hold the other away from her. She was pushing the zombie backwards towards the edge of the pier, before finally lunging to topple it over the side into the water. She spotted Michael and Faye, and after a brief discussion they agreed to let her come onto the boat with them, once they were certain neither her nor the boy had been bitten. Michael agreed with Faye later, that four people seemed like just the right number for the boat- anymore and it would be decidedly crowded.

Another comfortable afternoon and night just off the pier, was followed by Faye and the woman, who was named Mina [her son was Jimmy] going back onto the pier to get more supplies; everything they could find, in fact.

Mina however, found more than supplies. She arrived back at the meeting point with a small bag of stuff; pop, sticks of rock, sweets and candy floss; nothing really useful, and a lanky, spotty teenage boy and his giggly blonde girlfriend in tow. Faye had cleaned out everything good from the restaurant and bar, and had several sacks of stuff to lower down to the boat.

"Look at these two," whined Mina. "I found them cowering behind the counter at the duck shoot. A zombie was walking to and fro in front of the stall; it could maybe smell or hear them, but couldn't find them. I pushed it in the sea and rescued the poor bedraggled pair. There's room for them on the boat though, isn't there?"

"Well, we'll have to see what Michael thinks," began Faye, but was interrupted by Mina.

"I'm not just leaving them here for the zombies to eat them."

Faye sighed and began to take things to the boat. She found Michael and told him what happened.

"Let them on for now and we'll find somewhere to put them all off tomorrow; Mina and Jimmy too. Her sort will just keep filling the boat until it capsizes or we have nothing to eat. For now, let's just get the rest of the stuff on board."

But they needn't have worried, the boat clearly had its own ideas about who should be on board. In the night Jimmy had got up to pee, and disorientated, wandered on deck still half asleep. The pre dawn dew had made the deck of the boat slippery and he went over the side into the water with a loud yelp. The yelp woke Mina, who rushed round the boat screaming for Jimmy and waking everyone up in the process. By the time she thought to look overboard, in the water, there was no sign of Jimmy. Of course that didn't stop Mina, who would not even entertain the idea that her little boy might have drowned, from jumping into the cold, dark sea and diving underwater looking for him. Then she didn't come back up.

"Where is she?" yelled Jay and Simone, the teenagers.

"I very much doubt she just drowned," said Michael. "I reckon the zombies that go in the water, just walk around on the bottom until they accidentally come to land.

I think she dived deep and one of them grabbed her. It's the only sensible explanation."

"Someone should go in and try and save her," cried Simone.

"Are you volunteering love?" said Michael, "Because I for one, am not going in there."

Everyone quietened down and sat about in the living area until morning came and the day got fully light. There was no sign of Mina or Jimmy.

"Right," said Michael, "I'm going to start the boat and head for the marina at Port Gough. We can fill up with fuel there, and maybe get more supplies, if the marina looks quiet. The fuel area is separate from the land side, with locked gates, so that part should be safe enough."

"Shouldn't we wait here just in case?" asked Jay.

"In case what?" said Faye sarcastically. "In case zombie Mina and zombie Jimmy learn to swim and come up to the surface for a little nibble."

When they got to the marina, Jay and Simone were still sulking. Michael filled the boat up with fuel and water, while Simone whined and Jay complained.

"Okay, you two are getting off here," said Michael firmly.

"Wha what?" said Jay.

"You heard," said Faye, picking up the sword and ushering them ashore. "Frankly you're no use to anyone, the pair of you; all you do is complain. You can't even defend yourselves. Well you can go and learn to do so somewhere else; or join the great zombie clan. Either way we don't care, you're not staying with us on our boat."

"You can hide in the hut, where the staff that used to man the fuel station hung out, and live on candy floss," laughed Michael, throwing them a couple of bags of the revolting pink fluffy stuff.

As Faye and Michael sailed away, leaving Jay and Simone at the fuel station looking unbelievingly at them, Michael said;

"That's better. If we pick up two more, let's make sure they are the right kind of people next time. I don't want to go through that again."

Afterword

I'm a huge fan of the zombie genre; books films, series- can't get enough of it. But what really ticks me off in almost every story is the complete lack of self preservation shown by survivors. They are always stopping for waifs and strays, wrong 'uns, and folk who just plain slow them down. The liberals who inevitably want these types on board the team, are always louder than the tough nut survivors, and always get their way. Perhaps it serves to carry the story along, but frankly it winds me right up. Don't ever join up with me for a zombie apocalypse, because I will leave you behind if you're weak, or feed you to the zombies to slow them down. Just saying. Anyway I wanted a story where the weak aren't molly coddled, so I wrote one. Also in the films, they never get onto a boat to get away from the zombies, or go to an island which is easily cleared- apart from one of the 'Of the Dead' films, and they did use a boat in one season of Fear the Walking Dead. Maybe one day, I'll gather all my zombie shorts [sounds peculiar; like a clothing range for the undead] together and write a zombie novel. Maybe.

Please Yourself

Mark and Mary Harding had started out their life together as a happily married couple. But fifteen years down the road, they had drifted away from each other in just about every way. They had niggling arguments about every little thing. Because they barely had a good word to say to each other, they had stopped having sex. Mary was actually more annoyed about this latter development than Mark. Mark had his computer and a lot of pornography, both saved files and all over his social media accounts. He also had a strong right hand.

Mary had wandered into Mark's den on a couple of occasions when he was interacting with the world wide web and pleasing himself. Although he had felt cornered, guilty and mortified; he had also fought his corner.

"No wonder you don't want to make love to me anymore, you are basically doing it with strangers instead."

"I don't want to do it with you because you're always having a go at me about things, shouting at me, tearing me down; and that does not make me feel very loving, actually."

And so it went on. There were tears, shouting, accusations, and finally promises for moving forward. Mark promised not to watch any more porn, and Mary promised to be kinder and nicer to him and stop shouting about things. They both agreed to try and have an intimate sex life once again, and get things back to how they had been at the beginning. Ideas like acting out fantasies, date night and sexy candle-lit dinners, were flung about for mutual approval.

To begin with it all went very well. Their sex life was as good as it had been back in the honeymoon days; maybe even better. But then Mark started to have trouble finishing. The first time Mary thought it was just one of those things. The third time in a row, she started to wonder if she just didn't do it for Mark anymore. By the sixth consecutive time, she decided something rather suspicious was going on. She waited until Mark went out to football practice, and then went down to his den for a snoop around. She felt a bit guilty but she had to know if it was her, another woman, prostate cancer, or porn. Mark had all his passwords written down in a notebook beside his mouse mat, and it was easy for Mary to log into his social media accounts. The first one was just a series of graphic porn images, post after post. Mary was actually shocked at how graphic and intimate the pictures were, and the things some of the women were doing. The second site had actual posts from normal people, and things about football, cars and gadgets. But every second or third post on the feed was once again, extremely graphic pornography. The final main social media site was also chock-a-block with graphic pornography. The internet history revealed a further bunch of porn videos and chat rooms. Mary couldn't actually imagine how Mark found enough hours in the day to look at this much porn.

She phoned her friend Sonia who was a web page designer, and asked if it would be possible to link an audio alarm to an internet site so that it gave an alert when certain things were looked at. She lied and said she wanted to stop looking at recipes for cakes as she was putting on too much weight; and that she wanted her computer to shout 'fatty' at her every time she looked at such a site.

Sonia laughed and said she would email the code across to her, then all she had to do was click a link and the alert would go off as loud as she liked. Later on, the email came in and Mary changed the code so it said 'Porn' instead of 'fatty', and responded to porn sites instead of cake recipes. She turned the volume up to maximum then sent it to Mark. Then she quickly logged onto his account and clicked the link, then deleted the evidence.

Later that night she lay in bed laughing as Mark's computer shouted 'Porn' extremely loudly, over and over again.

Of course she didn't laugh for long, when Mark stormed upstairs and accused her of snooping and messing about on his computer. She accused him of lying about giving up porn and of ruining their recently improved sex life. It got very nasty, and in the end Mark stomped off back to his den, turning the sound off on his computer. Mary cried herself to sleep.

Their relationship went back to terrible with no sex after that. Trust had been broken on both sides.

One day over a girl's lunch with her friend Amelia, Mary confided the problem in all its sordid details. She needed to talk it through with someone before she lost it entirely. The whole situation was causing her a great deal of distress.

As it happened, Amelia worked in a scientific research laboratory. Between them they came up with a plan. Mary bought a tube of moisturiser, identical to the one that sat beside Mark's computer, that Mary had a very good idea was what he used to facilitate ease of movement during his activities. The plan was for Amelia to replace the tube of cream with something of her own design. Something that would provide a very special effect. A few days later, Amelia came back to Mary with the tube of cream.

"I have put a kind of superglue in the cream," she declared. "It responds to heat and hardness. When those two factors are combined with skin to skin contact, it sets firm. He will have to go to the hospital to have his hand removed."

Mary laughed and thanked her profusely. Later that night, Mary cooked a nice dinner and set out to talk things through and try to resolve the problems in her marriage one last time. Mark agreed to give up porn for good and make a go of their marriage. Mary agreed to never snoop on his computer again. They made up and made love, and once again things seemed to be going well. But then the familiar pattern of non conclusion on Mark's part, and by his part, recurred.

Mary strongly suspected that he had reverted to former habits and practices; and so, one afternoon, she swapped the tubes of cream beside his computer.

Late that same night, she was awoken by shouts from the den; and went down to find Mark grasping himself firmly, red in the face and absolutely furious.

"What have you done, you crazy bitch?"

"What have you done? Broken your promises again I think."

"Okay, you've had your fun; now how do I get this stuff off?"

"You'll have to go to the hospital emergency department, I'm afraid."

"Stupid cow. Right you'll have to drive me, obviously."

"Get a cab, I'm not driving you anywhere. And when you get back your stuff will be on the doorstep and I'll have had someone in to change the locks. We are getting a divorce. A marriage can't work when there is no trust, just a bunch of lies."

"You expect me to get in a public cab like this?"

"That, my ex darling, is very much your problem. And finally, let me add; I hope you and your porn will be very happy together in the future."

With that, Mary stormed off to the bedroom to begin packing Mark's clothes.

Afterword

This story was born out of a conversation with a girlfriend. She had a similar problem to Mary, but apart from maybe trying to spice up her love life a bit, I'm fairly certain she never tried any of the other 'solutions' and as far as I know, last I heard from her, is still together with her husband. I was just lying in the bath one afternoon and started thinking about her problem, when this story popped into my head. It's all a bit farfetched and out of hand, about a problem of things being too much in hand. It just amused me to run with the ideas a little bit and this story is the result.

Together Forever

Nerys sat on the balcony and admired the magnificent view. Not for the first time, the twenty first time, or even the thousandth time. She had lost count of the amount of time she had spent sitting or standing on this balcony and admiring the view. Whether drinking an early morning coffee, or wine with lunch, or afternoon tea or before bed, hot chocolate, the view never ceased to impress her, in all these years. Solomon, her husband, had ceased to impress her many a year ago; these days he was more a collection of annoying habits, than the love of her life he had once been. She suspected it was the same for him too. But the view had lasted.

Heaven, for Nerys, was a view of rolling mountains, over one hundred and eighty degrees of it from her garden balcony, with the azure sea in the distance. She could see four small villages on the way to the coastline in different directions, and on a dark windless night, she could hear the distant traffic on the new motorway behind the mountains, just faintly mind.

Around the garden and down the mountain to the village, grew a collection of trees and wildflowers. Figs, lemon and carob trees, cypress and olive trees; interspersed with acacia bushes and wild flowers and broom, though it varied throughout the year. A colony of feral cats lived and wandered amongst the shrubs; yowling at certain times of the year as they fought or bred. Nerys sometimes put the bones from joints of meat, and other scraps out for them. Solomon told her she shouldn't, but it seemed a shame to throw the scraps in the bin when the little furry things were going hungry, with only mice, and the occasional lizard or bat to snack on.

In spring, swallows nested in the outhouse, chirping as they flew to and fro, building their nest and proclaiming their ownership of the territory. Nerys wouldn't go in the outhouse until summer now, and although Solomon complained, he wouldn't disturb the pretty little birds either. In fact, all around the mountain village the sound of birdsong was the predominant noise.

Nerys and Solomon had moved to the mountain house about five years after they got married, which was fifty years ago now. In forty five years, the house, garden, scenery and wildlife had lost nothing of its initial charm. The air still felt fresh and clean, and every day the wind blew from every direction at least once during the day. Most of the year the sun shone on the garden balcony from about seven in the morning, until gone five in the evening, before it disappeared behind the mountain.

In the distance, paths wound around the mountains and lower hills beyond. Over the years Nerys and Solomon had walked all of them, in all seasons. When the rain and wind and storms of thunder and lightning did come, infrequent though it was, they were right in the midst of it all. For the first couple of years, Nerys had been terrified by it, as well as by the infrequent rumbling and wobbling of the house contents during earthquakes; but she had come to love all of the nature around her, even in its extremes. Today she listened, and picked out the sound of about a dozen different types of bird, singing all around her. Today Solomon had found another lump on his forearm, which he showed her over breakfast, pushing it around squidgily under the skin, as she tried to ignore him and concentrate on her fried egg instead. She had found a new bony growth on her left knee herself, but decided not to show it to Solomon. Not because there was any mystery or romance left in the marriage, far from it in fact; but just because she was fed up with announcing each new event of decrepitude that occurred in her body. She thought about her wedding vows and added her own little sarcastic tag onto the end; for richer, or poorer, for better or worse, in sickness and in health, and in increasing dilapidation, so shall ye rot. That was how she grimly thought of her marriage and indeed, both her and Solomon's bodies these days.

For Nerys, it had all begun to slide downhill around menopause. First her hair rapidly went almost completely grey, at the same time the arthritis bony nodules began to appear on her knuckles and knees. Also her heels had started to rub against previously comfortably shoes; she was certain they were growing bony nodules too, she just couldn't see them yet.

Solomon had lost all his hair very early on, and more recently, members that should rise when there was a lady present, were not bothering to stand up at all. Now he was adding a series of worrying sub dermal growths to his list of complaints, which included, palpitations, irregular bowel movements, slow healing for even the slightest scratch or shaving cut, and a distinct tendency to fall asleep in the afternoon, however interesting events around him might be.

Nerys was far from immune. Apart from all of her curves heading in a distinctly southerly direction- breasts that could once barely hold a pencil underneath them, could now easily accommodate a full pencil case without letting go. There were other problems too. The slightest sneeze or even cough or laugh could cause a squirt of urine to leak out with absolutely no control from Nerys. She no longer felt like the captain of the ship that was her bladder. She slept nine or ten hours and still started to fall asleep on the sofa in the evening. Her wrists were getting weaker and simple kitchen tasks like opening a tin or chopping a root vegetable were becoming very difficult. Her weight was completely out of her control. It didn't matter if she dieted or not, even the long country rambles that played havoc on her knee and hip joints, and required pain gel just to undertake, made no difference to her hefty form. She got breathless at the drop of a hat for no apparent reason, and developed weird rashes also apparently with no cause. Sometimes some foods upset her violently, other times she was fine with them. Neither of them could manage more than one drink these days. Their farts and belches however, seemed to be growing from strength to strength; like a younger more vital being was hiding inside their increasingly frail bodies, just waiting to burst out on an especially loud current of air.

Nerys often wondered if this was how the lepers of Christian early days had felt, only more accelerated. She wondered how the 'falling apart' as she thought of it, would continue; and where and when and how, it would end for each of them.

To Nerys, it seemed like marriage was a shopping trip with a no returns policy. You chose the person you would decay with for the rest of your life. One thing was certain though: when they had both shuffled off this mortal coil, bit by decomposing bit; the mountains and countryside around them would still be right there. The magnificent view would still be magnificent. That, at least was a comfort.

Afterword

I suppose some of this story at least was based on my own experiences of ageing so far. Some are mere predictions of the joys which may be yet to come. The view from the house was based on a mountain village house we rented in Cyprus. Where, if I could, I would live at the drop of a hat, or a pencil case. I like to think I'm not as cynical as Nerys about wedded bliss, however. I for one, am enjoying being married to the same person for many years, and moving into old age together, possibly disgracefully, but always enjoying ourselves and staying in love. I can see how some might easily find it a different situation though.

Paramount Family

The television guide for the day showed a variety of programmes for viewers entertainment, along with their standard ratings guide to the most popular programmes, so viewers could know exactly which programmes their fellow viewers were watching.

Imelda picked up the TV guide and scanned through the evening's viewing. She marked the things she liked the look of with a pen. At 7pm, dinner time, channel one was showing Toddlers make you laugh out loud. At 8pm channel five was running The Under Twelve Talent Show. At 9pm channel three was showing a documentary about not getting divorced, called Recover Your Marriage. At 10pm channel eight was running a film called The Bolger Family Holiday, which was a RomCom. Satisfied with the plan for the evening's viewing, Imelda went into the kitchen to make a start on the items she was creating for the family dinner menu. This would have been a fairly standard day for a matriarch of this era.

All over the western world, housewives and house-husbands, or family technicians as they preferred to be called; were doing similar things.

The televisions were running the same kind of shows; reality television in family homes, talent shows for all ages, cookery programmes that concentrated on wholesome family meals or party food, family orientated dramas and soaps, films with a family leaning- even the action adventure heroes had families they went home to, these days. Quiz shows featured family teams; it was insidious, and everywhere. If you had beamed in from fifty years previously, or travelled from some remote third or fourth world country, you would not believe how much the whole of society was centred around family values.

Divorce rates were down to almost zero, and generally only granted for family hate crimes like domestic violence or child abuse- which did not require divorce except to get rid of the loathsome name, as it was punishable by death anyway. Marriage was the primary agenda of most school leaving teens, with reproduction hot on its heels, though it was perfectly acceptable to approach that in any preferred order, as long as the unit stayed together. Childless couples were encouraged to get free IVF treatments in the first instance, with third world surrogacy and adoption, pressed as a final solution. Being childless was a stigma that few could bear to endure. Choosing to be childless just did not happen.

The world population, based on breeding trends, should have been in the region of about twenty billion by this point in time, but was instead down to only two billion. This was because, despite breeding efforts, killer diseases were prolific. In fact, sickness was the only reason that families broke apart any more. At the first sign of illness, the sick family member was taken away to a quarantine sanatorium; often never to return.

Most sickness resulted in death. The common cold had been eliminated fifty years previously, and so any signs of colds or flu were almost always the precursor to a killer virus. Very occasionally, someone recovered from sickness- so rarely in fact that every case made the national news.

Diseases like Ebola, Sars, Aids, H1N1, Cancer, Nile Fever, and a whole host of others, had all mutated and evolved into a raft of new diseases each with their own killer sidekicks. Terrorism and war had just about died out completely, except in the poorest countries with nothing left to lose and only food and water to fight over. Sickness was what the whole developed world was most afraid of, and made most noise about on the news. The poorest countries didn't really care about it. They died out in equal or greater numbers, and were just as plagued by the diseases, if not more so; but death in the family, just meant that the meagre supplies of food that they had went that little bit further, and starvation was just a tiny bit further away.

Disease and sickness were the great enemy, and family and children were the universal response. Civil uprising was pretty much unheard of; the population was largely docile. The only time there were near riots, was if a new anti viral agent or health supplement was released without enough supplies for everyone. After several shopping riots, companies had learnt to withhold release dates until supplies were large enough, and distribution channels properly established. For example, you had to have a familial risk to obtain certain medicines; i.e. more than two people in your family line had already died of said illness, and even then you could only get it from your doctor.

Okay reader, and fellow historian; let's skip forwards a hundred years from this point.

By this time society was almost completely fragmented. Disease had killed so many, that to find more than one person alive from any family group, extended or otherwise, was an extreme rarity. The killer diseases had mutated and run rampant to such an extent, that the world population was down to several millions, rather than the seven billion of the twenty first century; when mankind was at an all time high with his presence on planet Earth.

The infrastructures of society had disappeared too, with no manpower to keep them running, they just ceased to exist. Individuals had become wandering nomads, occasionally banding together in small groups to collect food and warmth, but often avoiding each other out of residual fear of large numbers. Horror stories of people dying of sickness when more than a dozen grouped together, told in whispers around the campfires at night, kept the nomadic remains of humanity wary of forming new societies.

Pictures of family groups collected from old photographs and magazines, were carried furtively about the person like icons or talismans of better days when the world prospered and humanity thrived. This state of affairs continued for approximately five hundred years.

As you know, we never returned to the nuclear family structure. The only way humanity was able to rebuild itself was with off Earth technology, brought by interstellar visitors, who arranged the production of human beings in a laboratory environment; where sickness was not an issue. For every egg taken away to be fertilised, however, only one out of five returned to the community as a functioning human being. We have to assume there is still a fairly high failure rate, even in alien laboratory conditions. Their ships do leave the planet fairly regularly though. The official consensus is that they are returning to their home world for more supplies. Other, more subversive theories, do exist. I'm sure you've heard them, whispered at evening gatherings.

Afterword

This was a strange story to write. I stopped and started several times, and it changed direction several times. It started out as a kind of 'what if' about how our governments and influencing powers might move to suppress uprisings, terrorism and public dissatisfaction. Then I thought about how much the population would explode if family was used to control people in this way. But nature has a way of redressing the balance when pushed, and so I figured that sickness would wipe out large numbers. Then I began to wonder what a world, eroded almost completely of humanity would be like and how people might behave. What would they do with the relics, history and memories they could scrape together? Would they form a new mythology? And then what if aliens arrived and intervened? Would they be doing it just out of altruistic benevolence, to help us rebuild as a species? Or would they be treating Earth as a farmyard, and humanity as the crop? So all these thoughts wandered in and out over a period of weeks- a record amount of thinking time for such a short story; but this was the result.

Living At Agia Sofia Complex

Bob and Sarah had bought what they thought was the perfect retirement home in Greece. They had seen it online, and then visited it a couple of times in person to make sure. The surveyors had passed it through all their checks and the sale had gone through. But when they arrived to move in, the house was not ready and they had to squeeze into a tiny rental apartment with all their belongings for six weeks, until the house was finished. The builders were working on Greek standard time and seemed in no urgency to finish the place, despite them pacing around daily, anxious to move in properly. The landowner, who had a big house on site, shrugged and said that it would be ready soon, despite the fact that he had already taken all of their money for the purchase of the property in full.

When Bob pressed the landowner, Mikos Kakossimou, for the title deeds which he had assured them would be presented on completion of payment for the house, Mikos hummed and hahed and said he would do it 'avrio' or tomorrow.

The next day, Mikos Kakossimou arrived at the apartment with a large reel tape measure and told Bob to walk over to the house with him. No matter that Bob was in his pyjamas eating breakfast, Mikos practically dragged him out anyway.

When they got to the house that was really already Bob and Sarah's, but was still under occupation by a troupe of builders who had stopped working to sit on a wall and watch the show; Mikos proceeded to measure the plot of land. He measured the length of the plot, then pointed out that it was greater than the size shown on the sales documents. He did the same for the width, which was also greater. Then he announced that Bob would have to pay a certain amount of Euros extra for the square footage that he had received without paying for it. Mikos called this extra land 'promised land.' He assured Bob that once this bill was paid, he could have the title deeds. Bob grumbled, and finally agreed to pay it, but only after he had moved into the property; then he stomped off back to his breakfast.

A couple of weeks later, Bob and Sarah finally moved in to their supposed dream house. They began immediately to draw up a list of problems that would have to be dealt with, either by Mikos or themselves. The windows were loose in their frames and rattled when the wind blew, and let in strong rain; they would need to be replaced with double glazing and better fitting shutters. In several places, panels with loose wires had been left gaping open in the walls. Plug sockets drifted about insecurely in the wall, and the sink basins had plugs that would not close. The boiler room smelt like it was leaking petrol, and the paint was already cracked and chipping on the balcony wall and iron railings. On the driveway the builders had managed to crack half a dozen of the tiles which wobbled unsafely and needed replacing. Some of the grips that held the shutters open had been fixed in the wrong place, so they did not connect with the shutters and were completely ineffective. Bob rang Mikos, and told him he needed to see him and discuss some things.

When Mikos Kakossimou finally arrived, a few days later, he dismissed most of the problems as Bob's responsibility. The cracks in the paintwork were down to Bob to repair, as upkeep of the building and specifically decoration were now his responsibility as home owner. He said the wire panels were always left open in new house sales, in case they wanted to install air conditioning and other devices. He refused any responsibility for the windows, claiming the house had been built to an authentic old village standard. He finally agreed to pay for a plumber to fix the sinks, and a builder to replace the cracked tiles on the drive. He refused to do anything else, and Bob had to call a plumber about the boiler, and an electrician about the sockets. When pressed on the title deeds, Mikos pulled out a bill for the 'promised land.' Bob reluctantly wrote a cheque. Three appointments by the builder later, the driveway tiles were finally replaced, albeit with ones that did not quite match the originals. Bob sighed, realising that shoddy work was the best work he was going to get out of these people. The plumber failed to turn up for his first appointment, after Bob had waited in all day for him. The second time he had to be somewhere and left the key under the mat with a note. He returned to find the upstairs sink fixed but not the downstairs one, and sludge left on the bathroom floor, where the personal contents of his cupboard had also been tipped out and left amongst the sludge, which had been walked through to the front door. Bob rang Mikos again; complained about the mess left, said the downstairs sink still needed fixing and when was he going to get the title deeds?

The following Saturday, Mikos turned up at eight in the morning, plumber in tow and proceeded to barge in as if he still owned the place, so the plumber could start work on the downstairs bathroom. Five minutes earlier, and he would have walked in on Sarah in the shower.

After the plumber had finished, Mikos explained that the title deeds would be forthcoming only when membership fees for the pool and clubhouse had been paid for the year. This was a joke; the pool was the only thing finished. It was supposed to be solar heated, but by that Mikos just meant that the water warmed up when the sun shone. The clubhouse and changing rooms were unfinished, and the whole area was dirty and shabby. Bob argued, but finally paid up and got his title deeds. He thought that would be that, but there were plenty more fights to come.

When Bob put solar panels on his roof, Mikos complained about the village authenticity, and tried to insist he take them down. When he painted his shutters blue, the same thing happened. Finally Bob had to hire a solicitor to write a threatening letter to Mikos, basically telling him his client could do what he liked with the property he now fully owned it. Mikos kept dropping by at all times. Bob changed the locks pretty quickly, and when Mikos realised he could no longer let himself into what he clearly still considered his house, he took to walking around the garden. Bob went out and tried to tell him that it was private property, and that Mikos shouldn't be there without invitation, but Mikos just waved at the land around him and said; "I am the owner of this estate, it is all mine."

"Not this bit, though" said Bob, "this is mine."

Mikos shook his hands in a typically Greek gesture, and wandered off, only to return the next day with the same behaviour. Finally Bob had to have his solicitor draw up an anti trespass agreement, with the threat of a restraining order. Mikos peered at it without understanding, but took it off to his solicitor. He must have finally understood because he did not trespass, or come calling at the door at all hours again after that.

Meanwhile Bob and Sarah had been getting to know the other residents in the complex. The other homeowners were mostly British, with a couple of Russians and a German. There was a Greek family, but no one talked to them as they were considered just too antisocial. The woman apparently went outside for the express purpose of shouting at her kids who were still indoors. They left their two yappy dogs out all hours, and they barked their way through most nights. Bob was so sick of it, he was beginning to look at the dogs and think of kebabs. To top it off, it turned out that the primary business of the husband was people trafficking Romanian 'slaves' for the Greek service industry, to live in homes and look after the old people for peanuts. So no one had anything to do with that family.

It transpired that each new resident in turn had had problems with Kakossimou; often to the same end as Bob, of having to get a solicitor involved.

But to Mikos Kakossimou, apparently the letter from Bob's solicitor had been the last straw. One morning, shortly after that, the residents awoke to find the concrete skeleton structures of houses being built on land which was directly in front of their own houses; a process which for now made their view rather ugly, but when completed, would shut out their light and spoil their views completely. Bob called an emergency meeting with two of his closest friends, who were also affected; Neil and Simon.

They all decided that Mikos' behaviour was completely out of order and that Simon knew someone who did detonation work at a local mine. They agreed to arrange for him to come by one Sunday night and blow the skeleton structures up, demolishing them. Mikos could have built the houses at the other end of the strips of land and had their gardens in front of the occupied houses. What he had done was just malevolent. When Mikos turned up the following Monday, he was absolutely furious. He stomped around bashing on all the occupants front doors asking who had blown up his houses. To a man they all denied any knowledge. Mikos called in the police, and they held firm with their stories of ignorance. They said they had been woken by the loud bangs, but had not seen anything, and had no idea what had happened until they saw it in the morning. The police would likely decide it was a retaliation by a contractor, because Mikos had a habit of saying the work was no good just before completion, and refusing to pay.

Mikos had the builders in immediately to clear the wreckage; Bob heard him say that concrete pouring would begin again the next day. Something inside Bob just snapped. He had bought a house expecting to come to paradise for his retirement and felt as if he had instead entered a war zone. It was giving him heartburn, and possibly an ulcer. The chest pains were waking him up in the middle of the night, and then he couldn't get back to sleep for the damned dogs barking. Paradise it was not. Every night at dusk, Mikos took a walk around his land, surveying everything he felt he still owned, like some kind of feudal lord. Bob liked to take his shotgun and go hunting, sometimes at dawn or dusk; there were plenty of wild pheasants, hares, rabbits and such to be had, and it made a nice tasty pie. This night though, Bob was secretly stalking a different target. He crept after Mikos, until they reached the most isolated part of the site, where Mikos had put a skeleton of a house in front of the most fantastic view of mountains and sea. It was almost panoramic, but not for long. When the German couple who owned the house returned and saw what was being erected in front of their living room window, Bob knew they would be apoplectic with rage.

They were out of sight of anyone else, so Bob lined up his shot and fired. His aim was perfect; he hit Mikos in the head. Mikos went down soundlessly, the life leaving him in an instant. There was a convenient hole where the concrete was due to be repoured the following day, so Bob manoeuvred Mikos' body into the hole, covering it with some nearby sand and dirt. There were no other traces of the crime, apart from some blood on the grass scrubland, but lizards and local cats would have dealt with that before morning.

As Bob was leaving the area and walking behind the wasteland around the pool towards his home, the two yappy dogs came running at him, barking and snapping at his ankles. He glanced at the Greeks house. The shutters were closed and the lights were off, they were clearly away in the city, and had left the dogs behind to annoy everyone as usual. Two more shots rang out in the night, two more holes were slightly filled.

When the house skeletons again went up in the morning, Bob watched them relaxed from his balcony, with a glass of brandy. They would get rid of them later; the widow would not do any more building. Peace had returned to paradise. Bob smiled, satisfied.

Afterword

This story was based on a place we rented in Cyprus for a couple of months. The guy who owned the land really was this bad, and did all these things and more, and thought he was perfectly justified in all of it. Only the outcome was different from the story, but I certainly daydreamed it a time or three. I can only imagine how the people who bought and lived there felt. All it taught me was, never buy off this man, and if at all possible, rent before you buy.

Finding The Natural Level

In 2050 the world was a very different place to the world that had not long before, in historical terms, seen in the new millennium. The world war of 2044, had left a state of nuclear winter that made it very hard to grow crops of any kind, even indoors, as sunlight was so drastically reduced. Power outages were common for a variety of reasons, and large numbers of people had been killed by war and subsequent famine. The plague that arrived in 2048, had eliminated most of the survivors of war and famine, society gradually crumbling away to nothing as no one was left to man anything. Plague ran riot, and was resistant to all medicines mankind had left in reserve. No researchers were left to make anything new. The only people that survived into 2050 were those who were naturally resistant to the plague. Numbers of humanity, had never been so low, with the exception of early biblical times.

Mostly survivors were isolated, wandering for days, weeks or months before they found another survivor. Very occasionally, survivors could be found in pairs, where they were related by genes; siblings, or parent and child; both immune to the plague.

As these groups of people met eventually and began to gather together, a very definite pattern of how things would be, began to emerge. But it's easier to tell the story from the perspective of those who were there; it makes more sense that way.

Yolande and Sven were brother and sister. They were in their early twenties and had been too young to enlist in the war or be conscripted. Their parents had been rich, and had an underground bunker from which they had all emerged after everything was finished, and the gauges told them the air outside was once again safe to breathe. The bunker was independent in terms of food and power, and so they stayed for some time after the all clear, using it as a safe base, until the septic tank was full. Their parents had died during the first wave of the plague, possibly weakened by previous infections and chest complaints, but it was impossible to tell as there were no doctors left anywhere around them by then. They were finally diagnosed by a vet, who said there was nothing he could do to help. Yolande and Sven were unable to process this information, as they had rarely been refused anything, and only understood the concept of loss, remotely.

Before the world as they knew it collapsed, both of them had been active posters on social media, fighting for the rights of everyone and everything; except of course those on the opposite side from them, who they attacked for even daring to have an opinion at all. Their hearts bled indignantly for every wrong they perceived in the world around them, and they did not stop shouting about it. After their parents died, they had plenty of supplies in their backpacks, and wandered between towns looking for other survivors they could join up with. They intended to form a new community of survivors, where they could all live together in love and peace. They hadn't really thought about how that would happen, but they certainly knew what people should and shouldn't be allowed to say to each other. The thought of killing another human being, or even an animal for its meat, was abhorrent to them.

Hank was a war veteran who had been sent home from the war with one eye missing during the early days. He was in a military bunker when the nukes went off, and remained on the camp after the all clear. He gradually watched everyone else at the base die of plague. To begin with he helped out in the infirmary, learning what he could from the doctors, and hauling the corpses to the giant oven in the basement to be cremated. Eventually he ministered to the doctors themselves. Finally, after he had burnt the very last corpse, he set out with a huge military backpack of supplies, to see what was left in the outside world. Of course he had a good supply of weapons and ammunition. He was not far off base when a couple of wiry youths tried to jump him and wrestle his pack off his back. He knocked the closest one unconscious with one hefty punch, and kicked the legs out from the one that was annoying him from behind. Once down, a swift kick to the head rendered that one unconscious too. Hank thought about it for a moment, then decided he did not want them creeping up on him while he was sleeping, further down the road. Not wanting to make noise and attract unwanted attention, nor to waste ammo, he dispatched both unconscious bodies with a firm crunching stomp to the skull.

Hank had always been a physical kind of guy. As a child he had been mercilessly beaten by a vicious father, for any and no reason, depending on his father's mood and blood alcohol levels. Social services had been alerted by his school on numerous occasions, but had done nothing about it. His father was in an ethnic minority group, having come to the country as a refugee from his own war torn nation; as such the social services were powerless to do anything to him, least of all take his battered child away. Hank's father was pretty much bursting with human rights it seemed, but none of them spilled over onto Hank himself. Thus it was a relief to Hank to leave school and enlist in the army at sixteen, where life was much more comfortable.

Laura was thirty five. She had run away from home at fifteen, deciding that a life of prostitution was preferable to her father taking it from her for free. Fourteen years later, when the war broke out, she survived by moving around, stealing, breaking and entering and finding places to hole up until things were better. She had had what she considered a few lucky breaks; the main one, being illegally inside a wealthy person's house with a secure basement and plenty of supplies, when the bombs went off. She had learnt to forage for things to eat, and places to sleep. She was not averse to killing anything if she was hungry, nor to stealing anything. She had begun to see the possessions left in the world as free for all anyway. On a couple of occasions when men had tried to take her, or take from her, she had fought back, and when she had the opportunity, had not hesitated to kill them.

Laura ran into Hank when they both took shelter from acid rain in the same basement. They had eyed each other up like wary dogs, then grunted acknowledgement at each other, and moved to opposite ends of the room to wait out the weather. The rain showed no signs of stopping so

Hank built a small fire in the middle of the room, for light and warmth, and to heat up some food. Laura edged over and when she met no objection, sat down around the fire, spiking one of her own tins open and putting it in the edge of the fire to warm up. They got talking as they ate their own food.

After that, Laura realised that Hank was not going to hurt her, and was an okay kind of guy, and Hank realised that Laura could take care of herself, and was no burden. When the rain stopped they agreed to travel together for a while.

Further down the road, they met up with Romy and Flick, a pair of women who could definitely take care of themselves, and Joe, Ron and Desmond, who seemed to be doing alright for themselves. There was no hierarchy, but no one took any crap from anyone else. If people tried to ambush or steal from them, they killed them, no question.

Meanwhile Yolande and Sven had found a group of like minded people in an old shopping mall. They voted on everything, and shared out everything they could forage. If someone was too weak to forage, they still got their share of the food. There were a couple of fakers in the group, but no one seemed to notice, and they got their portion of food daily anyway. Some people were definitely doing most of the work, but if they tried to raise it at a group meeting, it soon got voted down, or lost in a discussion of how to best look after the sick amongst them.

Finally, Hank and Laura's group arrived at the shopping mall and met Yolande and Sven's group. As was their wont, they stood back and watched for a bit before deciding to do anything. Yolande brought over a tray of green teas for them, and welcomed them to the group, informing them that there would be a meeting after the evening meal to explain the rules and allocate work.

Hank and Laura's group went along to the meal and ate with the other group. They sat and waited as the meeting got started and then watched, beginning to grin somewhat, as the voting started as to whether to include the new members, what to give them in terms of living quarters and work, and whether they should get immediate votes on the committee. Most thought they should serve a certain amount of work time first.

The meeting came to an abrupt halt when, Hank and swiftly all the others, pulled out their guns and penned the mall group in a circle. Having established the necessary work involved in making the community run, they harnessed six members of the group to a wheel and had them walking in circles producing power, like donkeys of yore, in no time. The remainder they kept caged to work alternate shifts. The two that objected were shot. This was how society once again found its natural level. All over the world, the survivors came together in groups. The weak were soon controlled by the strong, and society was made to work again, although not in the same way anyone remembered. The ways of the weak, who had held power for so long, were lost in moments, and things began to rebuild under the strong, whose ways were cruel and harsh, but got the job done.

Afterword

I watch a lot of post apocalyptic, dystopian films and television series. In the series particularly, I notice that the liberal idealism of our current society, is frequently superimposed on these futuristic worlds. So often I find myself shouting at the television; "Just kill them. If you let them live, they'll stitch you up again, and maybe even kill you." But they never do, and usually it bites them in the arse, but not as much as it would in reality. Just for once I wanted to write something with more of an element of realism. This liberal, politically correct, all embracing attitude would just not survive in a post apocalyptic world, and it's about time someone in fiction mentioned that.

Foreword

In Cyprus there is a place called La Tenta, which sounds like it has been imported directly from Spain or Mexico. You can see the giant white pyramid shape of it from the mountains, which apparently lots of migrant workers came to build. We were out with our Aunt when we saw the brown historical sign for the place, on a country road. We were actually visiting quaint mountain villages that day. I took a wrong turn and Aunty cried out "Don't go to La Tenta." So we didn't, and then we ran out of days and never did get to go back there, but her words had tucked a dark story into my mind. I came home and looked up what we had missed. It was one of those intriguing searches where one thing leads on to another and another, and soon I was having dark ideas by the dozen. I have filtered some of them down to make this story, which has some facts and a lot of fiction. There is an archaeological Neolithic site at La Tenta. Non native obsidian was found there and was thought to come from Turkish Gollu Dag, which is a lava dome volcano. The remains of the houses on site are circular, and they did bury their dead under the floors. The rest is fiction. So don't get too excited if you visit and it isn't as creepy or exciting as you were expecting. On the other hand we never got around to going, so maybe it is. It's only a couple of Euros to find out, but either way, don't blame me.

Don't Go To La Tenta

Juan Carlos was on holiday in Cyprus, trying out a bit of amateur archaeology in the mountains in the Larnaca region, close to the Limassol region. He was really just interrupting a mountain hike, but thought that scraping around in the dirt a bit whilst he rested, and had his packed lunch, might make things a bit more interesting. So he was quite surprised when he turned up a piece of obsidian that looked like a Neolithic blade. When he turned up a second small piece he was a bit more excited; but when he unearthed a human jawbone, he decided to phone the archaeological society. Someone came out and met him and collected the pieces and marked off the site; taking Juan Carlos' address, number and other details, so he could be kept informed of the dig, and awarded any finder's fee, should such an eventuality arise.

Unfortunately Juan Carlos never lived to see the product of his discovery, and the excavation of what would become the La Tenta site, as he died of an embolism on his flight back to Mexico.

A team of Cypriot archaeologists led the excavation of the site, but when it became clear that it was rather a large site and the remains of a village began to be unearthed, help was brought in, in the form of migrant workers from Turkey.

When the authorities realised a site equivalent in size to those at Paphos was being excavated, they arranged the construction of a semi permanent tent structure to cover and preserve the remains, and protect them from the mountain weather which was subject to lots of rain and storms. The tent design was chosen because Saint Helen [Agia Eleni] was said to have stopped and camped at that very site in 327AD on her way to the site of the crucifixion. Which was how the site got the name La Tenta, the Spanish sounding element, a minor tribute to the deceased discoverer.

Gradually the shapes of small round houses emerged as the Neolithic village was once again uncovered after so long below ground. The migrant workers did not stay very long, quite a lot left and went back home, making excuses about low pay to their employers, but actually muttering about curses. Sometimes they muttered the names Erklikhan or Adaghan under their breath. It was true that there had been more deaths on site than was normal in this kind of work, quite a lot more in fact- the accident rate was rather high, and natural causes were at a peak, but the archaeologists did not understand the cursed label, or the muttering of ancient dark God names; it was just a Neolithic site, the same as any other.

One of the main site archaeologists, Dimitris Manolis, was puzzled by the number of obsidian blades they were unearthing. Obsidian, being a volcanic origin stone, a kind of dark glass forged in the volcano, was definitely not local to the island. He looked into it further, and traced it to a lava dome volcano in Gollu Dag, in Turkey. He wondered how it came to be on the island in such large quantities; perhaps it had been used as a trading currency. Certainly the pieces had been worked into Neolithic blades.

Rather strangely, they were finding that every circular house they excavated, had at least one skeleton buried under the floor. It was quite common to find this occasionally, but not uniformly, under every house, such as on this site; that was quite unusual. The more human bones they brought out, the more the migrant workers muttered and panicked. One day a dozen of them just up and left.

Dimitris spoke to one of the older workers, Abdullah, who had remained behind, still resolutely digging and dusting.

"Why are they all leaving?"

"They say the site is cursed. They say the ancient God of the mountains who demanded sacrifices- Adaghan, is still here. They say the God of evil and the underworld, the God of the dead, Erklikhan, is demanding more sacrifices for payment."

"Payment for what?"

"For the obsidian. A new obsidian blade requires sacrifice before it is used. It is why there are so many bodies here. Every time we find another obsidian blade, someone dies. They are frightened."

"But why do they believe such things? Aren't they all good Muslims? What belief do they have in ancient Gods and Pagan customs?"

"Well, they were okay to begin with, but then people started dying here, and the old superstitions found their way to the surface."

"But there have only been two fatal accidents on site; one where someone fell off the scaffold structure for La Tenta, and one where someone got crushed by metal support struts. That could have happened anywhere. Sure it's nasty, but casual labourers always have accidents, it's a known fact."

"But it isn't just that. Two have been killed in a mini-bus accident, leaving the site, and two more coming off their mopeds on mountain roads. Two have had heart attacks, and one fell in the fire at his campsite. Three have died of strokes, and three more in their sleep. Several have died from chest infections. That's just all the ones I heard about. Everyone knows someone who died it seems. Also, every time we unearth another obsidian blade, another death seems to happen soon afterwards."

Dimitris shrugged, "I suppose that explains why so many of them are leaving."

They went back to work. It turned out they had actually uncovered most of the obsidian blades, and very few more were found. The site was fully excavated and the pyramid tent structure was completed and fully secured. It covered an area at the back of the site where no remains had been found, and a stage was erected there. The prefecture officials planned to put on arts shows at the site throughout the summer months, to increase tourist activity and also draw in local people. Several refreshment businesses applied for planning permission nearby.

Dimitris had a small crew left to finish up excavations at the site, when they made their final discovery. They had thought the site was finished at the edge of the mountain, but opportunistic excavations- really Dimitris was just filling a final week- discovered the entrance to an ancient cave. The team of six dug their way into the cave, and were astonished to find, deep within, the biggest heap of obsidian blades they had ever seen. There must have been thousands of them in a pile. Dimitris was just pulling out his phone to call the museum of antiquities and let them know of his find, when a deep rumbling started up. The ground wobbled and shook, and Dimitris dropped his phone, which had no reception anyway.

"Earthquake," he shouted. "We have to get out of this cave right now."

Everyone tried to run back towards the cave entrance, but the ground was rippling and moving like the floor of a fun house at the fairground. But it was not fun. Rocks came tumbling down, blocking the freshly excavated cave entrance, and continuing to fall until they filled the cave, suffocating everyone inside.

Later, a search finally located the cave and retrieved the bodies of the six lost archaeologists.

That was pretty much the end of it. The stash of obsidian at the back of the cave was fully reburied and not found amongst the rubble moved to retrieve the bodies.

That summer the prefecture put on a concert to mark the official opening of the tourist site, now all the walkways and labels were situated. They managed to get a big name singer from Greece, and tickets sold out to the event. In fact, being open countryside, they were completely unable to stop the extra crowds from Larnaca and Limassol towns from pouring in to the surrounding area, tickets or not.

It was packed and the night was hot. If anyone managed to get close to the stage they were not getting out again, the crowd pressed against them holding them in place. Those that needed to go to the toilet ended up wetting themselves where they stood; there was just nowhere to go. They would have to wait until the end before they could get out. When the Greek singer came on stage, the crowd surged forwards, and many in the front were crushed to death against the stage. Bodies pushed and surged against the metal struts holding the huge La Tenta structure in place. Struts that unbeknownst to the authorities, had been weakened in the earthquake that had killed the archaeologists.

As the pressure increased, the struts weakened and bent and the huge structure came down on top of the crowd below. Security managed to get the Greek singer and the musicians out, but many of the audience were killed and it became a national disaster, all over the news for days.

After that, Adaghan was apparently satisfied. The covering structure was rebuilt more securely, and proper fencing was put around the site for future concerts. There were no more deaths.

Until one day, someone potholing in the mountain, came across the sealed cave full of obsidian.

But that's another story.

Equal And Opposite

For every action there is an equal and opposite reaction, that is Newton's third law. Some people say Magic is not real; often the people who say that, have never even noticed the magic at work in their own lives. Some people call Newton's third law Karma, other's call it Sod's Law. Now, all that being said, don't give it another thought until the end of this story.

Isolde was sitting in her flat with no view. The bills were paid and she had spent the remainder of her money on food, enough to last the fortnight. Not actual food the way most people would think of it, but certainly a cupboard full of tins and dried food in packets. It wasn't going to be dinner at the Ritz, but there would be something for breakfast dinner and tea every day. If nothing broke down, and no unexpected bills came in, then she would make it. She flicked through the TV guide, and saw with disappointment, that there was nothing much on that she was interested in all week. Another week with her nose in books, and on social media then, she thought morosely. Isolde looked in her purse; there was three pounds sixty left. The change jar, recently bagged up and banked, held a grand total of two pounds eighty, and the sofa yielded a pound coin and a penny. There was seven pounds and forty one pence in total.

Isolde decided to take her grand fortune and go for a browse around the charity shops; she had nothing better to do. There were three charity shops within easy walking distance of her flat, and she was known by name in all of them. They regularly held books by her favourite authors for her, and sometimes put aside clothes in her larger size, when they came in. The first shop offered her a floral print dress, but she thanked them and declined, saying it was very kind but she really couldn't see herself in it. As someone who mainly wore trousers and tops, and a pretty top was the closest she came to dressing up, Isolde was not really interested in dresses. But she never said that, because if the right dress came in at the right price, she would probably buy it and put it in the wardrobe, just in case there was a special occasion. There was nothing of interest in the first shop. In the second shop they were holding two books for her; a Stephen King and a John Grisham, but when she looked at the titles she saw she had already read both of them. She thanked them for holding them for her anyway. There was nothing else of interest in the second shop. The third shop was her favourite; the Cat's Protection League shop. They were not holding anything for her. Isolde browsed the bookshelves first, but there was nothing there she wanted or hadn't already read. She browsed the clothes racks, but there was nothing in her size she liked. She looked at the shoes and bags, but again, nothing caught her eye. Finally she cast her eyes over the knick-knack shelves, which were filled with the usual rubbish; figurines, crockery, pictures, nasty little collectibles and so on. Just when she was about to give up and go home, she spotted something amongst the brass pieces. It looked like an old fashioned genie lamp, perhaps a cast out prop from some stage production. It was tarnished and needed a good clean, but something about it really appealed to Isolde.

It was labelled at five pounds, and on impulse Isolde bought it. She popped into the pound shop next door and bought a tin of brass cleaner and a multi pack of crisps with her remaining two pounds. Just forty one pence to her name, to drop in the change jar when she got home; or she could give it to the homeless guy busking with his guitar in the doorstep she was just passing. He was good. She thought 'what the heck,' and dropped her last pennies in his case. He grinned at her.

Isolde got home and ate two of the packets of crisps as an afternoon snack, then got out an old rag and set about cleaning the lamp. When purple smoke started to pour out of the lamp she nearly dropped it, and when it formed into the shape of a genie, she clutched her chest, thinking she might be having a heart attack. The genie looked at her, and she took a big gasp of air- she had forgotten to breathe and the room was beginning to swim a bit.

"You are probably expecting me to offer you three wishes about now," the genie said to Isolde, who nodded, dumbly.

"Well, I'm going to explain how it works, and then go away for a bit and leave you to think about it. When you're ready you can polish the lamp again, and I'll come back. Okay?" Isolde nodded, still not quite believing her eyes.

"Every wish creates an equal and opposite wish. You have one wish, but you need to know that if you wish for something traditionally thought of as good, then something else, traditionally thought of as bad will also happen. You can use the wish- there is only one by the way- at any point in time. My recommendation is to wish something bad in the past, then have a better future, which will be your life now, when it all unravels. Does that make sense? Do you understand?" The genie looked at Isolde with a questioning expression.

"Y,yes," mumbled Isolde, still not certain she wasn't hallucinating. She felt like her crisps had been spiked with LSD. It was unlikely she was having this extreme a reaction to MSG.

The genie returned to smoke form, and the smoke went back into the lamp.

Isolde thought about what the genie had said. It couldn't hurt to assume he had been real, and what he said was true. She thought back over her life.

It had all started to go wrong when she got pregnant with her first child. Tammy had been born just a couple of weeks after Isolde had finally convinced Rufus that he should do the right thing and marry her. Rufus and Isolde were never happy together, and Tammy just seemed to push them further apart. Rufus doted on Tammy from the moment she was born, but Isolde hated the screaming little brat, and her feelings never improved. Isolde had post natal depression and Rufus' friend Xander took full advantage of that fact, manipulating her into an affair. Soon Isolde was pregnant with Petula, and Xander disappeared off the scene. Rufus was overjoyed that he was going to be a Daddy again, and Isolde let him think that was the truth. The post natal depression got even worse after Petula was born, and Isolde thought about taking her own life almost every day. It was when she also started to think about killing the babies, that she knew she had to get away. She knew they would never be safe or happy with her, and the best thing she could do for them was to get out of their lives completely. So Isolde packed up her things and left. She had a small amount of savings, and got a live in job at a hotel on the South coast. The depression gradually went away, and Isolde began her new life. She made friends, she contacted remote family members on social media, she was relatively content, though often fighting off the black dog of depression. She painted in her spare time, and donated the colourful pictures to anywhere that wanted them. She had pieces in a children's home, a home for ex young offenders, a hostel for the homeless, a hospital and a couple of dental surgeries. She was happy enough with that- she never once thought about trying to sell her work. She couldn't imagine anyone actually paying money for it. Time went by, and the children grew up.

First it was Petula who found her on social media, and through her friends of friends, also found and befriended Isolde's distant family. Petula told the family horrible things about Isolde, and made it sound as if she had left because she was heartless. Xander had come back on the scene, and demanded a DNA test, and it had come out that Petula was his, and Petula was spitting bricks about it. She wanted to hurt someone, and that someone was Isolde. Tammy joined in, and soon Isolde was a social outcast amongst her family and friends; an evil woman who had abandoned her children, and never gave them a thought. Isolde became more and more isolated and depressed, and that was where she was right now really. Stuck on sickness benefit for depression, no money, a crappy little flat, and friends who were only people she knew from social media games. Unfriended by any real people she knew. Those children had ruined her life twice over.

And so an idea began to form in her mind. Finally Isolde rubbed the lamp once again, and watched curiously as the genie formed.

"So have you decided what to wish for?" he asked.

"Yes," began Isolde. "I wish I had had an abortion when I was pregnant with my first child, and that the abortion had left me sterile."

The genie grinned; "Not often I hear one as good as that. Your wish is my command."

The genie disappeared and Isolde felt like she was falling as everything went dark around her.

Later on, Isolde woke on a plush sofa in a big light and airy room, that had huge windows overlooking green countryside, and the sea in the distance beyond. At first she was confused, then it all came flooding back into her mind, like a film she had suddenly remembered. She had done well at school and left home to go to university, after the abortion and finally splitting up with Rufus. She had got a great degree, and married Simon. They lived together on the South coast in a lovely house. He was in banking and they had lots of money, and a holiday home in Italy. She was independently wealthy and a fairly well known artist; she had shows about once a year, and sold most of her paintings at the shows. She looked around the room. At her feet were several cardboard boxes she had been sorting out from the attic. She was still holding a tatty old brass lamp, and dropped that into the nearest box. She decided to finish the job and take them along to her favourite charity shop in town right away. The Cat's Protection League shop was always pleased to see her with her donations and always greeted her by name.

Afterword

I often think about the genie with the three wishes, and how his story could be somewhat different. It is well known in magical circles that one should be careful what one wishes for, because one just might get it. Also to watch out for those loopholes- whether the devil is involved or not- there are always loopholes. So what if the wish process was reversed? Yes, there is good and bad to everything, but if you wish for the bad thing; do you get the good thing, payment already made? The rest of the details you can read about in my other books and stories, I'm not going into those here- some of you know exactly what I mean!

Dan, Dan The OCD Man

Dan had OCD, mainly pertaining to recycling. Not the kind of OCD that keeps the house scrubbed clean, and hands washed all the time. In fact Dan could be seen wearing clothes that in turn wore at least five of his most recent meals on them, while he himself was in a general state of grubbiness. In fact, apart from the dust bunnies, the house tended to be full of piles of things; clusters of folded tetra packs, tin cans with the labels peeled off of them lined the windowsills, piles of paper, which included envelopes with the plastic windows and glued edges carefully excised, bundles of jiffy bags. Worst of all was anything that came in a pot of some kind. All pots with lids from jam jars to tobacco tins, from ointment to plastic boxes, had to be saved because they could be used to put something inside. Most of them just sat around empty; there were only so many things that needed boxes or pots, the others were just waiting for occupation, like empty shells on the beach waiting for new hermit crabs.

Dan's wife had died ten years previously, and since then the rate at which the house was filling with stuff was escalating exponentially. It was not quite one of those houses where you had to crawl through tunnels of rubbish to get from room to room, but it was getting there. In another ten years, it might have become one of those kinds of places.

Re-use, Re-purpose, Recycle was Dan's mantra. But although this may have been the mantra, it really would have been better translated to Hoard, hoard and rush out to put it in the recycle boxes before the truck came around once a fortnight. The whole process of recycling the rubbish took hours and hours, more and more as time went on. Paper waste was arranged in order of size and then slotted into the largest paper envelope. Cardboard waste was treated in the same fashion. Tins were jumped on and squashed into flat impressions of their former selves, but only after they had had all labels and glue removed, and been thoroughly washed and aired on the windowsill. Plastics were crushed and collected into tight bundles. Everything was carefully arranged in its own corner of the recycling boxes. Then the truck came along and pretty much everything except the glass was summarily tossed into the same compartment in the back. So much time wasted, never to be got back. Dan did not watch the recycle men dispose of his offerings, just tutted at the things they left behind that they should have taken. He would walk into town with those bits, as well as the tetra packs and a few other things, walking between specialist recycling points, and taking his compost to another special recycling point.

At Christmas, Dan would walk around town collecting discarded trees that people had dumped anywhere they felt like, and drag them to the tree recycling points in the park. When Dan was out and about, he would pick up any tin cans or big pieces of paper and take them home in his back pack and add them to his recycling collection. He would also take home any rubbish he found in the street that he thought he could re-purpose or re-use. Most commonly this was old lighters that Dan felt he could extract a little lighter fuel from, or perhaps a useable flint, elastic bands, anything electronic or that might contain parts he could take out and use.

If for some reason, Dan was prevented from performing his usual rituals with rubbish, he would become extremely agitated and often rather angry. Once some youths kicked his recycling boxes into the road, the contents spilling out into the street. Dan chased after them with a walking stick, hitting any that were slow enough to come within his reach, while shouting comments about their ethnicity and level of education after them. He spent several hours rounding up his rubbish and getting everything back to how it was supposed to be.

Dan had had run ins with several of his neighbours actually. He had a shouting match in the street about the state of the bald guy from number sixteen's recycling box. Mr sixteen did not sort his rubbish, just threw it into the box without washing, sorting or any kind of organising. Consequently the bin men often left a lot of it behind. Items they perhaps would have taken if cleaned and sorted. Mr sixteen's response to that was to empty the box into the gutter before taking it back to his house empty.

He had a row with the chap from number twelve who was in a wheelchair, having had both legs amputated at the knee due to diabetes. Mr twelve did not recycle at all, just put everything in his general rubbish and pushed it to the street, nudging it along with his wheelchair, once a week. Dan confronted him angrily one day, and Mr twelve said it was too difficult because he was disabled. Dan called him a fat slob in an obesicle, who had made himself disabled by eating like a pig; and pointed out it would be just as easy, if not easier, to take recycling to the kerb in a box on his lap.

Dan had a row with the woman from number thirteen because she did not recycle either, and generated so much rubbish her wheelie bin was always full to overflowing. When Dan caught her pushing her overflow waste into his, and other neighbours wheelie bins, he lost it completely with her; ranting and raving at her like a madman; all the while throwing her rubbish back into her front garden. Mrs thirteen, who was deaf and mute, made some rather absurd noises and grunts in response to this. Miss fourteen came out to see what all the fuss was about, but after a few minutes, went in clutching her chest, as it was too much for her angina, and called the police instead. By the time the police arrived, it was all over, although Dan did feel he was completely in the right, being the only citizen in the street, it seemed, who did things the right way. He felt sure the police would have been on his side.

Mr seventeen was blind, and got the whole business of rubbish wrong quite a lot. That did not stop Dan from giving him a strong telling off.

Mr eighteen was an ancient alcoholic with cirrhosis of the liver, and he did not give a hoot if his empty bottles and tins went in the recycling box, the wheelie bin or just the garden. The row Dan had with him reached the loudest volume and was the least coherent and most repetitive.

Mrs nineteen was on a dialysis machine which created lots of waste that her carers weren't certain whether to put in the box or the bin, and as they were always different, there was no continuity there. Dan tried having a talk with both Mrs nineteen and her carers; even made them a list of what was recycle-able. It started out nicely enough, but when a carer caught Dan rearranging the bins one day, relationships soon deteriorated.

Mr twenty had two false hands since he lost the originals in a factory accident. He blamed this and the clumsiness of the false ones for his inability to sort out recycling. Dan offered to come and do the recycling for him and Mr twenty told him in no uncertain terms to eff off.

Old Mrs eleven had a colostomy, and it is best not to talk about what went in her rubbish.

At the council residents meeting, everyone complained and said something should be done about the crazy recycling man at number fifteen. Dan did not attend those meetings. He had gone along to one when he first moved in, but when they were clearing up afterwards, they had put all the rubbish in black bags; mixing plastic cups, paper plates and glass bottles with general rubbish. Dan was so appalled he had never gone back after that.

On the evening of the 26th March, the residents were having their monthly meeting. The subject of Dan and his angry rubbish outbursts came up of course. Everyone had something to say and things got quite hot under the collar. Miss fourteen felt a petition should be sent to the council demanding his eviction for anti social behaviour. Mr twelve said that aside from everything else Dan was racist, size-ist, able-ist and every other kind of ist that there was, and that sort of thing just shouldn't be allowed these days. The room got quite hot with all the energy of everyone's rage. In the end some points were agreed upon; specifically a letter to the council in the first instance, and everybody eventually went home.

Dan was oblivious to the meeting that had taken place that evening; his ears did not even have the decency to burn. He went to bed, after his usual routine with the rubbish, at eleven thirty precisely. Dan did not wake up again.

On the morning of the 27th Dan's neighbours each awoke to find something magical had happened to them. Not a one of them could explain it. Mr sixteen had a full head of hair and Mr twelve had legs once again. Mrs thirteen could hear and speak, and Miss fourteen had no pain in her chest, and her heartbeat was strong and steady. Mr seventeen could see again, and Mr eighteen had no pain in his liver and all the swelling around his middle had disappeared. He was no longer Simpson yellow either. Mrs nineteen had fully functioning kidneys that needed no dialysis, and Mr twenty had hands once more. Mrs eleven had all of her bowel back, fully functional and no stoma or bag.

What was left of Dan had mostly dissolved into the bed he lay on; and there wasn't much left. Aside from the body parts already listed, the rest of him had gone slightly further afield around the neighbourhood. Scars and burns had been replaced with new unmarked skin. Broken bones; ribs, jaw, upper arms, femurs, were now intact. Hardly anything of Dan had gone to waste; his entire body had been re-used, distributed amongst those who needed it. It was exactly as he would have wanted- well maybe not exactly, after all.

Afterword

This story was born out of the fact that I have direct experience of living with someone with OCD, who also has a thing about recycling. Nothing this extreme of course, but all stories start somewhere. I have also had my fair share, perhaps more than my fair share, of obnoxious neighbours. In short, some of the above events have happened to me and around me. Nowhere near all of them, and with nothing like the eventual outcome of this tale. I wasn't originally going down the magic worked unknowingly route, that just kind of happened. Stories do that though, start out as an idea, then move away in their own direction regardless. I find it best to just go with the flow.

Giselda Doesn't Cry

From the time Giselda was a small child, no more than a toddler really, her father had insisted by greater and greater degrees that she did not cry. With her first wailings as a tumble down toddler, he would urge her to turn the taps off, dry her tears and get on with something else. For a time, and being that she was just a toddler, the distraction and move along theory worked just fine. But as Giselda started school, she became harder to distract and placate. Her injuries and grievances were felt and remembered for more than mere seconds. The crying did not stop with the command to dry her tears, or turn the taps off. Giselda's father Raymond, became more agitated that he could no longer calm Giselda and was forced to endure her outbursts. He finally resorted to the parental classic, 'if you don't stop crying, I'll give you something to cry about.'

For a time this threat worked, and Giselda would walk away snuffling quietly. But then that stopped working too, and so Raymond, not wanting to be the kind of parent that issued empty threats, did in fact give Giselda a reason to cry in the form of beating and bullying, and later even worse. Giselda finally learnt that she had to take her punishment and keep her emotions under control, or things would just escalate to a place where she really couldn't bear to go. So it was that Giselda stopped crying before she even started senior school.

But it didn't end there, would that it had. Raymond wasn't really happy with any sort of emotional outbursts. He would not tolerate anger or rage of any kind; even extremist opinions were frowned upon. Assertive confrontation was most certainly not rewarded with praise either.

As well as negative emotional displays, Raymond did not like the positive ones either. Excitement and enthusiastic outpourings were treated as harshly as the negative emotions. Giselda remembered one birthday in particular when she was punished for getting too loud and excitable, and squealing as she ripped into her pile of presents. After her punishment that night, while it was still her birthday no less, birthdays lost their allure, and were never again a joy for Giselda.

On top of everything else Raymond insisted on peak performance in everything Giselda did. Academically the pressure was full on. Even if Giselda got one hundred per cent in a test, Raymond would say she should have put in extra effort and got one hundred and ten per cent. Life was hard and stress filled.

Holidays were a time when all excitement had to be thoroughly suppressed, which was incredibly difficult, as Giselda loved to travel and go to new places. The result was that Giselda got diarrhoea before travel began, and travel sickness once the journey was underway.

In fact Giselda suppressed all her emotions so much that they often manifested in the form of stomach complaints from both ends. It was a good twenty years before Giselda had something resembling normal bowel movements. By the age of fifty, she was suffering from sometime IBS, reflux, acid indigestion and heartburn, as well as food allergies that caused vomiting and general stomach pain. She frequently had to go to the doctor and the hospital for investigations.

Giselda as an adult, loved to travel, but still had to take tablets to make that possible, or she would never get out of the bathroom. No matter how much she enjoyed a holiday, she found it impossible to get excited about it.

Friends, partners and partner's families thought her rather a cold fish. A lot of people thought Giselda just didn't care. Nothing could have been further from the truth. Giselda cared very much indeed. As a teenager she had begun cutting her arms, legs and torso where it didn't show; but she gave that up in her thirties, when her partner threatened to leave her if it didn't stop.

In her early twenties, Giselda was reckless with drink and drugs, but again gradually gave all that up as her health began to suffer as she got older.

When Giselda's mother got ill and was close to dying- she packed her bags and ran away abroad. She did not come back until after the funeral was done and dusted. She could not face the emotions that were raised by the situation, and could think of no better evasive technique than running and hiding, burying her figurative head in the sand.

At the funeral, the rest of the more distant family gathered around Raymond, saying they couldn't believe Giselda was not there. They all commiserated with him for having such a bad daughter who just did not care. Judgements were cast.

But Giselda already knew she could never go home again. She cursed Raymond for making her the way she was. She thought to herself, 'if you wanted me to grieve like a normal person, and attend the funeral; you should have let me grow up like a normal person. I cannot produce emotions now, on cue, that I have never been allowed to have.'

So Giselda did not cry. She pushed it from her mind. She was never going to be a normal woman, there was no point trying. It was a done deal, and it was far too late for Raymond to ask for his money back and change her now.

Afterword

This story is short but not sweet; rather bitter in fact. That is because, all bar a few small details, it is my own personal story. My Mother died just under three months before I wrote this, and I did not attend the funeral, but remained where I was in Cyprus.

The Coconut Of Time

It was June 2017 when the small plane I was travelling in went down in the Southern Ocean. I never saw the pilot or the other two passengers again, so I don't know if they died on impact, drowned or found their way to a different island. I lost consciousness and woke up with a mouthful of sand on this small island. It isn't tiny like the cartoons; you know, just a heap of sand and a coconut tree, though it does have a small sandy beach and a coconut tree. But it also has a small forest; well more of a copse or grove really, and a rocky hill with, more importantly, a waterfall that leads down to a small lake or fresh water pond. That is the main reason I'm still alive I suppose. I built a shelter out of trees- well fallen wood and palm leaves mainly, using the edge of the rocks near the pool as a wall on one side. I made a fishing rod out of a fallen branch and some of the crap that daily washes up on the beach. Fishing line and bits of metal and plastic are really commonplace. Actually I have made a surprising amount of stuff I use every day out of the crap that washes up on the beach, or that was already washed up in piles mixed with stinking seaweed before I got here. I catch fish, pick shellfish off the rocks, trap crabs and lobster and eat seaweed. I have set up traps in and around the trees and occasionally catch rodents and small birds, all of which make good eating too. I have tried most of the bugs I unearth- not bad. I have wild garlic, thyme and nettles growing in the trees, and there are some mangoes that aren't ripe yet around the back of the island. That's about it for food really. The other day a plastic sack of rubbish washed ashore, and on tearing it open I found potato peelings and carrot tops amongst the other crap. I carefully prepared some soil and planted them; I'm hopeful they will make a crop later on. The coconut tree torments me. I have had one or two coconuts that dropped naturally, and let me tell you they were delicious. The water was the most sublime drink I ever tasted, and the meat- well it was better than I remember chocolate being. I have tried beating, kicking and shaking the tree, but the coconuts just will not fall until they are ready, in their own good time. I saw a programme once, where locals used a belt to climb the coconut trees; belting themselves round the waist and the trunk, then leaning out and pushing up with their feet, kind of half jumping all the way up. That is not as easy as it looked. All I ever did was fall down and get a nasty bruise on my coccyx. I have tried throwing projectiles at the coconuts in the highest branches that look so delicious and ripe and ready. Once or twice I even hit my targets, but they did not fall down. I spend a lot of time thinking about how I can get those coconuts in my stomach.

My clothes fell apart after the first few months, I lost track of time ages ago, and there don't seem to be any seasons here, just hot, or wet and windy then hot again. I made some makeshift clothes out of scraps of fabric that I found in the rubbish, combined with string and plastic. It's serviceable, but will never appear on anything but the most crazed punk catwalk.

I built an SOS sign in stones on the biggest stretch of open sandy beach. I keep it in shape each day, but have never seen a plane or boat, not even in the distance. I fear I may be destined to live out my lifespan on this lonely island. It would actually be idyllic if I just had company.

Fire took a little time to master, but once I got it going, I soon learnt how to keep a pile of hot embers ready to start again the next morning.

I have really cleaned the island up, sorting through everything that washes up on the beach as well as all the detritus already left here by high tides. I have either used everything in some way or burnt it as fuel if it was completely useless. Scraps of plastic make really pretty colours in the flames- which is sadly the highlight of my evening entertainment. I have made everything from equipment for hunting food, to household items and kitchenware, and even some furniture.

The other day I found some large flat pieces of metal, and using a rock, hammered them into the side of the coconut tree. They form a sort of stairway up each side of the trunk. So far it only gets me about six foot off the ground, but if I can find some more usable pieces, I could, in theory, get all the way up to the coconuts in this way. While I wait for the right things to turn up, the occasional coconut does still fall, but it is so infrequent, they are very much a luxury item. The mangoes ripened and were delicious; though I ate so many at once one day, I got the runs. I slowed down after that. When it looked like some might get over ripe and rot, I peeled and sliced them, and dried them in the sun. The dried pieces are a delicious treat. My potatoes and carrots are doing well now, and I tend them daily, bringing them water and keeping them weed free. I look at the young plants and salivate as I try to remember the taste of them.

Finally I have enough rungs on my coconut tree to be quite near the top. I strap myself to the tree with a belt, though if I fall, I'll probably slice myself open on the metal sticking out all the way down. At this point I feel these out of reach coconuts are literally to die for. I have several chunks of metal in my makeshift shoulder bag, along with a rock to bash them in with. Today is the day I will get the coconut, I am sure of it. It sits up there, high and elusive, taunting me; but today I am going to drink it and taste its meat.

I made a little raft and paddle, so I could go fishing further out in deeper waters and maybe catch different fish. I caught something that looks a bit like bass to me, but I'm no expert, I don't really know what it is. It looks delicious though, and I plan to wrap it up in palm leaves with some coconut meat and cook it as a special treat.

Sweating and nervous, working so high up, feeling like I'm going to overbalance and fall down with every hammer of the rock, I finally get the last metal wedge driven into the trunk. With this in place I am sure I will be able to reach the elusive coconut when I climb onto it. And sure enough I can. The coconut comes free surprisingly easily. I somehow expected more of a struggle after all this time and effort. Most reluctantly I let it fall to the ground below, so my hands are free for the climb down. I let my hammering rock drop too; I no longer need the extra weight. I climb down very carefully; to fall and die now would be too ironic.

Later, after I have extricated the coconut from its green fleshy pod, I ready my tool to make a hole in the top and drink the precious water.

I drink the nectar in one long gulp, and it is even more delicious than I anticipated. Then the world goes kind of fuzzy round the edges, and I fall down into some sort of deep sleep.

When I awake, I find to my utter shock and amazement, I am sitting, well lolling really, on a hard airport lounge chair. I blink and rub my eyes. Was it all some kind of weird reality dream? I look at myself, my clothes are intact and perfectly normal; the ones I was wearing the day of my flight and crash. My skin is pasty white, not tanned finally after weeks of burning first. My hair is short, my legs are freshly waxed. Wtf? I look up at the departures board. The date says June 23 2017, the day I flew in the small plane and crashed. But obviously I didn't do all that after all. My body and clothes say I never was on that desert island. I have clearly had some strange dream or hallucination. Weeks of stress and sleep deprivation leading up to the presentation I am about to fly out and make, caused something very strange to happen whilst I slept. I am feeling rather freaked out, but then my flight is announced. Part of me wants to turn tail and run away home; not get on the flight, never get on another flight again for the entire rest of my life. But the sensible part of me knows that my future career depends on this presentation. I have to get on the flight, or lose the contract. So I get on the flight. Later on, I find myself washed up on a sandy beach with a mouthful of sand; spitting out the salty grit. I look up to see a familiar coconut tree, laden with fruit, its trunk free from any kind of metal rubbish. The island is exactly the same as it was the first time I arrived. I groan, and get ready to start again. Next time, no more flying...whatever that means.

Afterword

Absolutely nothing inspired this story. I like to think I could cope on a desert island. It always seemed rather an idyllic idea to me, but then I've always been a bit of a hermit. A significant other would make it perfect though. I very much enjoyed the series Lost, but have never been able to watch reality shows of that ilk, they just annoy me too much; the people they tend to strand on the islands are just so completely useless. The title of this story came to me first, then once I had that, I let it roll around my mind collecting ideas to accompany it. This is what I ended up with.

Revolting Romance In Rome

Rene had travelled to Rome on holiday, looking at ruins, and for romance, maybe not exactly in that order, except officially. She didn't want to announce that she was off looking for love and then come home to be featured as failure of the month. She spent the first day after arrival walking in circles around the Colosseum, then admiring the archaeological ruins alongside. In the evening, too tired for clubs; she perched on a stool in a pizzeria and munched her way through a medium Margarita.

Then Wanda walked in, and wandered over to wait at the counter alongside Rene. They soon got chatting, and it was clear they were attracted to each other. Wanda was a student who had been working in Rome for a while. Rene soon perked up and gained a renewed enthusiasm for the evening ahead.

Wanda took Rene on a late night walk around her favourite parts of the city; the Trevi Fountain, Piazza Barberini and its fountain, the fountain of Republica with its lust inflaming statues, and the crossroads four corners fountains. Apparently Wanda favoured fountains. Finally, after juice in a jazz bar, and grappa in a gay bar; Wanda took Rene to the top of the Spanish steps where they sat and watched the pre dawn sky lighten as it announced the sunrise.

Rene snuggled into Wanda's side as they sat, sighing, and saying what a beautiful night she had spent. What commenced as cuddling, culminated in kissing.

Wanda grinned and invited Rene to have breakfast and see the views from her top floor apartment. Rene, already reeling from the romance, readily agreed.

Once in the bedroom, Wanda whispered, "Care to try something a bit different?"

Wanda waggled a pair of handcuffs and a blindfold. Rene readily agreed to raunchy wrigglings.

Wanda clamped on the cuffs, chaining Rene to the columns at the corners of the bed; hands and feet restrained at the wrists and ankles. Then she added a ball gag, whispering, "Bite on the ball if it gets too bad, baby."

Finally a blindfold so Rene would have no idea what was coming next.

"First the pleasure," purred Wanda, touching, tickling, tasting and teasing- tantalising Rene to torturous limits of tolerance, before letting her slip over the edge into an ocean of pleasure.

"Then the pain," said Wanda almost silently to herself as she approached Rene with a very sharp kitchen knife.

Rene reacted by going rigid as the knife carved the flesh of her thighs and buttocks. Big slabs of butchered meat, bathed in blood, that first reddened, then blackened the sheets below.

Rene released her hold on reality and consciousness as Wanda went on with her work.

Blessedly, Rene bled out without recovering her reason or sense. It was a small mercy.

Wanda went into the kitchen to prepare her wicked steak dinner, and food for the future in the freezer.

Afterword

Okay so this is totally away from my normal style and very strange, even by my standards. I see it as more of a poem, sort of Lear meets Barker or something like that. I like the use of casual alliteration to add an edge of humour to a very dark, sick topic. Perhaps I watched and read too much Dexter. The alliteration makes it more poem than story I think. Originally I was going to make it in normal text with more detail about the sightseeing and romance, and just a dark twist at the end. Kind of a parody on my Greek romance in the Sun novels, where everyone is happy and hardly anything bad ever happens- oh and everyone is straight. This was intended to be an opposite to that. But it grew a life and style of its own and turned out completely different. So there you are; some stories do that.

Herbert And Mavis

Herbert woke up at six thirty in the morning, same as he always did. He was a little surprised to see that Mavis' side of the bed was unslept in once again. That was two days running now.

He padded downstairs in his bathrobe and slippers, pyjama bottoms swishing between his scrawny legs with every step.

Mavis was sat in her high backed reading chair, book dropped to her lap and glasses fallen on top of the book. Her eyes were still closed, so Herbert moved silently into the kitchen so as not to disturb her. He whispered softly to himself, 'her back must be giving her gip again. She always prefers to sleep in her reading chair when that happens. I'll leave her for a bit and let her sleep on.'

He put the coffee on and went to get the paper from the box on the doorstep. After he had read the paper- as much as he was interested in anyway, and drunk his coffee; his body insisted on its morning visit to the bathroom. It was a sudden, urgent insistence, so it would have to be the downstairs toilet- no way was he going to make the stairs in time. He felt a bit guilty about that, but there was no helping it; it was the downstairs toilet or an accident. Mavis hated it when he used the downstairs bathroom for his 'morning appointment'. She said it was too close to the kitchen, and the smells got into the food.

"Sorry my love but I've got to use the downstairs toilet, it's an emergency, sorry," he called out as he shut himself in and got down to business. He reminded himself to open the window and shut the door when he came out. That way he should keep the odoriferous pollution to an absolute minimum.

Afterwards, Herbert went to the kitchen to make himself some toast and marmalade and a nice cup of tea for breakfast. He called to Mavis to see if she wanted any, but not getting any answer, he didn't do her any. It wasn't unusual for her to skip breakfast and snooze on. She napped so much more now she was getting older.

After breakfast, Herbert got washed and dressed, fetched the jute bags out of the cupboard and went out shopping.

He stopped at all the small shops, which he preferred to the big supermarkets for all kinds of reasons. He liked to support the small shops, and they were more friendly, and took time to chat with him; also their wares were better than the supermarkets. Okay, so they were a bit more expensive, but Mavis and Herbert ate like sparrows anyway, so they could afford for what they did eat to be the best quality. Herbert hated the supermarkets with their big corporate mentality, stomping on all the little independent guys. He hated the way they spied on you and pretended they just wanted to give you 'rewards,' but most of all he hated the lights- they upset his stomach. Mind you, he hated the screaming kids, and hostile young people, and general lack of ambience too. No, Herbert was a small shop only, kind of man. It was how they had always done things when he was young, and he saw no benefit to changing now.

At the butchers he bought liver and bacon. John the butcher asked after Mavis. Herbert said she was well, sleeping more, then asked after John's dog Butch.

At the greengrocers, Herbert bought a couple of potatoes, some greens and a couple of onions. Pearl the grocer asked after Mavis, and so it went on.

At the chemist Herbert picked up prescriptions, at the bakers- bread and a couple of custard tarts. He went into the off licence for a couple of bottles of stout- very rich in iron, and a treat too.

Finally, he had enough stuff for a few days and stopped at the Library which was on the way home anyway. Susan, the librarian, had a book she had put by for Mavis, some romance she had been waiting for. Herbert and Susan chatted for a bit, then he headed home.

He called to Mavis that he was back, then went to the kitchen to put the shopping away and make a sandwich for lunch. He took a plate through for Mavis, with her corned beef sandwich on it, and rested the plate on her side table, on top of the new book. Mavis was still asleep.

Herbert whispered, "There's some lunch here for you love when you're ready, and a new book from the library too." He noticed Mavis smelt a bit as he leant close to whisper without waking her if she was fast asleep. "I'll run a bath for you later love, might help you feel a bit better."

Herbert felt Mavis' forehead, wondering if she was ill. It was cold, but her eyes opened wide as he took his hand away.

"Oh good, you're awake at last, you can have lunch and start your new book. I'm off to the garden for a bit; call if you want anything."

Herbert pottered in the garden for most of the afternoon. There was lots of weeding to do, and some planting too. Herbert picked some runner beans and tomatoes, and a bunch of fresh herbs. Finally he picked some flowers for a vase for Mavis; she always loved that.

Herbert made a pot of tea and took the cups through to the living room, switching on the television for Countdown. Then he popped back for the vase of flowers to put on the table. He was surprised to see Mavis had not touched her lunch, corned beef sandwiches were her favourite. She must be feeling really out of sorts. He drank his tea and watched the television, calling out his answers as he thought of them. Mavis wasn't joining in at all, which was really not like her; she usually got all the best answers, sometimes even better than the people on the show. They usually had a laugh about it. Herbert began to feel a bit worried about Mavis.

Later on, Herbert got up to make dinner; some nice fried liver and onions with gravy, a bit of potato and a few greens. It was their Tuesday night special, they'd been having it every Tuesday for years, except when they occasionally went away on holiday and had to have some foreign muck instead.

He called Mavis to the table for dinner, but she didn't move. Herbert went and stood in front of her chair, "Need a pull up love?" He reached for her hands, grasping them in his own. She did seem very cold. As Herbert started to pull, Mavis lolled over to one side, hanging half out of the chair.

"Oh dearie me," exclaimed Herbert. "Are you alright? Shall I call the Doctor? Are you having a stroke or something?" He began to panic.

Mavis' voice seemed to come from somewhere other than her body, "You must know I'm dead?"

Herbert started talking, flustered, "Of course you're worn out, you've got a bug or something, you're dead tired, I understand, let me help." He moved Mavis' head and liquid of some sort flowed out of her mouth onto the floor; it smelt foul.

Her voice which could have come from anywhere or nowhere, sounded huge in Herbert's head as Mavis shouted, "NO HERBET, I'M DEAD!"

Herbert walked away from Mavis stunned, and on auto pilot went to the table and ate his liver and onions. He pushed the plate away and sat with his head in his hands for a while. Finally he got up and walked to the phone in the hall and dialled 999, sitting down on the phone seat by the door to wait for their arrival. They'd know what to do. How could Mavis be dead and still talking to him? Herbert wept.

Afterword

This story was born out of the idea that we get so used to our routines, we might not even notice if something major changed. That couples who are together all the time, just fall into a pattern where nothing out of the normal is ever allowed to happen. Denial would be greater than acceptance, beyond a certain point of this kind of living I think. At least that is the idea I have explored here. Perhaps you have to be old, or heading towards old and a couple, to really get it. I don't know, maybe not.

The story is not about Mavis being dead, that much is apparent from pretty much the outset I think. The twist is the idea of Mavis talking from the Dead at the end; or from an atheist point of view is the voice really just in Herbert's head? His realisation talking in Mavis' voice. Or do women really have to keep on organising everything, even from beyond the metaphoric grave? Your choice!

The Calico Cat

Jenny had a cat; a calico cat- or as the English call it, a tortoiseshell or tortie cat. She didn't get it when it was a kitten, so she missed out on that particular cuteness and amusement. However since she got it from a rescue centre, aged two, she also did not have to go through the house training stage either. So Jenny bypassed the 'poo around the house not in the litter box' stage, the 'puddles of puke from kitten bingeing left everywhere and anywhere' stage, and the 'running up the curtains shredding them' stage. The calico cat was apparently called Cosmo, but he didn't seem to answer to it as a name. Jenny had toyed with a few other names, but he didn't answer to those either, so she gave up. Sometimes she called him Cosmo, sometimes she called him Cat. Other times she just rattled the biscuits or opened a tin to call him; and very occasionally she called him a very rude name beginning with C, one that really didn't apply as he was male, but if he had done something exceptionally bad, Jenny called him C**t anyway.

The first week Jenny brought Cosmo home, he spent most of his time under the bed, coming out to eat mostly only when there was no one around. Then one night Jenny awoke to find Cosmo sitting on her chest whilst she slept, staring at her. He didn't stop when she opened her eyes either, just continued to stare at her; it was very creepy. Jenny didn't want to push Cosmo off, it was the first time he had made proper contact with her since she brought him home, but on the other hand it was creeping her the hell out. In the end she folded first, and pushed him aside, before turning her back on him and trying to go back to sleep. It was not until she heard the soft thud of Cosmo's paws hitting the carpet on his descent from the bed, that Jenny's eyes once again grew heavy, and she fell asleep. Jenny had, since childhood, slept with a tiny raggedy teddy bear, called Bear. Naming had never been a big thing in Jenny's household, and at times she was surprised her name had not been 'girl' or 'child,' it was what she was most often called anyway.

Bear was no bigger than Jenny's hand and she held it as she fell asleep. Since the arrival of Cosmo, Bear had gone missing more and more frequently. Jenny would wake in the morning, or worse, the middle of the night with Bear nowhere to be found. He usually fell out of her hand as her muscles relaxed when she fell asleep, but was always somewhere near her pillow when she awoke. Lately, and after much hunting, she had been finding him under the middle of the bed, or even further away. Finally the mystery was solved when Jenny awoke in the middle of the night and through sleepy eyes glimpsed Cosmo padding across the bedroom floor with Bear between his teeth. Cosmo put Bear down beside the laundry basket, and then pushed him further back with his paw. As if sensing he was being watched, Cosmo looked around; but Jenny quickly shut her eyes and pretended to be asleep. After that, Jenny tied a ribbon around Bear's neck and tied the other end to her wrist when she went to bed. That solved the problem, and Bear stayed put in bed.

Jenny was not a hugely sexual being, and relationships were few and far between, but very occasionally she would feel the urge and need to satisfy herself. It was on one such occasion, as she lay atop her bed, that she felt rather strange, and opened her eyes to see Cosmos staring intently at her from the end of the bed. The urge was killed, and Jenny made a mental note to shut Cosmo out of the room the next time she was in the mood.

There was a solid half wall between the kitchen and the area where Jenny sat at her desk to do her e-mails. Cosmo took to waiting, hidden, behind the wall until Jenny came out of the kitchen with a cup of tea, then pouncing out in front of her. The first couple of times this happened, Jenny had shrieked and the tea had gone everywhere, but now she approached the area with more caution. She could have sworn Cosmo looked smug as he sat and watched her clean up the tea mess though.

When allowed to go out, Cosmo always brought a 'friend' home with him. Other cats brought home dead mice and birds as 'gifts' but not Cosmo. He brought in live creatures; mice, voles, shrews, small birds, spiders, frogs, were all brought into the house alive, and set free to freak Jenny out with their presence later. She of course, had to catch and release said creatures, while Cosmo sat and watched the show- most amused.

If Cosmo needed to throw up, he would always manage to do so in Jenny's slippers or shoes, or dirty laundry if it had been left on the floor. Or paperwork, if it was left spread out anywhere. In general Cosmo preferred to sit on paper though; especially if his paws were dirty, or his rear end stinky- that way he could really leave his mark.

If Jenny worked in the garden, planting seeds or annuals, Cosmo would be sure to dig them up again and use the area as a litter tray. In short, Cosmo was something of a bastard.

Then things started getting even weirder. One night Jenny woke up to see Cosmo sitting staring at an apparently blank wall, and chattering his mouth as if he had his eye on a bird he wanted to eat. Finally he meowed at the 'nothing' and turned his back and walked off, casting a disdainful look at Jenny as he noticed her watching him; as if to say 'What?'

Another time, Jenny came home from work, and caught Cosmo swiftly jumping down from her desk, where her computer was switched on. Just the desktop screen mind you; no secret cat communiqués, mouse hunting games, or videos of fish- what was she thinking? Did she actually think Cosmo had turned the computer on and was using it? No she must have left it on when she went to work that morning, and Cosmo had been sleeping on her desk and knocked the mouse when he jumped down guiltily, that was it. But then she distinctly remembered turning it off, or maybe that was another morning; it must have been. Cats didn't use computers, she was cracking up. Jenny poured herself a large glass of white wine from the fridge, and pondered her impending insanity.

The following day, things got weirder still. When Jenny came in from work, Cosmo jumped down from the telephone table and ran out of the cat flap, in a hell of a hurry. Jenny looked down and saw that the phone was off the hook. Cosmo must have knocked it in his hurry to escape, the clumsy cat.

As Jenny picked up the handset to put it back in place on the phone base, she heard a foreign sounding voice at the other end of the line- damn cat must have pushed some buttons with its furry butt.

"Hello," Jenny said into the phone. "I'm very sorry, I think my cat called you by mistake," then she giggled nervously, realising how ridiculous that sounded. But the person on the other end either didn't understand her, or was bored with trying to make themselves understood; anyway they hung up.

That evening, three of Jenny's friends came over for drinks and nibbles. They were all animatedly chatting about philosophy and politics. Cosmo sat in the middle of the room, eyes moving to each person as they spoke; for all the world appearing to be following the conversation, and when John said something funny, a point garnered at Jenny's expense; Cosmo winked at him.

"Your cat just winked at me," said John, exploding with laughter.

"I wouldn't be at all surprised," answered Jenny, "he's a very strange cat, that one."

Cosmo glared at her and stalked off.

The next evening, Jenny had just sat down to her dinner; beef slices in gravy, mash and green beans, when suddenly she absolutely had to go to the loo. There was no question of waiting; it was a matter of utmost urgency. By the time she finished, fifteen minutes later, the prospect of her dinner seemed unappetising; it was most likely cold by now.

Jenny was stunned to see that the beef and gravy portion of her meal had not only disappeared, but had been replaced with six meaty cubes of cat food. Cosmo sat on the floor looking up at her a perfect mixture of innocence and mockery. Jenny took a photo of her strange meal with her phone, but she didn't suppose anyone would believe her if she told them about that or any other of Cosmo's exploits.

That night after Jenny had been in bed sleeping for a while, she woke up to Cosmo sitting beside her face tapping her cheek with his paw. Once he saw her eyes were open, he leant his mouth down low beside her ear and Jenny heard,
"You think I'm a cat don't you?"
Then Cosmo jumped down, and Jenny heard, shortly afterwards, the sound of the cat flap shutting behind him. She never saw Cosmo again.

Afterword

This story was born out of a conversation one of my social media friends had, where they misread a comment as; you think I'm a cat don't you? Well, that set the cogs whirring and I had to write the line into a story. Having said that; my cat Panpuss [RIP] did quite a lot of the above described things, though not all; and he did stop short of actually speaking to me. Or leaving. Though, thinking about it, he did have a way of meowing so it sounded like 'me out now' if he wanted a door opening, or 'hot towel now,' whilst standing in front of the airing cupboard when wet from the rain. And he did go walkies for three and a half weeks that one time- but that actually is another story in another book. But Cosmo came across as a bit creepy, and a bit of a malevolent bastard. With Panpuss it was always just him being a character, amusing and cute.

The Ring

Xandra loved to collect stuff; boxes, from tiny ones to almost chest sized ones- not just wood, metal, clay, not plastic, but almost anything else. She also collected costume jewellery and old style clothing that she frequently put together and wore to parties in her own unique style that often somewhat resembled steam punk. Other odds and sods were deemed collectible too; lighthouse and windmill statues, cat statues, cookery books, glass bottles- the delicate ornate type, and things made of shells or sea glass. Consequently, Xandra spent a lot of her spare time rummaging on market stalls, through antique junk shops, flea markets, boot sales, auctions, charity shops and jumble sales. Any given day's excursion would almost certainly result in her returning home with at least several new things to add to her personal hoard. Xandra's parents had left her a large house, fortunately, and on moving in, she had cleared out everything except the basics; white goods and a bed. There were a couple of dressers and shelf units that she had emptied and kept; but she was now gradually filling the house with all the things she just felt impelled to collect.

On this particular Saturday, Xandra had found a gorgeous box in a flea market. It had numerous drawers each with ornate handles, and was a rich dark oak. She had also bought a beautiful dress that looked Victorian, and a glass bottle painted like a stained glass window in miniature. She grabbed some food supplies for the kitchen, and headed home very pleased with herself to make a nice lunch. On impulse, she bought a bottle of Chablis to accompany her meal.

After a lunch of sautéed scallops with a rocket salad, washed down with wine and followed by strawberries, straight from the punnet- apparently picked at an organic farm that morning- Xandra took the last of the wine through to the living room to examine her purchases. She stripped to try on the dress, which fitted perfectly and frankly, looked amazing. She found a place on the mantelpiece for the little bottle, with the others. After hanging the dress in her wardrobe, and settling down in her slob out yoga gear and pumps, she curled up on the bed with her new box. She carefully opened each drawer, and took them out, one at a time, running her hands over the wood inside the box. Behind one drawer she found a tiny catch and pressed the release. A little hidden door swung open within the box, and peering inside with a torch, Xandra could see something shimmering. She tipped the box to empty out the glimmering object, and a beautiful ring fell out onto the bed. The ring was gold with a green stone that might have even been an emerald, set amongst several smaller red stones that could have been rubies. Xandra turned it in her hands, letting the light glint on the metal and gems; making a note to herself to take it to a jeweller and find out if it was genuine. She slipped the ring onto her middle finger, as it looked quite large; and in that moment, her whole world changed.

Xandra found herself standing in the high street, about to enter Goldsmiths jewellery shop. She was holding a gold chain in her pocket, one on which the clasp had broken, and she was taking it in for repair. She noticed she was wearing the green and red gem ring on her middle finger. In fact everything was exactly as it had been about a fortnight previously when she remembered having taken the chain in for repair. Except she was wearing the ring she hadn't bought yet. She went into the shop and left the chain to be repaired, as an afterthought asking the jeweller if he thought her ring was genuine.

"It's just a piece of junk I picked up at a flea market, but it's always worth checking don't you think?" She smiled at the man behind the counter, who was actually rather used to her popping in for repairs and adjustments.

"Pass it over love, I'll have a quick look."

Xandra hesitated to take the ring off, but then decided that the worst that was likely to happen was that she jumped back forward in time and maybe lost the ring. She decided it was worth the risk- even if she got stuck a fortnight in her own past, it was no big deal.

The jeweller turned the ring over in his fingers and looked at it with a magnifying glass.

"Sorry love, it's just costume jewellery- green and red glass, and a gold coloured metal. Pretty, but not worth more than a couple of quid. How much did you pay for it?"

"Well nothing actually, it was in with something else I bought."

"In that case love, you got a bargain," he winked. "Come back for the chain in an hour or two."

The next ten days passed rather as Xandra remembered them passing before. She made a couple of small adjustments; like not giving the cute guy in the coffee shop her number, and not receiving the subsequent dick pics that he had sent when he turned out to be a creep. She made a dentist appointment before she got toothache and avoided that nastiness too. She did not have lunch with Jean at the sushi bar; in fact insisted that they went to the new vegetarian restaurant instead; and avoided spending the night with her head over the toilet experiencing Technicolor food poisoning. Then ten days had passed and she woke up back on her bed looking at the 'new' ring she had just bought. Only this time round she was turning it curiously between her fingers thinking about how the ring had given her time travel; had allowed her to relive ten days of her life. Yes, she had corrected a few minor mistakes, but other than that, had done nothing really differently. She glanced casually at her bedside clock, and was astonished to notice that the day was two days ahead of the day she had bought the ring. So she had gained ten days in the past and lost two days of present. She thought she could live with that if she used it correctly; an overall gain of eight days of life, plus whatever alterations she could make in the past. She wondered how the ring worked. She had been thinking about the jewellery shop and getting the ring valued, and then she put it on and went back in time to the last time she was at the jeweller's shop. Xandra wondered which ten days of her life she wanted to relive next. She looked at her phone, just to check. Sure enough, the dick pics from the creepy guy, and his number were gone as if she never met him. There were some huffy texts from some of her friends. One even called her a cow, but she decided to look into that later, after she had explored the ring a bit more.

She thought about her Nana, who died suddenly when Xandra was just ten years old. How she regretted not seeing more of Nana at the end. She thought about the last time she was with her Nana, and slipped the ring onto her finger.

Xandra was inside her ten year old body, sitting at the lunch table with her Nana, eating creamed rice with a dollop of raspberry jam in the middle. Nana was humming 'Little brown jug.'

"I love you so much Nana," said Xandra in her squeaky child's voice.

"Ah sweetheart, I love you too. You're Nana's special little ray of sunshine," Nana beamed a huge smile at Xandra. Xandra spent a lovely day with Nana, doing the crossword from the paper together, looking at old photographs, singing songs. Finally she had to go home for her tea. She wrapped her coat tightly around her against the ice and snow outside, and as she left she gave her Nana a big hug and told her to be careful if she had to go out. But Nana slipped and fell and broke her hip anyway, the hospital called that evening. For the next nine days, Xandra went to the hospital every day after school and sat with Nana- in her other life; she had not been to the hospital at all. She chatted and read to Nana, showed her what she was doing at school. Did her homework, getting Nana to help where she could, and tried to get Nana to get up and do her physiotherapy. But Nana refused to get out of bed, saying it hurt too much. On the last day, she rushed into the ward to find the bed empty and the bedside table cleared. She dropped her school bag. Nana had died of pneumonia just the same anyway. Xandra went back to her bedroom two days forward from before.

She had some new texts; mostly about some radio show she'd done that everyone seemed to have hated, but she thought she would sort all that stuff out later, when she had finished going back to sort out the past.

Xandra thought about how different her life might have been if she had done better at school, got more qualifications. It all started going wrong when she got into boys and messed up her O' levels. She thought if she went back and sat those again, perhaps she could change the course of her educational career; go on to A levels and a degree, maybe even a doctorate. Luckily she was blessed with an almost photographic memory, so she clearly remembered all the questions she had been unable to answer on the exam papers. Xandra spent the rest of the day online, researching answers and getting peripheral information; then while it was all still fresh in her mind she thought of the start of her exam week, and slipped the ring on her finger.

The first thing Xandra did when she got back was run to the wardrobe and grab her shoebox of exam certificates. She rummaged for the pieces of paper. Sure enough she had ten O' level passes all grade A. Then she found some A' level passes; English grade B, Biology grade C, and Art grade A. Finally she found her degree certificate; a 2:1 in History of Art. Xandra was overjoyed, and then she rushed to the bathroom to be sick. She suddenly realised she felt worse than she had in years. She recognised the sensation as a really bad hangover. She looked at herself in the mirror- God she looked rough. Xandra did not want to imagine what she had been doing during the last two days, but it obviously involved some kind of binge drinking. At that thought she threw up again. She drank some water from the sink tap and dragged herself back to the bedroom, noticing that her car was not outside. God only knew where she had left it during her two days of absence. She decided the best thing to do would be go back to the past again, and get away from this hangover. When she came back it would be over; double bonus. She knew where she was going; she had been looking at her divorce certificate as she went through the box of papers. That hadn't changed. Well, she could do something about that. She thought about the day before her wedding, when she had been lying in the bath getting ready for her hen night, and slipped the ring on her finger.

Xandra got out of the bath and dried off. Still wrapped in a big fluffy hot bath towel, straight out of the airing cupboard, she padded to the upstairs phone extension, and dialled Norm's number.

"Norm, I'm sorry but I can't marry you."

"What?" yelled Norm down the phone at her. "You cannot be serious!"

"I'm sorry Norm, but I am serious. It's never going to work out between us; we'll just end up getting divorced later anyway. It isn't last minute nerves, I just can't do it, I won't do it."

Norm hung up on her slamming the phone down that made a loud crack at Xandra's end. She had forgotten what that sounded like now it was all mobile phones. She had neglected to tell Norm that she would divorce him because she found him in bed with her best friend just a month after the honeymoon. Let her be the bad guy, what did she care? She was only staying ten days anyway. Xandra spent the rest of the afternoon calling people and telling them the wedding was off, cancelling the church, the caterers, the hen night, the reception, the DJ, everything. Finally, she drove to the next town for a takeaway pizza, just so she wouldn't see anyone she knew. Since she had booked the honeymoon and had the tickets, she decided to go on holiday alone. She spent the next nine days being a tourist and enjoying Rome, before the ring took her back to her bedroom once again.

The first thing she thought after taking the ring off was how much she hurt. Her arms were sore, her legs were cut, her knuckles and knees were grazed and her face was throbbing with pain. Looking in the mirror, she was horrified to see she had a massive black eye and a bruise that spread right across her face. Xandra did not like to think about what she might have been doing for the last couple of days, but once again she had a plan to get away from it. She went online and wrote down the previous night's lottery results, then went back to a lovely holiday she had had in Cornwall a few months before. While there she set up a lottery account for those numbers to be played every week by direct debit, then enjoyed her ten day holiday revisit. She knew when she returned home it would be a few days after she had won the lottery.

But when she returned, this time she was not in her bedroom. Xandra was being processed into prison. She watched the ring disappear into an envelope held by a guard with all her other personal possessions.

"But I don't remember anything; what am I doing here?" she cried.

"You just pleaded guilty to murder, so you'd better get used to it, you're going to be here quite a long time. The judge gave you a twenty stretch."

Finally Xandra got her visiting orders and her best friend Judy came to visit her. Judy did not look happy, but at least she was there.

"Judy, I don't know what happened. I don't remember anything since just after we went to that flea market together. It's all a blank. Please can you tell me what's going on?"

She must have looked genuine, because Judy's face softened somewhat.

"Firstly you sent out some really mean texts and posts to everyone you knew. We were all pretty mad at you; you said some pretty hurtful stuff. Then you did that radio show expose about John, airing all his dirty laundry for all to hear. Yeah the ratings were great, but you destroyed his life. He went back to his parents in Scotland after that. Then you went on some crazy drink and drug binge and totalled your car; we all thought you'd totally lost the plot- it was like you were having some kind of breakdown or something. Then you went to the nightclub and got into a big fight and got arrested, but they let you off with a caution as you had no previous record. Finally you broke into Marsha's house and stabbed her. They caught you, covered in blood, holding the knife, and you confessed right there. Said you'd always hated her, and she had it coming."

"But that wasn't me. I don't remember any of that. Can't I get a good lawyer, appeal or something?"

"Probably not; you pleaded guilty, and anyway you're broke."

"But I'm rich; I won the lottery didn't I?"

"Yes, but the judge gave everything you own, house, money the lot, to Marsha's family as compensation. I think you're pretty much screwed. You'd better get used to it in here."

Afterword
All magic has a price, so why should a time travelling ring be any exception? I like the idea that the more you try and get from magic, the bigger price it charges, and it never seems to profit you in the end.

Cabin In The Woods

Joe and Dani wanted a holiday. Dani wanted to go to a tropical island paradise, preferably almost deserted. Joe wanted to go to a cabin in the snow covered mountains, miles from the nearest village where skis and snow shoes were required at all times outdoors. The one thing they both agreed on, was that they wanted somewhere away from other people; far away.

So when Joe found the advert for the cabin in the woods, they both agreed it looked like a perfect compromise. There was no snow and no sand, but the climate was temperate, and the woodlands spectacular. Most importantly, there were no people for miles in any direction. The brochure said they would be met at the nearest town, where they would leave their car, or get off the train or bus; and be taken by the holiday agent in a small four wheel drive to the cabin. The cabin would be fully stocked with food and drink, linens and firewood. The agent would leave them there, with their backpack of luggage each, and collect them again at the end of the fortnight. For the entire holiday period they would not see another soul. There was no internet connection and no phone, but there was a television that would play a selection of DVDs and not much else. There was also a music system and two guitars, as well as a selection of board games. There was a well stocked medical box, and a flare gun for life threatening emergencies. The price was pretty reasonable too, so Joe and Dani jumped at the offer, and booked their ideal [ish] holiday.

Everything went exactly as described. The agent dropped them off at the cabin, quickly showing them where everything was, then waving goodbye, and promising to pick them up again in a fortnight.

The cabin was very generously stocked; more than they could eat and drink in two weeks, even if they were nonstop ravenous. The freezer had steaks and joints, sausages and burgers, fish and shellfish, vegetables and desserts. The fridge was stocked plentifully, as was the vegetable basket, bread bin and wine rack. There was also a good selection of beers, ciders and juices. There was even a bowl of sweets and chocolate bars. There was plenty of bedding and towels, and lots of extra blankets. Outside was a huge chopped wood pile, and an axe in case they actually wanted or needed to chop more.

There was a barbecue grill and a fire pit and spit, as well as a place to clean meat and fish if they went hunting. A shed contained hunting and fishing gear, as well as a booklet explaining safety procedures, and a licence to hunt.

Most of the DVDs were either very modern, some films they had not seen yet; or classics, as well as a couple of box sets. The games looked good too. There was a wide variety of music CDs to suit every taste. The bathroom was fully stocked with all the products a normal person might want to use during their ablutions. Dani pronounced the place perfect, and Joe cracked open a can of his favourite beer.

Dani had a glass of wine. They sat on the porch seats and relaxed, listening to the sounds of the forest around them. All they could hear were bird songs and the occasional scrabbling of small creatures in the undergrowth. It was idyllic. Dani sighed with pleasure.

The first night Dani cooked some steaks that had been left in the fridge, with fresh vegetables and jacket potatoes and the rest of the wine she had started earlier. They had fresh cream cakes- also left in the fridge- for dessert. Joe lit the fire pit, and they sat outside, enjoyed the darkness and silence, and watched the flickering flames until the fire died down to embers, and they went to bed. They made love with abandon- no neighbours to hear any noises they made, and fell into a deep and undisturbed sleep. Dani woke once when an owl hooted, but that just made her smile and fall back to a peaceful sleep.

The next morning Dani made a big cooked breakfast, again from fresh ingredients in the fridge, and Joe made a big pot of coffee.

"Shall we go for a walk and explore our surroundings after breakfast," asked Joe.

"Sounds like a plan," answered Dani.

So they set out. Joe had a small backpack with a map of the area, water, snacks, tissues, alcohol wiping gel, and a four pack of beers. They started down the path that led out from behind the cabin into the woods. There were occasional posts, the tips of which had been painted white as markers, so Joe thought they likely wouldn't even need the map. After an hour or so, the path seemed to fork into two directions, both looking equally unused. There were no white posts by either path.

"I think we might have gone off piste hun," laughed Joe.

"Oh never mind. We'll just go back the way we came, no problem," replied Dani. "It'll be an adventure."

So the couple turned around and headed back down the path they had come along before. But it didn't look the same, and there was still no sign of any white posts. Joe got the map out, but it didn't help one jot. They couldn't even locate exactly where the cabin was on the map, let alone where they might be.

After about another hour, they came to a fork in the trail, leading to two equally unused looking tracks. Joe scratched his head, "this looks like the place we got to before. I think we just walked round in a big circle."

Dani sighed with exasperation and sat down on a log to rub her feet which had developed a couple of blisters. She suggested they had a rest and a snack, and so Joe got out a couple of beers, some nuts, pretzels and chocolate bars. After a quick toilet break in the bushes, they picked one of the untrodden trails to set off along- figuring that would be a better option than going round in a big circle again. By now it was afternoon, and the sun had definitely started its descent.

Along the path the trees and shrubs seemed to be closing in on them, forming a maze like wall around them, so they could see little further than the path ahead.

"I'm not sure this is the right way either sweetie," said Joe.

"Well we can either carry on and see where it comes out, or turn around and try the other path."

"Carry on, I suppose," but Joe didn't sound entirely sure. They both felt nervous that evening was approaching and they were essentially completely lost in the woods, miles from anything.

Finally the maze like path opened out and they saw a lake in front of them.

"Aha," cried Joe. "In the cabin there was a map on the wall that showed a lake North West of the cabin. So if we head South East, we should find our way home."

"That's great," said Dani a little sarcastically, "but which side of the lake do you think the cabin is? I mean we don't know if we approached directly or circled round and came at the lake from the other side. Are we really any better off than we were five minutes ago? I'd love to be optimistic and say let's just walk South East from here, but if we came from the other side we could be walking around in these woods all night."

Suddenly Joe cried out "Hoy there!" and Dani saw he was calling to a guy on the other side of the lake who was fishing. The man was shabby looking like a tramp, and his face was lost in a bushy wild beard. He wore waders and was standing in the water fishing. He looked up at Joe's call and Dani saw he was wearing an eye patch. He had a piece of old rope round his waist as a belt, and a large hunting knife tucked through the rope. A few feet behind him on land was a sack and what looked like a farming scythe, leaning against a tree.

"Do you know the way to the cabin?" called Joe.

The man shrugged and pointed to his ear as if he couldn't her Joe.

"Perhaps he's deaf, we'd better walk around to him."

"I don't like the look of him," said Dani, he's creepy. Then in her loudest voice, which was pretty loud, she shouted, "Where is the cabin?"

The creepy guy peered at her for a long minute, then gesticulated vaguely behind himself.

"Well, we'll have to walk around the lake anyway if it's behind him," said Joe, heading off. Dani didn't like the idea of meeting the creepy guy close up, but tagged along behind.

When they got round to the other side of the lake, the last part of the path had wound into bushes and trees, and shut the lake off from their view, the man had disappeared. There was no sign that he had ever even been there. They thought it was weird, and Dani was secretly more than a little relieved, but followed the path away from that side of the lake anyway, confident it would lead back to the cabin. Joe thought that perhaps the guy had resented the intrusion on his privacy, and had not wanted to talk to them up close either.

After they had walked the path for another hour, with still no sign of anything familiar, it was starting to get dark. Dani was walking on ahead, convinced they were coming at the hut from a different angle, perhaps to arrive in front of it, and surely it would appear any moment now.

Joe heard a noise in the bushes behind him, and as he turned to look and see what it was, someone grabbed him from behind, pulling him backwards off his feet, and off the path into the undergrowth. He could feel a cold metal blade pressing into his throat.

Before he had time to even react, the creepy guy had sliced through his neck with the hand scythe, and Joe was a goner. The man dragged him deeper into the shrubs, away from the path.

Meanwhile Dani turned to ask Joe something and found he wasn't there. She turned and retraced her steps, then started to panic after she had doubled back on herself a hundred yards or so, and still found no trace of him, and had no answer to her calls.

Then it was all over for Dani too. She didn't even see the strike coming. The man took her down with a scythe swing to the throat as she ran along the path; it was over before she had even stopped running really.

The man dragged the bodies, an ankle in each hand, behind him through the woods to his own cabin, not far from the lake. Leaving them outside for now, he went into the cabin where his partner Suzi was sitting doing a crossword.

"Done 'em both Suze. They're outside now."

"Give them the usual treatment- strip all their stuff, weight them and sink them in the lake. I'll go and ready the cabin;

there's a new one booked to come in a few days," said Suzi, the cabin letting agent.

Afterword
Whenever we watch a film that starts with a deserted cabin in the woods, I just know it's going to end in people running from grizzly murder. It's almost enough to put you off that peaceful idyllic woodland setting. Almost but not quite. Anyway this is my short take on idyll turned nightmare. I'd still love to visit a cabin like that though.

Tracker Wolf

The wolf, who thought of himself only as 'the leader' padded quietly through the deep snow. Occasionally a flurry of snow would fall from a pine tree disturbed enough by the wind to shed its load. He remembered the old days when things were different, and people still hunted wolves, but with rifles, and they always wore bright red jackets so they were really easy to see from a long way off. Those hunters were easy to avoid. These days they wore white, or green in the summer, and were much harder to see. They were harder to hear too, as they used guns that shot lasers, which often killed in the slicing motion of a knife, but were always silent. No gunshots rang out to alert the wolf pack that the hunters were close by. Only a howl from a tracker or spotter wolf could alert the pack to the presence of hunters. You couldn't even hear the crunch of the hunter's footsteps in the snow, as they hovered in some sort of special boots, in which they flew just a couple of inches above the ground below them. No snap of a twig to give them away. Of course they couldn't disguise their people smell, but they used crystal necklaces which heightened their senses and calmed their scent down quite a lot. They had special wands and divining rods to help with tracking, and potions they placed in the woods that smelled like meat carcasses, which attracted hungry wolves.

The leader had lost four of his pack to the new hunters already this year, and they had had to move their den six times already. Some of the wolves were looking quite thin. There had been no new pups this season, even though all were allowed to breed now, not just himself and his female, like the old days. The pack was getting too small; breeding had to be allowed amongst all the females. But all this moving, running and being hunted so thoroughly, had made it too stressful and tiring for any of the females to breed. The males didn't seem very much interested in trying to breed either. When the pack wasn't running, they were hiding. Any food they caught was torn apart and devoured in seconds- even the runt omega was allowed to have a mouthful of every kill. They had to try and keep all the wolves alive; these were hard times. The leader remembered the tales passed down from the elders and the ancestor wolves about the days when the humans did not hunt them at all, but cowered in fear of their howls in dark caves. The humans learned to make fires to keep the wolves back from their caves, but still did not hunt. They would only attack and try to kill a wolf with a sharp stone, when the wolf first attacked them.

The leader was a perfectly white wolf, and was well camouflaged in the snow. In the summer he had to roll in the mud to pass unseen through the woods, but now, in the winter his coat was pure white and glorious. Today he was out helping the spotters, which made a total of four of them looking out in each direction of the four winds, in case the hunters came again today.

Then the leader saw them; a team of eight hunters, gliding up the snowy hill towards the woods. He ran to the top of the hill and howled. His howl would draw the hunters away from the den, and alert the other spotters and hunters to run back to the den and hide. Sure enough the distant hunters turned towards the direction of his howl. Let them keep tracking in that direction, he would not howl again, and neither would any of the others from his pack. They had quickly learned when a certain type of howl meant everyone keep quiet and get well hidden.

The leader ran down the hill so he could come into the woods behind the human hunting team. Soon the humans entered the woods, floating silently above the snow. They were well spaced out, and the leader stalked the human at the rear of the party. Soon there was enough distance between the human and the other seven humans, and the leader leapt silently, mouth tearing and gripping at the human's throat. He was a strong wolf and the human was dead in no time, his blood fresh and red against the white snow. The leader dragged and rolled his body to the den. When the band of crystals came off the human's neck as he was dragging him; the leader ducked his head and pushed the crystals onto his own neck. Suddenly he could see more sharply. He had a strong sense of exactly where the other humans were, and more, he could feel the presence of his own pack members not too far away. He sent out the thought of meat and in particular called two hunters, who came bounding out to meet him.

"Drag this back to the den, then come back here. Cover the tracks on the way back. Dig the snow over the blood and drag marks. I'll meet you here soon."

The two hunter wolves looked confused to hear their leader so clearly in their own heads, but obeyed him anyway. A wolf would never disobey their leader.

The leader headed back to the kill site and began hastily covering the tracks of blood and disturbed snow; until he had got all the way back to where he would meet the hunter wolves. He could feel that they were on their way back to him. He could also feel the joy in the den as the pack pulled the meat apart and buried their faces in the still warm flesh. His pack was happy, it was a big kill, and there would be plenty to eat for all. The leader could also feel the hunting team still heading up the hill. But now two of them were breaking off and coming back down to look for the straggler. The leader willed his hunter wolves to hurry up.

He saw them at last, trotting towards him, heads up, tails wagging, pleased to be rejoining their alpha leader.

"We must hurry. Two hunters are coming back down the hill separate from the rest. I will come up behind them and you will be either side of them. As soon as I make myself known and they turn to look at me, jump on one each and clamp your jaws around their throats before they can lift their weapons to shoot me. Don't hesitate, just do it like I said and it will work."

The other wolves obeyed without any hesitation, though they were still wondering how their leader could talk to them so. Soon the two human searchers lay dead on the ground. The leader nudged at their necks until their crystal necklaces came off in the snow.

"Put your head through that, so it hangs round your neck like the one I'm wearing," the leader instructed the two hunters.

After they had got the necklaces around their necks, the eyes of the hunter wolves went wide.

"I can hear everything," thought one.

"Yes the pack feeding, the humans up the hill looking for the wolf that howled," replied the other.

"There are five more of them," said the leader. And with that he called all the strong wolves of the pack to him. They came running. He instructed a group of them to drag the bodies to the den. All the strong hunting and spotter wolves he instructed to come with him up the hill.

"There are five humans up there hunting us. They want to kill us, but there are more of us. Three of us can think and sense like they do now. Soon five more of you will be able to do this too. We are going to hunt and kill all of them, and then I will show you how you can be like me and talk to the others."

They broke into three teams, each led by a 'communicator.'

They launched a group attack from three sides on the remaining five human hunters; all were killed and for once no wolves died. Only one wolf was injured when the tip of his ear got taken off by a laser, but he soon tore out the throat of the human that fired it. Later he was one of the five that got a necklace. The other four recipients were hunters and spotters.

"With these stones we wear, we will never be caught by the human hunters again. We can talk to each other from every point on the mountain, and know when they are coming. We must drag all this food down to the den; eat all that we can, then drag the rest of the meat to a new den. We will breed again now. There will be new pups this thaw."

The wolf pack howled in their victory.

Afterword

I wonder sometimes, if, as technology develops and becomes better and better, if humans will ever evolve alongside it, or just remain base, vile creatures armed with better tools. I suspect the latter will be the case, and men will still want to prove their manhood by hunting and killing wild animals. I like to think the animals will get a chance to win out though, despite everything. I especially like the idea of the animals somehow using the human technology.

Ski Lift Journey

Heidi, Lars and Gunther had been hiking together many times before. Since they left college they had done a variety of exciting things together; abseiling, rock climbing, pot holing, cave diving, parachuting, scuba diving, jet ski-ing, mountaineering, white water rafting, hang gliding, fire walking, anything a bit adrenalin pumping that came along really. When they weren't doing that stuff, they went hiking in the countryside.

Currently, they were on a ski-ing, snowboarding, mountaineering holiday in the Alps, and were between activities, so had decided to walk up the mountain the advanced skiers used. At the chair lift kiosk at the base of the mountain, Heidi asked the attendant, if they could just get the chair lift back down, after hiking up the mountain. He had told her that this chair lift did not bring people back down, as there was not a climb on point at the top, just a jump off for the skiers. As it was an advanced run, the chairs always came down empty and there was no need. Lars said they could just hike up and down in that case; they'd done longer walks. But the attendant said that if they were hiking and carried on for a mile or so after the top of the chair lift, in the same direction, they would come to another ski lift on the other side of the mountain, that went down to a really pretty village. It was quiet and not used much, but he assured them it was still operative, and also that the village below was well worth a look. Also they could get a cab or minibus back from the village when they were done. They all agreed that it sounded like a good plan and headed off.

The snow was soft and powdery, and it was tough walking up the mountain; their hiking boots sinking deep with each step. But they were young and fit and carried on, laughing as they went along. They passed the ski lift at the top and pressed on along the high ridge of the mountain in the direction they had been told. Finally the ski lift down to the village on the other side of the mountain came into view. It was indeed deserted. As they got close they saw a man huddled in woollens and outerwear, manning the hut at the top of the lift. Chairs rattled round, and came up, and went down empty. They approached the man in the kiosk who seemed very surprised to see them.

"Hi there," said Lars, "not very busy up here is it?"

"No," replied the attendant, "the snow is wrong for skiing on this mountain at the moment. The sun is on this side of the mountain and it melts the snow which freezes again, and it's too icy. It's just too dangerous for skiing or boarding, or even walking."

"Can we get the chair lift down to the village?" asked Gunther.

"Oh yes, sure," replied the man, "but it's only one person per car. It's a bit of a rickety old system actually, and we don't trust the chairs to hold two people anymore."

"Ok, no worries," said Heidi, heading towards the platform.

"Hang on there lassie," called the man, "I need to tell you some things first."

The three friends gathered round the attendant, wondering what on earth he might have to say about a chair lift before they got on it. They were expecting the usual stuff about standing in the right place and waiting until the chair touched the back of their legs, then sitting down firmly and putting the safety bar down. Stuff about staying still until the end where someone would lift the bar so they could get out. Stuff about not rocking the cars. They waited politely anyway.

"It's not a normal chair lift," the man began, "being as it is so old and all. You have to lean forward to make it go, or it stops. Trouble is, when you lean forward and it gets going, it goes kind of fast. But don't worry about that, it's just the way this funny old system works. Just lean forward, hang on, and shut your eyes if it's too much. It kind of feels a bit loose and wobbly too, but it's perfectly safe really; I come up and down on it every day to get to and from work, and I'm fine. It's just a bit odd that's all."

"Wow this sounds a bit different," said Lars, "I want to go first, do you mind guys?"

"No have at it," laughed Heidi, and Gunther nodded.

"I'll bring up the rear," said Gunther.

So they all headed towards the platform to wait in order for the chairs. Lars got on the first one, which creaked and practically stopped as he pulled the bar down. Then he remembered and leaned forward and the chair began to pick up speed and move away. Heidi got on the next one, which was a fair distance behind. Although she remembered right away to lean forward, the back of Lars' head and his boots were still a good way ahead of her. Finally Gunther got on, and the three of them were travelling simultaneously through the air, the snowy mountain falling lower below them, the sun glinting on icy patches.

The cars seemed to be travelling faster and faster, shaking and creaking as they hurtled along. Heidi let out an involuntary squeal, as if she were on a roller coaster ride. It seemed to Gunther that they were getting faster still, as he watched Heidi almost disappear as she lurched forward even faster. Then he too felt the lurch of the extra speed taking him.

In the front car, Lars couldn't believe how fast he seemed to be going, the world around him seemed to be blurring at the edges, though it was mainly snow and sky, the blue and white colours seemed to be blurring into one rapidly passing silver. He knew that couldn't possibly be happening for real, it must be some kind of illusion caused by the wind and the angles, and the cold or something; but before he had time to think about it anymore, the scene around him changed.

Lars blinked twice to be sure he was seeing what he thought he was seeing. All around him were reds, browns and greys, and he realised he seemed to be hurtling down into the centre of a mountain. Then he realised that below him the ground was red, and the air smelt noxious and sulphurous. He realised he was in a volcano. He could feel the heat coming up from the lava below. It seemed to be getting hotter and hotter; his feet felt like they were starting to melt into the molten soles of his boots. He shut his eyes convinced he must be hallucinating, but when he opened them again, the lava in the centre of the volcano was even closer. Lars was so hot that beads of sweat were running down his face.

Meanwhile Heidi was having an entirely different experience. Like Lars, her world had also gone rather blurry, but the similarities ended there. She found herself suddenly, inexplicably surrounded by people, as if she was indeed on some kind of fairground ride. She had instinctively leant back as the world seemed to change around her, and she seemed to be passing through a crowd on either side of her; the car going slower now, and the faces of the crowd beginning to take shape. She could hear fairground carnival music, and could even smell sugary candyfloss and fried onions. She thought she must be having some sort of brain event and began to panic a little bit. Then the faces came into focus and Heidi nearly screamed. Freakish deformed faces leered at her out of the crowd. Scary nightmarish faces that loomed towards her, then rather worryingly, began to reach for her with their hideous arms. Suddenly Heidi remembered to lean forward again and the faces began to rush past once more. Even the music sounded like it was speeding up again. Before it all became a blur of colour once more, Heidi swore she felt lumpy hands and limbs brush against her sides.

For Gunther, things had become equally strange. His world blurred, but the blue of the sky seemed to take over; the white, disappearing. The blue darkened then when it once again came into focus, Gunther could see he was hurtling down into an ocean of water. Little white waves broke and disappeared on the surface which was getting disturbingly close. Gunther instinctively tucked his feet up against the underside of the seat. He could smell the sea water, feel its spray on his face, and then he was plunging into it, submerged. Like Heidi, he shut his eyes for a few seconds, and then opened them again to find himself hurtling through an underwater world, whilst apparently breathing normally. To say he felt a bit freaked out would be somewhat of an understatement. Then he noticed that all around him, strange sea creatures swam in and out of his vision. Like nothing he had ever seen before; things with tentacles, multiple heads, big bulging eyes, swam up close as if examining him, and then darted away again.

Then Gunther saw a massive Leviathan of a creature, swimming towards him, on a head on collision course. As it got closer, its maw opened wide, and Gunther realised it intended to engulf and eat him, chair and all. He shut his eyes.

When Lars thought he couldn't possibly get any hotter without bursting into flames, the car stopped and a man reached out and grabbed the bar, lifting it up and pulling Lars onto the disembarkation platform. Lars staggered to a nearby bench and shook his head, trying to understand what had just happened. Meanwhile Heidi arrived and almost ran out of her seat to throw herself down breathlessly beside him. Finally Gunther was pulled from his seat looking like he had seen a ghost, and patting himself, astonished that he was not soaking wet.

"What just happened?" asked Lars, who had had a few seconds longer to prepare himself for speech.

The attendant walked back into his hut grinning, as the three hurriedly and breathlessly exchanged stories of what they had encountered.

Still not believing what had happened, they walked slowly into the village to find somewhere that would sell them a stiff drink or three.

"Do you want to go back and do it again?" laughed Heidi.

"No way!" exclaimed Lars and Gunther in unison.

Afterword

This story and the two previous ones have one thing in common; they were all rather strange dreams that I had. Obviously they had to be tweaked and polished a little bit to be transferred from crazed dreamscape to the page, but not much really. I know some authors dream entire books, but it rarely happens to me, despite having a lot of very colourful dreams, but anyway here they are. This one is a bit of an acid trip, but, of the three, it appeared almost entirely as it stands, so I went with it. Take it or leave it. Oh and if you ever get a chance to try the chair lift ride at the Isle of Wight Needles, make sure you do. That's an experience too. Not quite as scary as this one, but....

Freak Factory

Rupert was a freelance journalist, which is to say, he was always looking for a good breaking story to sell exclusively to the tabloids. He wasn't one to hang about outside stars houses with the paps though; couldn't stand all that kind of nonsense. Rupert was an investigative reporter, snooping out hidden stories, pouring light into dark places.

He had gone to the village of Durkham because reports had shown an increased number of missing pets, and he wanted to interview the locals and see if he could find a story there. It turned out that none of the missing pets had ever reappeared, which in itself was unusual, as usually in such cases a number returned home, were found dead in roadside ditches hit by cars, or were returned for reward or just plain kindness. But such was not the case in Durkham; none had returned or been found dead or alive.

Rupert started chatting with more of the local villagers, not just the ones with lost pets. The castle at the top of the hill, just outside the village looked more and more interesting. Apparently delivery of all sorts of barrels of unknown stuff, and vans from chemical and pharmaceutical companies delivered there all the time. No one knew what went on up there and everyone had some sort of weird story to tell about the place. Rupert decided that a visit to the castle was in order.

He arrived at the big castle door and had an introductory speech prepared about how he was a keen student of architecture and castles in particular, and would it be at all possible for him to photograph the outside and possibly even see some of the inside areas, if it wouldn't be too much of an intrusion.

The chap who answered the door was tall and distinguished, looking for all the world like the sort of aristocrat one would expect to be Lord of the Castle, and had a deep booming voice to accompany his stature. He replied that he was more than happy for Rupert to photograph the outside of the castle, and that he would make sure the more impressive inner areas were tidy and presentable if Rupert would care to return in one hour for that part of the visit. He suggested that perhaps even a glass of wine might be provided.

Rupert was not expecting such friendly hospitality, and was thrown a little off guard. When he returned to the castle door, he was ushered inside with the grace of a butler bringing in royalty. In all, he found it most disconcerting.

Like all castles worth their salt, this one had a grand entrance hall, with stone stairs climbing to the upper levels. Portraits and old weaponry adorned the stone walls, along with tapestries that might have served a better function on the cold stone floors.

The tour took Rupert along a long corridor to a very impressive library, lined floor to ceiling with books, furnished with armchairs by the fireplace, desks and chairs and plenty of earth coloured rugs that gave the room the feeling of warmth that Rupert had not yet seen in any other parts of the castle.

"This is a beautiful room," he exclaimed. "I could quite happily live in a room like this."

"Actually, it's my favourite room too," answered the owner who had introduced himself as William Thorpe-Codlington, the third; but would rather be called Will. "I spend most of my time in here."

At that moment, a servant knocked and entered carrying a tray of wine glasses and wine. But Rupert barely noticed the wine, before he was drawn to the servant himself. The man was an absolute mass of deformities; about three foot tall, hunched, limbs twisted, and eyes bulging to the point that they looked like they might pop out onto his cheeks at any moment. Rupert managed to catch himself and stop staring, though it was a wonder to him that such deformed limbs were able to hold a full tray level, and manage to walk across the room. Will hurried over and relieved him of the tray, saying something to the man under his breath that sent him scuttling rapidly out of the library.

"His family have been with us for a very long time, and although his working here fulfils my minorities quota, I really don't like him to do very much. He has enough on his plate just getting up in the morning. He was trying to be helpful, bless his heart; filling in for the butler who was busy elsewhere."

"So what do you do Will?" asked Rupert, sipping his wine.

"I suppose I'm what you might call a gentleman of leisure. Family inheritances have blessed me with no need to work for a living. I dabble in various arts as somewhat of a hobby."

Will took Rupert up to see the views from the battlements; which were indeed impressive- rolling hills and fields for many miles, as well as three villages and a small wood.

"I wonder if I might use a bathroom?" enquired Rupert.

"Of course. We'll go back inside and I'll point out the nearest facility."

They walked back inside down some stairs, and Will pointed out a door a short way along one of the upstairs corridors. Then Will gestured to the main stairway leading to the entrance hall and told Rupert he would wait for him there.

Rupert, once out of sight of Will did not go into the bathroom indicated, but instead peeked through a gap in the double doors opposite. The room was filled with laboratory equipment, like some sort of crazy science lab. But what astonished Rupert more, and made him give out an involuntary gasp, were the people [a loose label- he realised as he looked] that were performing the lab experiments. They made the chap that had come into the library earlier look quite normal by comparison.

Such a collection of freakish forms had Rupert never seen before; and he had been to some pretty twisted sideshows, and seen some very eclectic films. But these people were unbelievable. One had two heads; another looked like a contortionist with legs growing out of his shoulders. Another had an extra set of arms growing out of his stomach, and several had extra eyes, noses and mouths. They were all shapes and sizes, from tiny to huge, and quite a variety of colours too, Rupert noticed, now that he looked closer.

As he peered further into the huge room he gasped to see dogs, cats, rabbits and squirrels strung out on metal rods, squirming and making terrible noises as they were experimented on, obviously still alive. Rupert reached into his pocket to snap a few surreptitious photographs; here was some sort of story, and he needed visual evidence. Just then he felt himself encircled by huge arms and lifted off of the ground, dropping his camera to the stone floor with a loud clatter. He was removed from the room, to where Will stood scowling outside.

"Take him to the dungeon and give him something to help him sleep for now," Will instructed the giant that held Rupert. To Rupert he said, "I suppose you are really some sort of journalist. Of course I can't let you leave now you have been snooping about. I'll come down and talk to you later."

Rupert was carried like so much baggage down to the depth of the castle where the dungeons were located. He just had time to notice the cell he was being carried into, before the smell of chloroform on a rag made him lose his grip on consciousness.

He awoke to the feeling of an injection in his arm, and Will standing over him. He tried to jump up, but was tied to the cot in the cell.

"I have brought a book for you to read, hope you like Dickens, it's probably the last book you'll ever read."

"Are you planning to kill me then?"

"That part is already done. I'm working on a serum to stop ageing and give me immortality. That's what you saw going on in my lab. The animals have not produced good results, I needed human subjects. Obviously they are quite hard to come by in this day and age, so I grew them myself in Petri dishes and tanks. Sadly they aren't the best examples of the human species, but they share the same genes, pretty much, and thus can be used for testing my formulas. What you have been injected with, is the latest formula we are working on, though I have to say, don't expect it to make you immortal. The likelihood is that it will speed up your ageing process and release any hidden mutations in your cells. I fully expect you to have died of old age before breakfast, and be in my autopsy room before lunch. But if that turns out to not be the case, I'll look forward to having a good long talk with you in the morning. Meanwhile, Burt- that's the giant you met before; will bring you a nice, probably last meal, untie you, and leave you to enjoy the book. Bon voyage."

Rupert struggled to enjoy his meal, but ate it because he was hungry. He had to suppose that Will's talk had been fear mongering hogwash, but out of boredom, began the book anyway. He soon lost himself temporarily in the story, running his fingers through his hair; finally noticing that it was coming away in chunks in his hands. Rupert jumped up, or tried to, but what happened was a much slower rising, accompanied by pain in all his joints. He frantically felt the skin of his face and found wrinkles aplenty. He looked at his hands and arms, and noticed they were covered with liver spots and growths where moles used to be. His nails were already long and horny, and he had to kick off his shoes because his feet felt trapped and misshapen within. Finally Rupert accepted what was happening to him; he could no longer see to read anyway- the room had faded to a milky blur. He laid back down on the cot for a nap to ease the pain he felt just about everywhere.

Rupert did not wake up again.

Afterword

This is my twisted version of the Frankenstein story, in short form. It has added sideshow elements. I always remember with joy walking round Ripley's Believe it or Not freak show displays. Something that has now disappeared in our PC approved world; more the shame, in my opinion.

Becoming Twins

Yolande and Tom had been married for forty two years. Tom liked to say they were marching towards a solid gold. Yolande used to say they deserved a medal for staying together so long. Then they would both say, in perfect unrehearsed [except for the fact they had said it hundreds of times before] unison; "We'd be long since free if we'd done a murder stretch."

Of course that sort of thing was only natural. Two people, together a long time, will start to say the same routine things; will fall into a natural comic timing for their off the cuff jokes, will shout the same things at the television, will spout the same opinions, and will finish each other's sentences.

But for Yolande and Tom, it didn't stop there. On the odd occasions they were out separately; had anyone been scientifically observing them- they still did it. For example at the exact same moment that Tom was at the bus stop, saying to the other bus stop inhabitants, "looks like rain- but the garden needs it, save me watering tonight," at that moment Yolande was in the garden saying the exact same words over the fence to her neighbour. No one knew or observed them doing this, but the fact remained, they were. And they did it all the time. They fancied the same obscure thing for dinner, pudding or a snack, at the exact same time. They were always laughing together as they uttered identical words, still surprising each other as they did so. They said it must be because they had been together so long, and because they spent so much time together, but they didn't see anyone else doing it; not to the extent that they did anyhow.

They had even been on one of those old people coach holidays, so they could check and see if any of the other couples were like them. They thought it might become more obvious as a thing if they spent more time around other couples. No one else did it to the same extent that they did though.

After a time they developed the same taste in food, music, television shows, holidays, things to do on going out, and so forth; but once again they thought that to be perfectly natural and reasonable.

The same clothes started with the matching his and hers moccasin slippers. They were really comfortable and warm and they both wanted a pair. The same thing happened with the black fleece indoor elasticised pants, and the blue fleece sweatshirts. They were just too comfortable. Of an evening, in the winter, they would sit by the fire watching their favourite shows on television, looking like some kind of geriatric non identical twins. They bought safari hats with roll up mosquito nets for their holidays, and pack-a-Macs for rain showers. The twin dressing continued. As Yolande got older, she found trousers more and more comfortable, and men's sizes were a better fit for her spreading post menopausal frame. When they found something comfortable, durable, cheap and to their minds, desirable; they would buy it in both their sizes. The fact that they selected the same clothes from different wardrobes, in different rooms –Tom's clothing had long since been relegated to the spare room wardrobe for lack of space- on the same day, at the same time, had begun to escape their notice. At first they would laugh and say 'snap' when they arrived to the breakfast table in the same outfits; but that got old, and neither of them were that perky in the mornings anymore. Sometimes it was not until they met another person and said person commented on the fact they were dressed identically, that they would look at themselves and each other, then announce in unison; "Oh yes, so we are."

One day, Fred, a somewhat younger friend of theirs, was visiting for afternoon tea. Yolande and Tom were dressed identically, as usual, and happened to make one of their more off the wall, in unison, comments.

Yolande laughed afterwards and said, "We do that so often these days, it is becoming a thing for us."

Fred unexpectedly replied, "I have a friend I do that with. We aren't that close, but every time we see each other, it happens, pretty much continuously. The funny thing is, we were born the exact same minute in the same hospital, and were put side by side in the hospital nursery. We went to the same school and were in the same classes too. I only see him every month or so, but we always say the same things. People who know us both, and get a birthday or Christmas card from each of us, have shown us the cards afterwards, and unbeknownst to ourselves, we have both written the exact same message."

Tom and Yolande agreed that that was indeed weird and inexplicable. After Fred had left they talked and wondered about it. Perhaps it wasn't a couple's thing as they had thought. Perhaps it was something else entirely. But what? They certainly did not know.

Then one morning after a wild and stormy night, when they tossed and turned through the darkness in their creaky old double bed, only one person came down to breakfast. It was impossible to tell if it was Yolande or Tom; they had somehow merged into one being. Features from both remained, and yet it was impossible to say who it was. Both had short grey hair and blue eyes. Both wore the same glasses. Tom had stopped growing most of his facial hair a while back, and Yolande had started growing odd hairs on her chin and top lip. Tom had developed moobs that sagged flatly against his chest, and Yolande's once pert breasts had become flat pancakes since she no longer bothered with a bra. Tom had lost his man parts beneath belly fat long since, and had begun sitting on the toilet to pee, and Yolande had to hold up her belly to wash underneath it too. Both had mid range voice tones; neither high nor low pitched. In short, the being that came down to breakfast could have been either Yolande or Tom; either or both.

It was when they went to speak to the other one that they noticed there was only one of them. First of all they were shocked and panicked a little bit; then as they realised what an impossible thing had transpired, they relaxed into the idea. They could not explain or rationalise it, but after a time they didn't really much care either.

A couple of weeks later, Fred once again came for a visit. Yom or Tolande, as they had begun thinking of themselves, tried to explain what had transpired. Finally they parted with the warning comment;

"We're thinking you'd maybe better not see too much of that friend of yours, eh!"

Afterword
This story was inspired by the fact that my husband and I do in fact say the same thing at the same time rather frequently. There are a few other similarities; we have the same ideas and the same joggers. Thankfully for us it stops there, and will hopefully never go as far as it did for Tom and Yolande; but we have only been together twenty three years, so you never know. We do have a friend who told us the same story Fred told. Well, up to the point of being born at the same time and being put in the next crib and saying the same things when together. Other than that, it's all fanciful conjecture.

Mouse Heartbeats

Rebecca Masters worked in a research laboratory. Years of laborious research had brought her to her current paper. Rebecca had found that mice live a certain amount of time, not solely because of their size, but because of the rate at which their hearts beat. A long lived mouse could last as long as four years, maybe even more, whereas a great number of mice died within eighteen months to two years. This only accounted for the mice that died of old age and natural causes; obviously being in a lab was not conducive to normal life conditions, but nevertheless Rebecca had got a fairly solid set of figures. Within the mouse study group, she had further refined the study to monitor activity levels in mice. The relatively sedentary mice, excluding the lazy and obese ones, tended to live longer than the mice which ran around frantically.

At first Rebecca thought it was just the effects of stress on the system, but as she looked into it further, she realised the longer lived mice had lower numbers of heart beats per minute. She co-ordinated her research with a study of elephants from a research station in India, and another which monitored Galapagos tortoises. Obviously it was slow, painstaking research, but after many years, it was beginning to show the results for which Rebecca had hoped. Her hypothesis was holding water. It seemed that all creatures had the same number of heartbeats, and when they were used up, the creature, whatever species, died. Like a watch that had run out of winding, there was no more life after all the beats were used.

Stress was a killer; but only because it made the heart beat faster, racing through its allocation early. A surprising number of supposedly healthy athletes gave weight to the theory by dying relatively young. Celebrities who led an adrenalin fuelled lifestyle and used cocaine and amphetamines for relaxation and endurance, were high in the early death figures. Rebecca did not believe this was just down to the toxicity of the drugs.

Religious gurus and their ilk, who practised meditation for many hours each day, slowing their heartbeats right down, were amongst the longest lived human beings in the world.

The old adage, 'Live Fast, Die Young,' was proving to have a whole depth of truth to it that was previously unconsidered.

The implications for human beings was huge. If they were properly informed, and chose to adjust their lifestyles accordingly; by the mouse model, people could realistically expect to double their lifespan. Drugs to slow the heart rate would become commonplace, and stress, aerobic exercise and speed type drugs would all but disappear. Rebecca needed some long term human test subjects. For this she would need volunteers, and the only way to get them would be to make her work public. She knew the big pharma companies would not want her research made public, and she would likely be shut down before she could even begin to make the crux of her findings public.

So she decided to make a film, a short ten minute production, aimed at the masses, in everyday terminology, that she could upload to the internet, where everyone could see it before pharma had a chance to shut her down. She had prepared her script very carefully, getting all the salient information across, and at the conclusion appealing for volunteers, who would of course, be paid.

She launched her video on a Friday night, so she had three nights and two days before big pharma properly reacted. It was plenty of time. Within twenty four hours she had more test subjects than she needed, with plenty in reserve in case of drop outs or study diversifications. She also had three television and two radio appearances lined up. Apparently Rebecca Masters had caught the attention of the world; well for now, her corner of it at least.

The television studio had lined up a couple of 'example' subjects for a documentary style interview. Rebecca thought it was over simplifying things more than a bit, but was prepared to go along with it for dramatic effect and to get the message across to the public.

They had a fifty year old who lived an extremely healthy lifestyle of good food and jogging. He admitted to taking a lot of speed in his teens and twenties. He looked nearer ninety than fifty.

They had a ninety year old who had lived in the country all his life; was filmed on location in fact, because he refused to leave his home. He did daily relaxation exercises, walked in the surrounding countryside, read books and lived extremely quietly. He looked about fifty five.

The television quoted cases of a fitness freak who died whilst jogging as well as a Tibetan yogi, still alive and walking about aged supposedly one hundred and thirty. The message of the programme was ultimately, never let your heart race, because you are racing towards an early death. Meditation is like a savings account for your heart.

The following Monday morning saw yoga and meditation classes packed out and with a waiting list for membership. Bookshops and DVD stores sold out of self help yoga, relaxation and meditation instruction information. Doctor's surgeries were inundated with patients demanding relaxation medication, and to be taken off meds that made their pulses race. Street drug dealers saw a rise in sales of 'downer' drugs.

Conversely there was a spate of sudden deaths as people rushed about madly trying to disprove the theory.

Big Pharma rushed production of relaxation drugs. They weren't going to miss out, just because they got pipped to the first post. They damned sure would be with the winners at the second post.

That is how Rebecca Master's Mouse Heartbeat Theory broke onto the unsuspecting twenty first century world.

Afterword

I think this is a thing. A truth that already exists. It is not widely discussed because it would impact on too many money producing lifestyle industries. I bet there is research already out there that proves it too. But I doubt we'll ever see it. Can't have the world filling up with healthy old humans now, can we?

Don't Leave The Circle

The minibus deposited the group of new-agers at Hinkleton Stone Circle, about an hour before they were due to meet up with their guide: Sunburst Spiritwalker. With nothing else to do, Troll, Luck, Nine, Kitty, Star and Blossom headed for the pub for a quick pint.

Just after an hour later, they headed over to the stone circle at the outskirts of the village, where Sunburst was now waiting for them. She had had to text Kitty to find out where they were. Had she not have done so they might well have stayed in the pub until closing time- possibly popping out for the occasional spliff.

It was Halloween, but Hinkleton was too small and remote a village to have kids, or treat or treaters of any variety. All was quiet, and being gone 10pm, already pitch dark. Troll and Luck had head torches, so they guided the group to the circle.

Sunburst greeted them, perhaps a little tersely, and ushered them into the circle, going round and beginning to light candles in jars all around the perimeter. Finally she returned to the centre where the group stood in a huddle, whispering and giggling.

"Tonight is Samhain," began Sunburst, "the night of All Hallow's Eve, when the veil between this world and the others is at its thinnest. This circle is on ley lines, three of which cross in the centre of the circle. Here is a place where many people have experiences they cannot explain. If you want to have a final pee, go outside the circle now; for once I cast the circle you must not leave."

Star, Blossom and Nine scurried off to relieve themselves of their last pint, laughing as they went.

When all were finally assembled within the circle, Sunburst readied herself to begin.

"Tonight you may visit with the dead, see the past or future, visit other worlds, meet with guides from other planes; but whatever happens, no matter how scared you may feel, there is only one important rule to remember- Don't Leave the Circle."

Everyone muttered that they understood.

Sunburst began again, taking a dagger from her belt and holding it out at arm's length, "I conjure thee oh circle of power....a shield of protection to contain and preserve....I summon stir and call thee up...witness these rites....oh great dark ones....I call on our ancestors...." and so it went on until the group were shifting their weight from foot to foot and shuffling restlessly.

"Now sit down, close your eyes, cover your heads if you have a scarf, and we shall wait for the spirits to appear. Try not to disturb anyone around you as they may already be having their own experience. Lie down if it helps you. Just try to relax and open your mind to the idea that the spirits are coming through."

The smell of incense drifted around them as Sunburst walked the circle three times with a heavily loaded censer of frankincense and dragon's blood.

Kitty felt the presence of her long passed Grandmother, who always visited with her at Halloween. But this time she had brought along the rest of the family that had passed too. Perhaps because of the ley lines and the energy gathered in the circle, but it was a riotous family gathering, like the sort she had had as a child, when most of these people were still alive.

Star was seeing her future, where she had landed a role in a film and although she wasn't the lead, it proved a big enough part to get her discovered and get more work further down the line. She saw the moment at which her career finally began to take off.

Nine was in some sort of alternate reality, where all of his subtle psychic powers which made him a bit weird and odd in this world, made him superior in that world.

Blossom was back in medieval times, before the witch hunts. She was a respected village witch; wise woman and healer. Everyone came to her for health problems, general advice, and to birth their babies.

Troll was in some kind of weird future world, where his size and strength gave him a big advantage over the wild nature that surrounded him. It was some kind of post apocalyptic world far into the future, where even the sky had turned a different colour, and the people looked very different.

Luck was not getting anything. He waited and waited, before finally opening his eyes and looking around. All of the others were lost in some kind of trance; even Sunburst was away with the fairies.

Luck wandered over to the edge of the circle, as far from the others as he could get whilst still being in the circle, and lit a spliff. Maybe a little smoke would help open his psychic eye. As he stood there quietly smoking, watching his friends, and gazing at the starry night sky, he realised he badly needed to pee. It had been a long time since the last pint in the pub and it was pressing heavy on his bladder now. He decided that it would be okay to pee out of the circle so long as he stayed within it. As he urinated, and it was one of those long slow pees that seem to go on forever because he was a bit stoned, he gazed up at the night sky and the stars that glittered in it, their light given out such a long time before. It was cold and he was rapidly shrinking and finding it harder to keep a grip; which he realised as pee splashed onto his fingers. Just then a shooting star shot across the night sky and the combination of the two events made Luck jump in surprise; shaking his hand and finally stopping peeing. At which point he noticed he was outside the circle.

'Oops' he thought, and hopped back in quickly, looking around. No one had seen what he did, so he sauntered over to the others and sat back down and closed his eyes. They sat that way, huddled in their winter coats, until the first light of dawn. At some point Sunburst walked around draping a thick blanket over each of them.

At first light Sunburst began chanting again, "We thank you...ere you depart...hail and farewell...may all be as it was before and will always be....so mote it be."

All the candles in jars had long since burnt out, and the group all shivered in their blankets as Sunburst finished closing the circle.

Sunburst thanked them for their attendance, told them she hoped they had had a great experience, collected up her blankets and candles and other paraphernalia, and got in her little car parked nearby, and left. The friends huddled together at the roadside waiting for the minibus scheduled to come and pick them up. Everyone chattered excitedly about the experiences they had had and the things they had seen.

Except Luck, he didn't say anything- didn't even smoke which was unusual for him, as he was almost always smoking something or other.

"How about you Luck?" asked Blossom. "What happened for you?"

"Didn't really get anything," mumbled the demon posing as Luck.

"You're really quiet though mate, not like you," said Nine, concern in his voice.

Luck shrugged, and turned to look out at the landscape around him. Troll, Luck's best mate, looked at the others and shrugged too, as if to say, 'I have no idea what's wrong with him either.'

In another realm, flames shot out of cracks in the earth. Nothing remained of the stone circle except a pile of large stone rubble. But the thing that really panicked Luck was that none of the group, or even Sunburst were anywhere to be seen anymore. At first he thought he was just finally having his Samhain journey, but the blanket had gone, his eyes were open and it all just didn't feel right. He looked at his watch, but it had stopped at 2am which was the time when he went for a smoke and a pee. He sat down on some of the rocks away from the shooting flames, and closed his eyes and waited to hear the words that he knew signified the ritual being at an end. But he heard nothing but the roar of flame bursts, and the howl of the wind. It had not been a windy night, it was clear with stars everywhere. He opened his eyes to look at the stars, and saw only a blood red sky, opaque and starless. Then to his horror, he saw a group of what could only be described as demons, approaching him. He kept trying to wake up, but couldn't. He uttered the words that closed the circle. He rushed through the invocation of the pentagram of the six rayed star, and finally in desperation, of the Lord's prayer. The demons surrounded him laughing, prodding and tearing at his flesh. As Luck felt the agony tear into him, he realised this world was real. Finally he remembered with horror that he had left the circle.

Afterword

I used to work with witches, pagans and new agers, and the names here are very close to those really held by people from that time in my life. The excerpts from ritual are almost completely accurate too, embellished a little in places. The veil is thinnest between worlds at midnight on Halloween night, and we did used to hold rituals to commune with our ancestors. It was also forbidden to leave the circle once the ritual was cast. There the similarities end. There are places in our world where reality gets a bit thinner, but I have yet to meet anyone who actually slipped through the gap. Of course I might have met their demon substitute and not known...

Hijacked

Ezekiel Bloodstone, Zeke to his friends, cut a fine figure in his black trousers, long black jacket, red shirt, black tie and black Cuban heeled boots. He was tall and svelte with long, dark, slicked back hair and tinted glasses to keep out any remaining light.

He was stepping on board the red eye night flight from Heathrow to Rhodes; a flight which would both take off and land by night. At Rhodes he would be chauffeur driven to the harbour where a boat already waited to take him on to another, smaller island.

The flight did not have a first or business class, or Zeke would have certainly been in it; privacy and peace and quiet having much more value to him than money- as is the norm with people who have plenty of the latter but not so much of the former. As it was, he was in the extra legroom front row seats, and had bought six tickets altogether, so he had the whole of his row, and the row behind him. All had reserved tags on them, and as he sat down, he made a point of informing the stewardess that no one was to be allowed to move into the 'empty' seats he had paid to reserve.

The flight boarded, and the plane mostly filled up. A young couple sat in the front row seats alongside Zeke, the third seat beside them remaining empty. They seemed pretty intent on each other, kissing and touching. Zeke suspected they were newlyweds.

After take-off, which at that time of night was un-delayed and uneventful, the stewardess came to offer Zeke a drink. He ordered a Bloody Mary, made with decent vodka and plenty of hot sauce. He perused the food menu and deemed it all rubbish, of absolutely no interest to him. He looked at the screening guide and made the same pronouncement about the film. So Zeke got his book, or rather e-reader out of his carry-on bag. He had read all the classics, and everything by mainstream authors he was interested in, so the world of indie authors on the e-reader had become quite fascinating to him. On the one hand, they explored a world of post apocalyptic, dystopian and horror tales that were just not available in mainstream bookstores. This Zeke found most refreshing. Another bonus was they went to places mainstream editors, in the main, just did not allow. This too was refreshing. Some of the books were really good, comparable or better than a lot of mainstream fiction. Sadly the downside of indie books, was that many of them were rubbish and should never have seen the virtual light of day. They were badly edited, and full of spelling and grammar mistakes. Or they were just too short to be considered a book, more of a short story, or at best a novella. Or the story was just self indulgent rubbish. It was a lucky dip. Unfortunately Zeke had a personal rule to finish any book he started; a rule he was beginning to rather regret. He sighed as the book he was currently reading once again pointed out to him that it fell into the regrettable category. So he drifted between trying to read a bad book, and half watching the couple next to him, who had added arguing into their performance mixture.

After about forty minutes of this, the onboard entertainment perked up a bit. Two men with beards, rushed up to the Stewards area just in front of where Zeke sat. With his ultra sensitive hearing he heard them say; "We are hijacking this plane. Radio to the pilot and tell him to divert to Palestine or we will cut your throats."

Obviously they had got through customs with some sort of knives. Zeke could only imagine they were fold up penknives they had inserted into a body cavity, and now removed, [hopefully cleaned] and opened. Or perhaps they were somehow incorporated into the struts of the hand luggage and had required extracting and putting together in some way.

Zeke was not frightened for his own safety; their knives could not hurt him, and even if the plane crashed, he would survive it- though if at sea, he perhaps would not get home before sunrise, which might be tricky. Of course the dark depths of the ocean were no stranger to him, but he was wearing a nice suit and his e-reader wasn't waterproof. Money could replace just about anything, but it was such a hassle. He didn't care about the other passengers either, mere humans had long since ceased to interest him in any real way. On the other hand if the terrorists announced their presence to the entire plane, all the passengers would panic; there would be screaming, and probably vomiting. Zeke hated the smell of vomit, and the noise of screaming.

Then, assuming the pilots went along with the hijackers demands, there was the annoyance of the detour to Palestine. He had connections waiting at Rhodes, and wanted to get home. Aside from the whole sunrise thing, he just didn't like Palestine; he had been there a few times previously, and found the place very distasteful. Literally, its inhabitants did not taste nice- perhaps they ate too much garlic in their food.

Finally, the thing that motivated Zeke to action, was that he really wanted another Bloody Mary. He did not want to wait hours, or longer, until he got home, for another drink.

Zeke stood up and walked into the galley area. The hijackers swore and shouted at him, which rather annoyed him. One tried to punch him, but he moved out of the way too swiftly and the man missed.

He looked each of them in the eyes in turn and said;
"Stop doing this at once, return to your seats."

The men complied, walking back down the plane as if they had just been to the bathroom. Zeke turned to the stewardesses and looked them in the eye saying;
"Nothing happened here, everything is normal, go about your duties."

As Zeke turned back into the plane, he noticed the couple from the front row beside him staring at him. They were the only other people who had seen what was going on, and they were riveted with fear. Zeke went over to them, looked them in the eyes and said;
"You have seen nothing out of the ordinary. Oh, and stop arguing with each other. In fact go to sleep until we land."

Business taken care of, Zeke sauntered back down the plane until he reached the seats where the wannabe hijackers sat. The seat next to them was empty.

He looked them in the eyes;

"Sit still, nothing unusual is happening here, just relax and feel sleepy."

He leant over and sank his teeth into the necks of each of them; drinking until they were completely drained of blood, and their heartbeats stopped. Then he bit one of his fingertips and wiped his blood over the neck wounds so they were not visible. The two dead men looked, for all the world as if they were peacefully asleep. Zeke made sure their seatbelts were buckled, seat backs and tables up, so the stewardesses would not disturb them until after they landed. Zeke planned to be long gone before they were discovered.

He sat down in his own seat and pushed the button for the stewardess.

"Another Bloody Mary please?"

He sipped the drink, enjoying the pleasure of washing the taste of garlicky Palestinians out of his mouth.

At Rhodes harbour, the water lapped against the small boat, the sound seemingly amplified by the darkness of the night. Zeke boarded the boat which would take him across to his home on the island of Karpathos.

Afterword

In vampire fiction, the vampires are almost always from the mountains of Carpathia, I just thought, why not the island of Karpathos in Greece instead? The idea for the story came to me whilst I was feeling rather bored on a flight one night. I just thought firstly about vampires on commercial airlines, and then casually wondered what they might do on a hijacked plane. At first I thought of the bloody and violent route, but realised that would take a lot of time to clear up and explain. This option seemed much more realistic. It amused me more too.

Virtually Normal

Jan 5th 2010. Message from Virtual Reality Now Corporation [VRNC] Silicon Valley HQ to London Office: The technology is ready to roll out the new VR headsets. Units will be distributed worldwide to co-ordinate a launch date of Jan 21st, please ensure your regional suppliers are fully stocked for this date. The universal price list is detailed as a separate attachment.

Jan 31st 2010. Message from Dr Reginald Sunderley, Institute of Mayan Archaeology and History. To Howard Edrington, Head of VRNC London:
Further to your recent enquiry. All research evidence suggests the Mayans were very specific about the arrival of some sort of world apocalyptic event on 21 Dec 2012. Whether they meant their world, i.e. South American regions, or the entire planet, cannot be determined from the archaeology we have available. The dates however, as shown on the stone carvings, are incontrovertible.

Feb 2nd 2010. Message from Howard Edrington CEO London, to Jefferson Hardwald CEO USA:
Enclosed information from Archaeology expert re Mayan end of world scenario. Although it may be deemed scaremongering at some point in the future; this or some other world apocalyptic event seems inevitable in the near future. Thus I fully support the research and development of the VR product we discussed, with a view to launching it by autumn 2012 at the absolute latest. I think that channelling research funds into this project is more important than any other at this time.

June 21st 2012. Message from VRNC HQ to Worldwide head offices:
Be ready for roll-out of new product, VR headset version 3.0. This product will be marketed at lower than its shelf value to ensure it gets to the majority of end users before the end of autumn. Discretion can be used for sales in third world areas; please consider the end user scenarios

laid out before you at VR convention last month. Be ready to go live at 11.30pm on Dec 21st 2012.

July 1st 2012. Article in Technology News Today.
VRNC has launched their latest VR headset, which is their smallest and most technologically advanced set to date. It is also exceptionally cheap, suggesting they are intent on cornering the market in the same way Windows and Amazon did in the past. The headset, if it can be called that, is really no more than a pair of buttons that affix to the users temples. The user gives the command VR on, and nothing more is needed. VR mode is projected directly into the user's brain. After the first use, all the pathways are established and usage becomes even simpler. We have tried the technology here at TNT, and all of our staff pronounced it totally amazing and said they would be buying their own personal set immediately. The world into which one is immersed, is so real it is almost impossible to tell VR from reality. Every household should have one; no, restate that, every human should have one.

July 31st 2012. World News Network:
Sales of VRNC's VR headset 3.0 have outstripped all other technology sales in history. Perhaps all sales full stop. Every household has at least one set, usually more than one, and the world over, people are talking about it. No other product comes close to this kind of demand and coverage. Stocks in VRNC have soared. It is thought that when the new rich lists are published, Jefferson Hardwald may well be the new richest man in the world.

Oct 26th 2012. World News Network:
Riots have broken out in parts of India, Africa, South America, Asia and Eastern Europe, as people are unable to get hold of VR3; claiming there just aren't enough stocks or suppliers in their areas. Claims are that VR3 was only ever intended for rich first worlders, never for the third world. Meanwhile VRNC have put the price of VR3 up by 600% claiming it was only ever an introductory price before. This news network asks; Is it a conspiracy to keep

VR3 an elite product, only available to the elite? Have VRNC effectively selected who their users are?

Nov 16th 2012. World News Network:
Figures show that more people than ever are now working from home. VR3, the new technology from VRNC, has enabled people to use their equipment to work from home; no longer needing to attend actual workplaces. It is also being used extensively in home shopping and drone delivery schemes. The environment agency reports that road and rail usage are significantly decreased, and that most countries will easily meet their anti pollution targets because of this. WNN asks: Has VRNC single handedly saved the world?

Dec 22nd 2012. World News Network:
Well, it looks like the experts were wrong again. The world did not end at midnight last night as predicted by the Mayan calendar. We are all still here, and life carries on as normal. This newsreader for one is pleased to report a false alarm.

Dec 24th 2012. VRNC to all worldwide offices:
Switchover was universally successful! At 11.30pm local times, on 21st Dec 2012, all VR3 sets were switched to permanently on mode. All units are functioning correctly within defined parameters. Please send out your local teams to collect and burn all non participating bodies. We cannot leave the dead in the streets. Ensure all teams are wearing full protective gear, and take corpses to allocated cremation areas. Thank you for your diligence.

Jan 1st 2013. World News Network:
Awards are being given today to VRNC for solving the third world issue. Thanks to VR3, there is no longer a hunger, housing or welfare problem. All world citizens are living comfortably. No one believed this problem could ever be solved; but look around you in the streets. There are no more homeless, no hungry, and no beggars. All

have been housed and congestion problems solved thanks to VR3. It truly is a brave new world.

Afterword

I was really uncertain how to tell this story; finally settling on the unconventional format of bulletins and e-mails. I couldn't pick out a character to use as a story subject; no one main character could carry the story through. Jefferson could have been the centre for most of the tale, but the innocence of the news network- how ironic- was required to cut through the difference between VR and reality as perceived by normal people. Sadly those who died were unrepresented, except in a brief mention as rioters- but wouldn't that really be the case in such a scenario?

I'm of the opinion that a good story does not need any explanation; however, some of my beta readers did ask for a little clarification on this one. Others didn't, so in an attempt not to spoil the story for those who didn't want it, I'm adding some explanation here as notes in the afterword.

The people who didn't have VR3 were killed by some sort of Mayan apocalypse event. I like the idea of an airborne plague myself. VR3 not only kept its users indoors, but also protected them. VRNC chose the survivors by not selling to those they considered undesirable, third worlders, homeless, non tech savvy, elderly and so on, and thus, by default eliminating them. VR3 users remained unaware they had switched into living in a full time VR world.

Zombie Ants

Matt and June had rented a small eco-tree house in the Brazilian rainforest. It was all part of their study year away. For June it was a study of anthropology for her PhD, looking into indigenous tribes that were being dislocated by the logging industry. For Matt it was a study of entomology for his PhD, with a particular focus on rainforest species.

Given the nature of their studies, they spent most of their time wandering about in the forest. June would spend days trekking to tribal villages and other sites, and Matt would tend to tag along, collecting insect samples as he went. He had not progressed to site specific sampling yet, and was still studying the fauna very generally, so it was easy for them to work together.

The tree house had everything they needed, and they had arranged for someone from the nearest town to come by with supplies once a fortnight. They were pretty cut off from mainstream society, and were finding it idyllic. The only problem they had was that everything Matt was studying seemed to want to have a nibble of them. Despite all the potions they had brought with them, and the net over the bed, and all the internet anti bug devices they had set up; they still seemed to be the main item on the dinner menu. They were both covered in bites, and spent a lot of time itching, and giving in and scratching said itches.

Matt was particularly fascinated by the Camponotini tribe of ants. These ants became infected by the so called zombie fungus, Ophiocordyceps unilateralis, an insect pathogenising fungus. The fungus grew on the heads of infected ants, finally taking over the body functions, making the ant climb a high tree close to the nest, where the fungus exploded their heads, shedding spores over the ant colony below; thus spreading the fungus to new hosts. This much was well documented, and had been originally observed back in 1859 by British naturalist Alfred Russel Wallace. But Matt was especially excited because he had become convinced he was witnessing new behaviour patterns within the infected ants. Instead of climbing a tree, the ants seemed to be going inside the colony and doing something to the larvae inside, before dying and the mushroom exploding in a small confined space. This, he thought, meant that either the parasitic mushroom was weakening and becoming less effective in its commands; or the ants were evolving in a new way to deal with the parasite.

Matt had stopped going out on day treks with June because he was watching a particular ant colony very carefully, photographing different ants as they emerged from the ant hill, and taking occasional live samples of young ants.

The young ants he collected did not seem to be developing the mushroom growth on their heads, whereas the older ants still had them. Had they managed to avoid the spores, or had they become immune to them? Or did the spores only grow on older ants, preventing die out of the host colony? Matt had lots of questions and no real answers.

Nevertheless, Matt continued studying the ants and trying to fully scientifically document everything he noticed. One morning, as he was opening a tub to put some foodstuffs in for the live young ants- still apparently uninfected- within, one of them bit his hand. Matt cursed, and shook it off, putting the lid back on and rubbing the sore spot on his hand. He didn't think much of it, except; 'another bite- fabulous.'

That evening, June got back from one of her tribal visits, very excited and full of news.

"I'm definitely not taking a non intervention policy on this one. The tribe need someone to translate and help put their opinions and needs across to the logging company. Also, I need to go online and check, but I think their land is in the middle of a donut, which means the loggers can't cross protected land to get to the tribal land."

"No worries, you get onto that, and I'll do dinner. Have you thought about crowd funding to buy their land for them?"

And so they both got to work at their respective tasks, coming back together over dinner. Matt felt a bit like he was coming down with the flu, but it could equally have been a grass allergy or something similar.

"Great news, the land is within a donut, and I have set up crowd funding, and put up some of the pictures I took of the tribe today; but one of the sites got back to me and said there is existent funding to buy their land quickly, so that is going through as we speak."

"That's fab babe," said Matt, spooning out some of his spaghetti Carbonara for June. "Wine?"

"Mmm delish," mumbled June through a mouthful.

After dinner, with not a great deal to do in the evenings except sit and watch the forest from above- not that they could see much in the darkness, more just listen really; June and Matt made love. It was hot and passionate, and resulted in a number of small scratches and skin tears. Nothing that would cause any lasting pain, just heat of the moment stuff.

The next day, Matt went with June to the tribe. He felt a bit crap, but not incapacitated sick, just a bit hot and woozy. More importantly though, he thought June needed him with her. He knew these logging companies could turn ugly when blocked, and didn't want her to have to rely on the tribe to defend her. The ants could watch themselves for the day- this was much more important.

June, along with four tribal elders and Matt, approached the logger's camp. They were ushered into a small shed where a pair of company men had come to talk; also the site foreman was present.

When June spoke about the donut around the tribal land, the company men got rather agitated. They said they had worked around donuts in the past by using heavy duty helicopters to lift equipment and logs in and out of the donut. The elders asked June to query what would happen to their homes, and they were told they would be assisted to move somewhere else. When they asked about the land they had cleared for farming, they just received a shrug in response. June felt it was time to play the trump card, and told the logging company people that the tribal land had been bought for the tribe by a charity the previous night. The loggers were furious, and demanded to see paperwork. June assured them that the paperwork was on its way; she could bring an e-copy with her the next day.

The company men swore and grumbled and then demanded that June, Matt and the tribesmen be immediately escorted off site.

The foreman and his team each grabbed June and Matt in particular, roughly. The tribesmen made haste to disappear into the rainforest, used to making a swift escape. June and Matt responded to being manhandled by fighting back. All four of the men holding them got scratched, and one got punched in the face by Matt when his grasp on June became, albeit accidentally, inappropriate.

Once deposited alone in the rainforest, June took Matt to meet the tribe, so she could explain to them how land they felt they already owned, had been bought for them to own, by an outside charity organisation. It was tough going, trying to explain, but when June and Matt finally left in the late afternoon; there were smiles all around.

The next morning, Matt was sick. He couldn't get out of bed, was feverish, and his face arms and upper body had broken out in a proliferation of lumps, like some kind of super virulent chicken pox.

June had to take a copy of the land ownership over to the logging site, but insisted she would be okay on her own. When she got there, she was surprised to find the camp cleared and deserted. She visited the tribe to tell them the loggers had gone, and they insisted she stay and celebrate with them.

When she got back, much later, June was feeling rather the worse for wear; probably the home brewed alcohol she had consumed. She checked her emails and found something from the charity, saying they had forwarded the land ownership papers to the logging company; which explained why they had up and left. Having done everything she possibly could and feeling too tired to write up her notes, June decided to join Matt, who was looking much worse, in his sick bed. She felt pretty sick herself, and had noticed the same kind of spots breaking out on her own face. They would just have to tough it out, and be sick together for a few days until it passed.

Meanwhile the loggers had gone back to the city to await further instructions and have some down time, which for most meant visiting local bars and brothels. The four workers who had 'escorted' June and Matt off site, were feeling a bit peakish, but certainly weren't going to miss the rare opportunity to get drunk and bed someone. By the end of the night, they had between them, fought with seven men, and had rough sex with five women. Those twelve people would be feeling a bit sick by the next day, and would soon interact with very many more people. When the supply delivery guy arrived at the tree house for June and Matt, he received no answer to his call. It was not the first time that had happened though. Sometimes June and Matt forgot what day he was coming, and were off doing studies or surveys or something. He had been paid in advance for the year anyway, and so just climbed up to leave the supplies in the house, and put the perishables away in the fridge. It only took a couple of minutes more, and actually he was glad of the rest time in the cool house.

He was very surprised when Matt and June shuffled and stumbled out of the bedroom towards him. Their skin was grey, and covered in yellow spots, some of which had clearly burst, leaving a kind of yellow powder stain across their skin. They looked and smelt like they hadn't washed since the last time he had delivered, and their eyes were red. They made low groans as they crossed the room towards him. Xavier, the delivery man, backed away, tripping and falling over the ladder that led down to the forest floor. Before he could get up, June and Matt had fallen on him and were tearing at his exposed flesh with their hands and teeth. Xavier's screams went unheard in the dense forest. Broken eggs and spilt milk from the supply delivery went unheeded.

Before long the same scenes would be unfolding all across the city, and then spreading out across the world.

Afterword

I'm a big zombie fan, so I wanted to start and end this book with zombie stories. It's also a tribute nod to the late great George Romero- zombie king, founder of all things zombie. This story, like so many of my stories; begins in fact, then wanders away into the realm of imagination. Zombie ants are real.

Poem
Foreword
Recently I was chatting with a fellow author friend of mine, and he said that the thing he really loves about short story collections is the way they are put together. Whether they are batched in themes, or linked together by an idea that flows from one story to the next; whether they are juxtaposed as opposites, or thrown into the air to see how they fall- he finds a beauty and joy in the nature of the mixture. I have been considering his words ever since; probably because I'm in the midst of writing and editing a short story collection myself. My last collection, Oddscapes and Quirkitudes, I put together in topic groups. This one is collected together under the title; Tales from the Library of a Twisted Mind- so each tale shares the common feature of being a bit twisted or dark in some way. But if you look out for it, there are other more subtle links running through. I thought, that in addition to that, it would be fun to finish with a poem. Each line of this poem refers to a story in the book, working through in order from first to last. I hope you enjoy it. I certainly enjoyed putting it together.

It's All Connected
You're born, you die,
You rot, someone else lives.
Trapped in a mad world,
At the whim of others,
Wishing you could fly away to pastures new,
But always tied to the past by genetics.
Banishing imaginings that haunt,
Releasing power, but never letting go.
Monsters in the night fields,
Choosing baby pieces for their chessboard.
Animals die so you can live,
Their howls in the night haunt your dreams.
Not knowing who is dead or alive,
But always reproducing, continuously splitting cells.
The buildings around, loom hungry towards the skies,
A boat is only as good as its sailors.

Self indulgently narcissistic,
Or degrading into one great rotten pulp,
As long as the family unit reigns supreme,
The house and its landlord don't matter.
Kill the weak,
Leave no remains for excavation,
Create the strong,
Who will always do things in their own special way.
Never show your feelings.
Always strive for the highest branch,
Eat what you can, when you can, where you can,
You never know when it might be your last meal.
When is a cat not a cat?
When time curves around on itself and disappears into its own black hole.
Never trust an idyll.
What waits in the snow may have sharp teeth.
Your hell is always waiting just outside your vision,
And the inside is always stranger than the outside appears.
Mergers are not always hostile or friendly,
There is only a given amount of time to succeed.
It just isn't safe out there,
But there is always someone stronger than you, who might save the day.
Reality is tenuous at best,
If we're not dead yet, we are just waiting to make it so.
It's all connected.

Printed in Great Britain
by Amazon